A HATEFUL WIND

by

Col. Lee Martin

I.E.R. MEDIA

Miami, Florida

A HATEFUL WIND

By   Col. Lee Martin

Copyright © 2011

I.E.R. Media

13874 SW 151 Lane

Miami, FL 33186

tbyrnes@ierworld.com

786-525-9487

ISBN: 979-8-9872241-6-8 (pbk)

ISBN: 979-8-9872241-7-5 (ebk)
Printed in the United States of
America

Acknowledgements

To the tribal warriors of South Vietnam, the Montagnards, who I had the privilege of training and operating with as a Special Ops advisor. To my Vietnam brothers-in-arms, some of whom gave their all.

A Hateful Wind is the third work of fiction in the McGowan Collection Series. The reader is encouraged to first read *Wolf Laurel,* where it all began, as well as its first sequel, *Provocation.*

NLM

CHAPTER ONE

It was altogether perfect, my new life. Here I was, two years married to a goddess of the angelic persuasion, teaching Criminal Justice two days a week over at VMI, which was scantly an hour's drive from my home at Wolf Laurel, and traipsing off to Washington every couple of months for a week at a time to help my former team profile suspected terrorists, both foreign and domestic. On three occasions, with Mrs. McGowan's permission, I also took part in terrorist smack down operations with my team. Two such take downs were in California where al Qaeda had covertly settled in and was operating training camps outside San Diego and just south of Yosemite. The third deal was in Mexico City where a newly discovered Taliban faction had found a way to bring subversives into the U.S. along with Mexican illegals through border weak spots. Our boss, the Birdman, had sent Zulu, our highly-skilled counter-terrorist team (CTT), into all these locations to neutralize any potential threats and to make the bad guys mysteriously disappear. The good thing that came out of these operations was that my body took on no additional lead. Most people have the same number of holes in them, such as seven in the head, the navel and a couple more south. If my memory serves me correctly, I think I now have a total of fifteen.

My name is Bruce McGowan. And yes, I had a great deal of apprehension about hanging up my spurs with CTT back in mid-2002, at least on a full-time basis. I had also experienced such reservations on at least two other occasions: when I quit the Army…Special Forces to be exact… and again twenty-one years later when I retired as an FBI Special Agent. So, most all my life I had been 'special' in one way or another. Much to my surprise, however, I had actually become adjusted to this new life of semi-retirement, mainly because of the beautiful Adrianna Wolf, inn proprietress, Greenbrier County, West Virginia socialite, lover and wife.

Adrianna was not exactly keen on my part-time duty those two years with CTT for a couple of reasons. First, she knew there was an element of danger to what I did and there was a very good chance I was going to come home with *more* holes in me…or not come home at all. Secondly, on two occasions I had brought that danger to Adrianna's own door before we were married. In 2001, an Islamic terrorist took her prisoner along with my brother and a guest just to get to *me*. Then a few months later there was that radical, domestic terrorist asshole from out of the sixties who also wanted a piece of me. And it was this second incident at Wolf Laurel that nearly proved fatal for Adrianna.

So, after a tremendously enjoyable career with the military, the Bureau and the State Department (CTT), I was more so enjoying the best couple of years of my life, ageing as I was. And it was mostly this woman, the new Mrs. McGowan, who had made it that way. Each day broke with new pleasures. Every once in a while in the wee hours of the morning when thunderstorms woke me from a sound sleep, I would get up and sit in the blue velvet sofa chair near the foot of the bed and smile when a flash of lightning that might continue for several seconds streaked across the night sky, illuminating her sweet face. The face of an angel. It seemed to me I had known her all my life. And maybe I did. I just didn't know who she would be.

I especially recalled that one night after dinner we walked along a trail by the Greenbrier River when the full blood moon was low on the horizon peeking through the branches of the cottonwoods and river birches, until only moments later it turned a bold yellow, finally coming into full view over the treetops. And then as we strolled slowly and quietly along the dirt path, the moon turned again, but to a brilliant silver that covered us like a street light and lay upon her cheeks like silk. I can never look at the full moon when I am away from her without thinking of that one sweet April night.

A perfect, uncomplicated life and sentimental romanticism aside, however, I must admit I did miss the day-to-day exploits that came with more than thirty-six years as an action man. Although my brain still needed it, my body had said "enough, McGowan. You might not be ready for the rocking chair on the front porch, but you can't run with the dogs like you did ten years ago either." And I knew the old bag of bones was right. My last mission in Mexico City proved that out. I was having just a wee bit of trouble keeping up with my much younger Zulu brothers running through the streets in a 106 degree temperature.

*   *   *   *

It was the early morning hour of May 19th when one of those aforementioned, unexpected pre-dawn thunderstorms was rumbling through, the light in my brain turned back on. Generally, once I wake up, there's no getting back to sleep. And it *was* while I was sitting in the old chair watching Adrianna stir uneasily and listening as the window-rattling booms followed closely after the lightning, my cell phone on the dresser rang, playing the first notes of *Jesu, Joy of Man's*

Desiring. Adrianna rolled over and looked at the red numbers on the clock radio.

"Good grief," she muttered. "It's three thirty. Who…" She stopped short and I knew she was wondering if perhaps somebody died. She sat up straight in the bed.

"Hello," I answered, myself apprehensive that something could be wrong at my brother's house or with my FBI agent daughter, Caroline, out in Denver.

"Bruce," the voice began. "Pardon the early morning call, and I am doubly sorry if I woke Adrianna."

"Lionel, what's the deal?" I said rather indignantly. "You couldn't call me some time after our rooster crowed? And do you have any idea what kind of dream you woke me from?"

"Spare me the pornographic detail. And again, forgive the rude awakening, but can you be here by eight?"

"Today? And I assume you don't mean P.M. You know I just left the team house two days ago. I thought we were stretching out my work. You remember the agreement…I would retire, give you a week here and there, and my wife would continue to let me come out and play with you all."

"I remember, but this is a different deal, Bruce. Something came down last night from the head shed. Something that involves a bit of travel out of country…like in two days."

The 'head shed' meant from the President himself. I had found out a couple of years before, although having assumed all along, that Lionel Byrd, the Birdman, CTT's director, did not answer to anyone except Mr. Big, the Commander-in-Chief. Even though Byrd's boss was 'officially' the Secretary of State, even *he* did not know what covert activity we performed. He thought we engaged government contractors who provided the government's security products and services. But, actually *we* were the government contractors. And the Department of State stayed out of our business. They only paid us. Except it wasn't nearly what we were worth. A secret fund maintained somewhere else supplemented the salary very nicely, however.

"I assume you've gotten everyone else on the team out of bed as well."

"No, Bruce. The task involves only you."

"Just a minute, boss." I then took the phone to the living room out of Adrianna's earshot. "Just me? Why?"

"I'll give you the run-down as soon as you get here. Kiss the wife goodbye and hit the road."

"Am I leaving country from there?"

"No, I have you scheduled to leave from Charleston on Friday. Marina has already secured your ticket. You will have a couple of days to put your affairs in order there."

"So where *am* I traveling to?"

"I'll tell you when you get here."

I took a moment for the cement to set in my brain and then said, "You know someone's going to be mighty pissed about this."

"Uh, yes. I expect so. But tell her I'll make it up to her somehow. Maybe when this is over she'd like to come up and have dinner with the boss."

"Mine or yours?"

"Both. It'll be a nice, private little gathering."

"And *your* boss knows it'll be *me* on this deal?"

"He especially singled you out."

"With all the talent out there? Why me?"

"Just *be* here, Bruce. I'll give you the complete run-down in a few hours." I then heard a click and he was gone.

So, I just stood there in my BVDs at the living room window with the dead phone in my ear, watching the lightning illuminate the dark…in a bit of a shock. The President of the United States knew who I was and expressly asked for me. I didn't know whether to be flattered or angry. Of course, it was Adrianna who would be angry. But I was also just a wee bit angry at the Birdman. We had an arrangement, dammit. I would get married, do a little part-time CTT work, maybe a couple of missions where needed, and then work on my golf game when I wasn't teaching cadets about the evils out there in the world. On the other hand, a FAG (Former Action Guy) like me only dreams of one day receiving a call to go do some kind of 007 mission for his majesty the Prez. As I continued to ponder Byrd's call and the opportunity, my virulence about the 3 A.M. call went away. Now, the hard part. Telling my usually understanding wife that I would be leaving her once again to go who knows where and staying who knows how long to complete a mission who knows what.

No sooner than I had laid the phone down on the coffee table, I felt her presence behind me.

"What's going on, Skip?" Skip was my nickname, and only *she* called me that. How I got it goes way back to when I was a kid. A story for another day.

I took her by the hands and sat her down on the couch beside me. My doing so caused alarm in her face. Maybe she *did* think someone died.

"You love me, right?" I said, putting a set of wrinkles in

my forehead that probably reminded her of a Shar Pei.

She sighed. "I think I'm not going to like this. Obviously, the call was from Mr. Byrd and he's pulling you in for something."

"Yeah," I replied in a sheepish whisper.

"But you just got home. And what about your class this week?"

"I'll get another professor to take the class till I return."

"Return from where?"

"I don't know."

"You don't know," she responded wryly. "Then how long will you be gone?"

"I'm not sure."

She closed her eyes and laid her head back onto the cushion. Pissed or not, she looked sweet in her white nightie and long dark hair pressed against the cushion. Her lips parted…not of course in anticipation of a kiss, which would have felt forgivingly nice…but in disgust. She had a right to be disgusted. And I was a disgusting kind of guy.

"What's this thing about?" she finally said.

I knew she was getting pretty darn tired of me saying I didn't know, but honestly, I didn't. Of course Byrd couldn't let out the subject of my mission over the phone, considering it had to be some kind of hush-hush deal that the President had in store for me, should I decide to accept it. And of course, I *had* to accept it.

"Lionel couldn't talk about it over the phone. Said he'd tell me when I got there."

She took my hand in hers, which under the

circumstance was a genuine surprise, and said, "You're breaking our covenant, you know. You promised when we were married things like this would not happen. You would work as a part-time operative for Mr. Byrd. Do you realize in the two years we've been married you have been away from me a combined six months?"

"Not so…uh uh," I replied like a six year old school boy.

She didn't say anything more for a while nor would she look at me. She then stood and walked to the kitchen to put on some coffee. I went in after her and as she stood at the counter measuring out the Maxwell House, I slipped my arms around her tiny waist and placed my lips on the nape of her neck.

"I'm sorry, sweetheart. It's that the President specifically asked for me to do this thing, whatever it is. I don't know anything more."

"And how does the President know *you?*"

"I'll have to answer one more time, 'I don't know.' Lionel Byrd seems to know though."

After a long, uncomfortable silence she finally said, "Well, then give the President my regards and that I will hold him personally responsible if anything happens to you."

I pulled her close into me. Her tight buns beneath the silken gown brought the soldier to the position of attention. I wished that I had had the time for a bit of Drill and Ceremonies, but I soon had to hit the road.

"You're leaving now, aren't you?"

"Only for the day. I have a meeting with Byrd and hope to be home tonight. I leave out on the mission on Friday."

"Do you have time for a little breakfast?"

I smiled a lecherous smile. "If I had time for *anything*, it wouldn't be breakfast."

I thought I caught a return smile as I peered around her. But maybe not. She continued to make the coffee and I veered off to the shower. In fifteen minutes I returned and found she had placed a sweet roll on a saucer beside my coffee mug.

I wolfed down the pastry and coffee and saw that it was four ten. I should be able to make it to CTT Headquarters by eight, barring any unreasonable traffic delays on I-66. Of course, *every* weekday proved unreasonable when it came to rush hour in Washington, D.C. I then strapped on my shoulder holster, checked the clip in the Glock and kissed my understanding wife goodbye for the day. She stopped me before I made it to the porch, however.

"I have a bad feeling about this one, Skip. Every time you take a trip it tears my insides up. You haven't even left on this mission and already my stomach is kicking like a mule."

"It's going to be okay, Adrianna. Every mission I do does not have an element of danger to it. I'll know more by the time I get home."

She nodded. "Okay, then. Be safe on the road today."

"Always."

*   *   *   *

As I drove along I-81 past Lexington, it was still dark. I would be somewhere near Winchester before the sky would lighten. Being the Road Warrior that I was, it always provided me the opportunity to do some serious thinking. What Adrianna was feeling, I had a little case of as well. The thing is, danger in my life is and always *has* been expected. It never makes me afraid. For some reason, however, I had a gut feeling about this deal. For me to be singled out by our Commander-in-Chief to pull a mission without Team Zulu, well that raised the hair on the back of my neck. Don't get me wrong. I don't avoid danger and I'm not afraid to die. But what I was afraid of was that Adrianna Wolf McGowan may someday find herself a widow yet again. Would this gig bring with it an even more profound sense of danger?

I had enough to worry about what with my daughter, Caroline, still assigned as an FBI Special Agent in Denver. There wasn't a day that had gone by in two-and-a-half years that I didn't wake up thinking about her and then trying to put my worries about her to bed when I signed off at the end of the day. I had had a few lengthy conversations with the good Lord about her, some even out loud while I was running my five miles a day. I've asked Him over time a bunch of questions and listened patiently for his reply. And I swear I have heard answers. Why is it that when we talk to God we're said to be praying, but when God talks to us, we're schizophrenic?

CHAPTER TWO

About seven forty-five I rolled into the rear parking lot at Terminal Enterprises and parked my ageing Suburban into a space beside the Birdman's Olds. For a dapper spy who dressed better and was ten times more suave than James Bond, a twelve year old Cutlass just didn't cut it. Maybe an Aston-Martin or a Jaguar. But as much as Lionel Byrd loved to dress well, he was an unpretentious sort who never put on airs.

I gave my usual finger wave to Voyeur, the ever scanning camera on the roof, and was buzzed in by Byrd's personal assistant, the lovely, buxom Virginia. As she had long since given up on the idea of divorcing her husband to marry me, she was finally retiring at the end of the year, much to the Birdman's dismay. Without her and his full-time master operative like yours truly, what was he to do?

But Lionel had hired a new receptionist a couple of months before, a pretty young thing about twenty-eight named Marina, who spoke four languages, and coming to us already having spent five years with the Company (CIA). All business, but very personable, she had become Byrd's new Girl Friday who would be replacing Virginia. However, Marina would be no Moneypenny as far as I was concerned as she lacked both Virginia's maturity and sense of humor, sick as it was, but fully compatible with mine. Marina's was the first face I saw just inside the door each time I dropped in.

"Good morning, sweetie," I greeted. "I guess you didn't expect me back so soon, huh?"

"I made your flight arrangements, Mr. McGowan, and you can pick up your tickets when you leave today."

"Oh, good. Where am I going?"

"I believe Mr. Byrd will be talking with you about that."

Like I said…all business. She was going to have to warm up to me a little more if we were going to have some fun around there.

As I sauntered down the hallway to Byrd's office, I literally bumped into Chuck (the Rock) Robinson coming out of the break room which was like running head-on into a Mack truck. Since I had been with CTT, I had been on more missions with him than anyone else. And he was the kind of guy you wanted to have your back.

"Bruce. Hey, old man, what're you doing back here so soon? Thought you just left."

"Thought I did, too, but looks like I have a new gig."

"I haven't heard about it," he said. "What is it?"

"I'm the Lone Ranger on this one, Chuck. It's not a team deal."

"What do you mean? We don't do that. At least we never have in the past. Where you going?"

"Don't know, my man. But I'd better get in there. Byrd is anal about promptness, you know."

"Yeah." He gave me a puzzled look as I turned toward the back office.

As I passed by Virginia's office, she winked and waved. "He's waiting for you, Brucie. Go on in."

Byrd rose as he always did to shake my hand, the gentleman that he was, greeting me like it had been eons since I had darkened his door rather than two days.

"Coffee, Bruce?"

"Please."

"Then close the door and take a seat. I'll get you a cup."

I didn't take a seat immediately as my legs still felt like rubber after the four hour morning drive. Byrd shoved the steaming coffee in my hand and went around to his side of the desk to take a seat in his rather large leather chair. He was dressed in a crisply-starched white shirt and a stunning red-and-white striped tie. His double-breasted Ralph Lauren Navy blazer with four small brass buttons on each sleeve hung neatly on the coat tree in the corner near his desk. After picking up his pipe, which was probably older than his Oldsmobile, he placed it between his teeth and started chewing on it.

"The President, huh?" I said. "And specifically, why did he select me for whatever this mission is?"

"Did I say it was the President who called me in?"

"Well, you said your boss put you on this thing and I know who you answer to…and it's not the Secretary of State. I'm a spy, remember, and a very good one at that; not your junior G-man."

"Let's get beyond that, Bruce, and talk about the job. Again, he asked for you to do this. He read your file…Army Special Forces, Vietnam, highly-decorated FBI agent, accomplished counter-terrorist operative who saved thousands of Americans from perishing at the hands of al

Qaeda terrorists…need I go on?"

"You needn't. But how would my file happen to fall into his hands?"

"I hand-carried it to him."

"Okay," I responded. "So the President now knows who I am. What's this all about?"

"What I am about to tell you, only three people will know…you, him and me. There are others who know the scenario, but don't know you'll be investigating the matter. You will become acquainted with two or three of them. You're going back to Vietnam, Bruce."

"Vietnam? I thought my two tours over there were enough. Are we planning on starting another little unpopular police action that will last ten to twelve years?"

"Go ahead and sit down, Bruce. This will take a while to explain it all to you."

So, I did, opposite his desk in one of the wingbacks.

"First, did you leave things in good order with the wife? I can't tell you how much I think of that lady, Bruce. As much as I was dismayed that you officially left our services for a beautiful woman like that, one could not blame you. I assume she has not disapproved of our part-time arrangement."

"Not much, but we have had some very frank discussions at times about the increased frequency of my work with CTT."

"Like your being brought back in two days after you left here."

"*Oh*, yeah. We had some *real* dialogue this morning about four o'clock."

"I'm…sorry about that and that I've had to ask you to do this thing for the boss. I know how this must be very demanding for her."

"Well, she's not really the demanding type, ordinarily. Never wants anything for herself, unlike my last wife."

"Darlene was demanding?"

"Well, you never had the pleasure of meeting the woman, Lionel. 'Demanding' is actually a docile word where it came to her. It was *all* about her. One day she blew up when I was tinkering on a Saturday with the Healy. She said "you think more of that thing than you ever did me. You can sport around in it looking so suave while I'm driving my beat up old Pontiac." I said, "I thought you liked the Bonneville." She replied, "It's all right for going back and forth to work, but I'd rather have something black, built low to the ground and will go from zero to two-hundred in less than three seconds." So, I bought her a set of scales. I was pretty much toast after that."

Byrd *wanted* to laugh, but as he had some very serious things to talk over, he moved on.

"Okay, again, you, me and Eagle One will know about this deal. However, we have also made contacts with three other people who this is all about and who you will interview. A seventy-seven year old retired Army sergeant-major, a Vietnamese male in Ho Chi Minh City and a Montagnard woman deeper in country. It will be more of a fact-finding mission than anything, Bruce. And I can't tell you how important it is to Eagle One that the information be obtained quickly and efficiently."

"Sounds mysterious…like secret agent stuff."

Byrd set his unlit pipe down on the desk and leaned into me.

"When you were with the Special Forces in Vietnam, you were with the Montagnard people, weren't you?"

"Yes, in the Central Highlands."

"In your area of operation were there also Catholic priests and nuns ministering to the people?"

"I knew two French priests, who I learned were actually CIA, and worked with several Swedish nuns who were also nurses, tending mostly to children who had contracted tuberculosis. I had heard that a couple years after I left that the priests and nuns were killed by the NVA when they captured Dak To and other major villages in Kontum Province."

"Yes. Well, more recently, graves of several religious people have been unearthed by farmer tribesmen outside the villages of Bin Vinh and Dak Trang near Quang Tri. And our information is that they were not killed by the NVA. The skeletal remains reveal that may have been hacked to death by machetes. Crucifixes were discovered on their neck bones. Their Bibles had been tossed in the mass grave with the bodies."

"How do you know it wasn't the NVA or VC?"

"Because there is a witness to the killings who has agreed to come forward."

"And who was supposed to have done this? Would it not be a matter for the U.N. to investigate...you know, war crimes and all?"

"No. That's where you come in."

"I'm confused," I said. "You're alluding to a crime that has been committed but not perpetrated by enemy troops. Has it not been investigated by the Vietnamese government?"

"They wouldn't be interested in something like this that happened over thirty years ago."

"So, this mission has nothing to do with terrorism and would not normally be the kind of investigation that lands on CTT's plate."

"This is a special project, Bruce. And Eagle One specifically requested *you,* considering your stellar history and keen interrogation skills."

"Well, the man obviously has good judgment."

"Mmm, right. Anyway, the former Army sergeant-major I mentioned, who by the way is now dying of cancer, decided to clear his conscience about an incident that occurred in 1972 in the Montagnard village of Dak Trang. His company commander gave the order to basically annihilate the entire village, claiming that it was not only 100% Viet Cong, but that several villagers had killed and cut the ears off an American GI who had slipped into the hamlet for a rendezvous with the village chief's daughter. The French priest and four nuns who operated a hospital within the village were cut down as well and buried in separate graves. About eighty of the villagers were dumped in a mass grave. The American company commander gave the order to shoot and kill anything that moved. That included women, children and the aged."

"I assume the sergeant-major is coming forward after thirty years now because he's trying to get into Heaven."

"Apparently, it's lain on his conscience all these years."

"Sounds like another My Lai," I said.

"Yes, except Calley claimed his unit took fire from the village and even children were supposedly found with AKs in their hands. In this case, the sergeant says that the village was peaceful as a Sunday morning and that the village chief had even invited our soldiers in for some rice wine."

"So, instead of firing on our soldiers, the chief intended to poison them."

"The sergeant-major also said there was absolutely nothing to the story about the GI having intercourse with the girl or that he was killed. It was a total fabrication."

I folded my hands and placed them under my chin. "Okay, let me get this straight. He's the only one out of perhaps a hundred to hundred fifty former soldiers in that company who came forward."

"That's where this all gets even more interesting. You see, Charlie Company of the Second Battalion of the 105th has gotten together for a reunion every five years since 1972 here in D.C. Everyone except the commanding officer, First Sergeant and his two lieutenants. According to the sergeant-major, the captain threatened that if word ever got out about the massacre, any of the company members still in the Army who told would be court-martialed. Or after they left the Army and wanted to relieve their consciences, they could still be charged with war crimes. Basically, the company commander put the fear of God in them. If he and his officers went down, *they* would as well."

"Do we know who this captain was?"

Byrd nodded. "The President knows. And *I* know. He asked me not to divulge the man's name as he wants to give him the benefit of the doubt. And considering *who* this man is, we need to be sure about the facts."

"You won't tell me, then. So, how am I to perform the investigation?"

"You know how to get this done. Anyway, you're bound to find out the captain's name after you nose around, but even when you talk with Sergeant-major Berryhill, he was asked by the President not to divulge it when he is interviewed. When you leave here and before you return home, I want you to go by Berryhill's apartment to interview him. He's one of three people you will speak with."

I nodded. "Specifically, how does the President…excuse me, Eagle One…know about this? How would this information ever get from an old retired sergeant-major to him?"

"By happenstance, Bruce. Glenn Berryhill has been active for years in the Washington Area Non-commissioned Officers Association and has on occasion given the invocation at the Annual Prayer Breakfast that the seating President always attends. He's actually had the President's ear the past couple of years. This year he asked for a private moment with the President, and much to everyone's surprise, was granted it. That's when he told him the story."

"Amazing." I then caught from the corner of my eye a small black spider on the leg of Byrd's desk, weaving a web to the leg of the other arm chair beside me. Metaphorically, it caused me to think how the story I had just heard was a thirty year old web that had been woven early on by this captain who had threatened his soldiers should they try to escape that web. It set me to wonder if any of *them* had experienced nightmares similar to what I continue to have about ending innocent lives. As much as my heart told me the woman and child I had killed some thirty years before had met their deaths by accident, the guilt pangs in my head would not go away. I could imagine what these soldiers had felt over the years having actually *murdered* the innocent. I am sure many of them had experienced PTSD. But why wouldn't just one of them decide over the years empty his conscience and go to the press? Certainly *someone* had to have gotten religion along the way.

I turned my attention back to Byrd. "And the FBI or Army CID have not been engaged to locate and question all the other members of the infantry company?"

"No. The boss wants as few people as possible to know about this investigation. Perhaps upon completion of your fact-finding trek, he will put one of the agencies on the matter. No one else is to know what you're doing until after you bring home your information. I was able to secure the list of all company members, and let me tell you, there is some alarming data about them. Out of the one hundred forty-two members of that company, thirty eight have died from natural causes."

"What's so strange about that? This happened over thirty years ago. People die."

"I'm not through," he said. "Another forty or so have fallen off the face of the earth, many reported as missing. I expect some became homeless like so many troubled Vietnam vets."

"Yeah, I was technically homeless for a while after my divorce."

Byrd gave me a laser beam stare.

"Sorry," I said.

He continued. "You're going to be astounded at this. "Twenty-four either committed suicide or fell victim to accidents, unnatural ends or…were murdered. That's over a hundred dead or unaccounted for."

"My God. If the remaining forty have figured out these stats, they must be somewhere in hiding. Sounds like this former captain and who ever remain loyal to him have been busy cleaning house. Maybe the guy *continues* being a mass murderer. But why would he resort to such extreme measures? Is it because people had been talking up turning the guy *in* over the years?"

"I expect so," replied Byrd. "When heads get together at re-unions, a lot of memories come out…a lot of bad memories. When the dialogue starts, people get charged up. Maybe this captain had a spy in the midst who took names and reported back to him."

"But if I'm one of these guys, when it became apparent that a lot of my buddies started disappearing, dying and such, I would get concerned, start asking some questions and press *some* law enforcement agency to investigate."

"At the peril of disappearing yourself…or maybe a member of your family? Knowing who this former commander is, he would probably go to extreme lengths to protect himself."

"I can't believe that *nobody's* come forward to advance the story of the massacre and get this guy tripped up. Stories have a way of anonymously ending up in the mailbox of the *New York Times.*"

"This man has far-reaching arms. A lot of people and entities are in his pocket. I think he could stop *any* story from reaching the streets by just a couple of phone calls."

"The guy has *that* much power? And you're not going to give me his name."

"It's important that you remain objective about this." He then changed focus. "Most of the infantry company's members who disappeared or died did so over the past ten years. This had a lot to do with the reason the reunions stopped."

"Likely because people were getting scared, especially if they were seeing their ranks dwindling after perhaps receiving threats," I added. "Did this sergeant-major say *he* was threatened or knew of others who were?"

"He personally was not, but did report that as recent as last year two of the men contacted him and said they had received alarming phone calls from an unidentified caller reminding them and their families to 'be careful when they are out and about.' One caller specifically said 'let the Dak Trang matter remain dead…or you *will* be.' As you can see, this is a wide-spread coercive attempt on someone's part to quell any chance that this incident gets out and brings this man down."

"This *important* man," I commented.

"He does enjoy a great degree of prominence."

"I would know his name if I heard it."

"You would. However, his name has changed slightly from what it was in 1972. You might not be able to correlate the two names."

I shook my head. "And you're not going to make this easy for me. You lay out the pieces of puzzle on the table, but keep one of the key pieces from me until I bring home what you need to know…"

"*Then* we complete the puzzle. Again, I want you to be able to maintain your objectivity about the mission."

"All right," I sighed. "Who's the contact in Vietnam?"

"A former ARVN sergeant named Luc Thanh."

"And what's his story? How is he connected?"

Byrd placed his elbows on his desk and leaned forward. "He's a fifty-six year old former South Vietnamese man who served as an intelligence sergeant in his headquarters and who was privy to the deal that went down between his commander and the U.S. company commander. And Berryhill, who was a platoon sergeant in that company at the time knew Thanh. Berryhill had previously worked in a G2

Intel section and was the company commander's go-to Intel guy. He was often dispatched to the 39th ARVN Division HQ to gather information from and collaborate with Thanh about enemy locations and activities. Both knew that Thanh's section leader by the name of Bao, a major at the time, had some kind of, as we find out now, an unholy alliance and were often seen talking and whispering with one another.

"A few years after the fall of Saigon, Thanh and Berryhill began corresponding with one another, remaining friends for over twenty years. Thanh is fully cognizant of the Dak Trang incident and is prepared to take you to that Montagnard village, which of course no longer exists, but will hook you up with a woman who was merely six years old when the village was razed. The last thing her mother did after the attack began was take her to the Dak Bang River and hide her in the weeds. The mother was then shot and killed, but the child was not found. The child was later located by a nun from another village and raised there for three years. But then she was placed in an orphanage when the nun died. The Montagnard woman is now working with an underground group to protect the Degar people from further persecution by the Hanoi regime which is bent on forcing the people from their land."

I was getting intrigued. "So, the little girl was actually a modern day Moses who was rescued from the bulrushes to become a leader for her people."

"You could say that. Good analogy."

"And Thanh knows where this woman is."

"Yes. They have met a couple of times. Both have similar agendas directed against the Vietnamese government. Liberation of the people from the Communist stranglehold."

"Wasn't there some kind of war fought about that back

in the sixties and seventies? I assume I'm supposed to go over there and start it up all over again."

Byrd ignored my moronic quip. "If this woman remembers the particulars of the raid on her village, she may be a valuable resource."

"It's doubtful she ever saw the face of the commander. Her mother probably whisked her out of there when the first volleys were being fired."

"We're not counting on the facial recognition of anyone, especially by a child. We just want the particulars of the attack itself to reinforce Thanh's story."

"But wouldn't Thanh's information just be hearsay, having merely corresponded with Berryhill?"

"Thanh knows more than you think. He overheard plans for the raid while Bao and the American commander were talking. You see, Berryhill took part in the attack on Dak Trang and was sick about it. You will be connecting the dots…getting statements from Thanh about overhearing the plans and from the Montagnard woman about the massacre. Then when Berryhill finally brings his story out, likely to the Bureau for a full investigation, you will have supplied the icing on the cake."

"And a super-spook from the CIA or FBI couldn't pull this investigation why?"

"I'll say this again; the super-spook that Eagle One wanted was you. *You* he can trust. He's not taking any chances this thing starts bouncing through channels and somehow reaching the ears of the man who this is about."

"Which says that if this guy is all powerful, he might have markers or IOUs out there even within the agencies."

Byrd maintained his stoicism and didn't answer that. His

silence *gave* me that answer. The stem of the pipe returned to his mouth. As hard as he crunched on that thing, I was surprised it had not been whittled down to a mere strand of plastic.

I had been taking notes as quickly as I could scribble. Mom had wanted me to take Shorthand along with Typing and Home Ec. However, not only did my military school not offer such life-sustaining courses, but if it did and I had signed up for one of them, my cadet peers would have checked me for lacy drawers. But I can't tell you how many times I would have benefitted from all three. I then sat for a moment with my fingers to my brow, looking at my notes and allowing the information to this point to digest. I think Birdman thought I had fallen asleep.

"Bruce?"

"I'm awake. Just mulling all this over, that's all."

"Uh huh. You're probably saying to yourself. 'How am I going to convey this to Mrs. McGowan?'"

"It crossed my mind."

"Well, you'll think of a way…without actually telling her what you're doing."

"Thanks for your help, Mr. Byrd. Maybe you should go back home with me and help me face the music. She won't hit me with you around."

"That sweet lady would not swat a housefly. You'll handle it, old boy. Now, enough of the whining. You'll leave here and drop in on Sergeant-major Berryhill before trekking back to West By God."

"I'll need his address."

Byrd then handed me a small slip of paper that read 285 Fontaine, Falls Church.

"Is he expecting me?"

"No. He knows nothing about you or that you'll be investigating the matter. You'll have to gain his confidence."

"You can't get Eagle One to call and announce me? Maybe he will think I'm someone who was sent to silence him."

"Once you start the dialogue, he'll know you're on the right side of things."

I gathered up my notes, shoved them in my briefcase and stood.

"And I leave when?"

"The day after tomorrow. You're flying out from Charleston, connecting in Chicago, then on to San Fran and across the big drink to Hawaii and the Philippines. You should be in Tan Son Nhut on Sunday morning. Here's your ticket."

I looked at it and cocked my head to one side. "One way? Are you anticipating I'll get plugged over there?"

"Didn't know how long this would take you or when you'd be back."

"Uh huh. Or if I *would* be back."

One corner of his mouth turned up in a stifled smile. "You made it back fine two other times."

"I had a gun then…and a fighting chance. Am I traveling on the pretense of a vacation or what?"

"You're an ex-GI that wants to go back in time and see some of the country that you missed appreciating before…just like hundreds of others do annually."

"Actually, I always thought I'd like to do that…maybe see if our old Special Forces Camp, Ben Het, is still there.

It's probably been replaced with condos and cat houses."

Byrd held out his hand and we shook. "If you have any trouble, get to the American Consulate in Ho Chi Minh City."

"Otherwise, if I'm taken prisoner for war crimes against their fathers and grandfathers, you'll dis-avow any knowledge of me or why I'm there."

"Exactly. But do us both a favor and try to keep a low profile, Joe Tourist."

"What happens if I *do* run into some trouble and get grilled about who I am and why I'm really there?"

"Officially, you and this mission, if somehow discovered, will not be acknowledged by the American government."

"Oh, great."

"*Un*officially, Eagle One has your back. Don't forget that. We'll get you out of there."

"Sounds like there's every probability something *could* go awry," I commented.

"There's always that possibility."

"When is my contact expecting me and where?"

"You're booked for one night at the Hotel Beaufain in Ho Chi Minh City. He will contact you there. After that, you make it up as you go along. He'll be taking you north into the Highlands."

"I see. Back to sleeping in the jungle. For some odd reason, I thought those days were over thirty years ago. Silly me."

"Enjoy your camping trip."

I nodded.

"And send me a status in a few days," he added. "Use Zulu code Zircon."

"Got it. Tam biet, ong."

"Hen gap lai ban," he replied.

On the way out I saw Chuck again who was talking and joking around in animated fashion with Marina at her desk by the rear door. The lecherous way he was looking at her told me that he obviously had designs on her and it wouldn't be long before this charismatic, muscle man would be muscling his way into her bed.

"Hey, Bruce," he said. "So what does Birdman have on your plate that don't involve the rest of us?"

"Wish I could tell you, but I'd have to kill you. *You* know how that works."

"All too well, my man. So, you really can't tell even us?"

I just shook my head to avoid further dialogue on the matter. "Watch out for this dude, Marina. Don't fall for any of his lines. I've seen him in action and he's slick."

"Why are you poisoning this girl's mind about me, Mac?" Sometimes he called me that…but never Skip. If he knew that was my nick-name, I'd never live it down.

"Your track record with women, old boy. Need I say anymore?"

Chuck glared at me. I think he actually had a case of the ass, thinking I was sabotaging his chances with the little cutie.

"I was just kidding, Marina," I said. "Chuck's a damn good guy…a little misguided at times, but as we've been friends for over three years now, I've gotten to know him pretty well. Prince of a guy. I'd trust him with my life…and have."

"I think he's nice, Mr. McGowan," Marina replied, giving Chuck a warm smile. Obviously, she was developing a crush on the big lout.

"Okay, I get it," I said. "I'll leave you two alone. I gotta get going anyway. See you in a week or two."

"Yeah, I'm not far behind you," said Chuck. "Gotta get my oil changed before it gets too late." He then gave me a two finger Boy Scout salute off his brow and went back to schmoozing Marina. He wanted to get his oil changed all right and maybe a lube job and front end alignment as well.

*   *   *   *

In a way, I was actually looking forward to the mission, finally returning to the country where I could reminisce those two wonderful years of combat, boredom, hot, steamy days followed by monsoon rains, rats, snakes and razor-like banana grass. Actually, I loved the Central Highlands and the people…both the Vietnamese peasants and of course, the Montagnards as the French referred to them. I remember that they were a happy sort, loyal to the bone, and would do anything in the world for a carton of cigarettes. And in handing out the cancer sticks, we Americans did our best to shorten their life expectancy even more.

CHAPTER THREE

It was already ten-twenty as I sat in the Suburban in the rear parking lot, basking in the rays of the May sun that poured in through the windshield like warm honey. Before moving out, I wanted to take a little time to mull things over…especially the part about having to tell Adrianna that this was not going to be a mission somewhere in the states that would be accomplished in short order. With travel, which would take a couple of days each way, plus time spent with this guy, Thanh, who would accompany me into the Vietnam highlands to locate the Montagnard woman and then back to Ho Chi Minh City, I was looking at a minimum of a week and perhaps two. Adrianna, of course, would not be happy about all this, especially the part about not being able to give her the particulars about my vacation.

After loading up the sergeant-major's address in my GPS, I backed out of my space, threw my hand up to Chuck, who was just exiting from the back door, and began following the sweet feminine voice that would tell me step by step how to get to my destination. I always wondered what these GPS gals looked like. The voice on my last system led me to believe she was a real bitty. She would get disgusted with my incompetence when I failed to make a turn or otherwise follow her directions. Like I was intentionally disobeying her instructions. She'd sigh, tell me what a contentious bastard I was, and say in a rather obnoxious voice, "Make the next legal u-turn." And if I didn't, she'd really get a case of the ass and infer in her tone of voice that I was just a typical stupid man who refused to take directions from a woman. And that set me to arguing with her. I wanted to make sure she understood I resented her telling me where to get off. Literally. But I liked *this* GPS gal. She was not only tolerant of my obstinacy, but had a rather sweet and sensuous voice.

I hadn't eaten anything substantial, so before I trekked on, I stopped at a Chevron station and got a pronto pup. Considering the fact that 'health nut Adrianna' had been making me eat properly these first couple of years of our marriage to get my weight down to where I was my old fighting self, I needed to sneak in an occasion grease fix and put a shot of nitrate in my system. After wolfing the dog down with a diet Coke, which served to balance out the calories to a net of zero, I drove on for a half hour until the voice told me I was nearing my destination. It was an average-looking neighborhood with a conglomeration of forty to fifty year old houses and flats that were scarcely an arm's length apart. Berryhill's house was a two story, rather shabby-looking duplex with a dark roof and screened-in front porch. I could see inside the porch that there were two doors leading to two flats. A postage stamp front yard was dissected by a narrow sidewalk with uneven, broken slabs leading to the front steps.

I pulled into the one remaining parking space on Fontaine, killed the engine and gathered up my note pad. As I stepped from the SUV onto the sidewalk, a black Crown Vic two spaces in front of me then pulled away from the curb and disappeared quickly around the corner at Preston Avenue. Redirecting my attention back to the house, I negotiated the broken sidewalk and climbed the five steps to the front porch. There was a sign over the door to my left that read 'Available,' and which made it easier to determine which apartment belonged to Berryhill. The door on right appeared well-worn with dirty smudges all over it which did not fit the mold of belonging to a career Army senior NCO whose place should have been spic and span. But, over the doorbell was a small nameplate that read *Berryhill,* so I pressed my finger on the button till I heard the familiar Westminster chime inside. After waiting a few seconds, I rang the doorbell again. No footsteps. As I knew he was not a well man, I figured he may be in bed or had to take his time getting to the door, so I waited patiently another half minute. Finally, I rapped sharply on the door glass. Still, no response. Perhaps he had gone out. I rued the thought that he was not at the point in his illness that he had expired during the night. And was there not a Mrs. Berryhill?

I then stepped off the porch and went around the side of the house, thinking perhaps Berryhill was working in a shed or in the small rose garden that came into view as I approached the back yard. No one was in sight. On a tiny patio outside the back door to Apartment B sat a rusted-out charcoal grill and a green and white webbed lawn chair that over-looked the dozen or so rose bushes that huddled up against the redwood fence at the back of the property line. An explosion of glorious red and yellow blooms, the first of the season, added life to the otherwise decrepit back yard that measured 25 wide by 40 deep. When I stepped onto the patio, I saw immediately that the back door to Berryhill's apartment was standing wide open.

Stepping inside, I found a small utility room with a sink and a pair of muddied galoshes beside a mop and pail.

"Mr. Berryhill!" I called out. "Sergeant-major, are you home?"

There was no answer or any sound of activity. Immediately, something didn't feel right. I pulled my Glock from the shoulder holster beneath my leather jacket and allowed it to lead me deeper into the shotgun style apartment. A long hallway connected a bathroom, a bedroom and a small living room on either side. On the hall walls were old photographs of men in uniform, a couple from the Vietnam era, and several pictures of an older woman standing beside a tall, heavy set man with a balding head I took to be Berryhill himself.

I called his name again. No response. When I swung the Glock toward the stairwell that led to the upstairs, it stunned me to see why there had been no response. Hanging by a telephone cord from the railing directly above the small foyer was the body of a seventy-something year old man still in his pajamas and wearing one bedroom slipper. His face, pale with a purplish tint, told me he had been dead for at least several minutes.

Nonetheless, I raced up the stairs to check the body. Placing my fingertips on his jugular, I found no pulse. The flesh had also already cooled. There were no marks on the sergeant-major, but I did check his hands like a good detective would. Three fingernails on his right hand were bloodied, one of which after closer examination I saw contained bits of flesh. It wouldn't take a genius, much less a medical examiner, to rule that Berryhill's death was not by suicide. Somebody had ruined the man's morning.

I then remembered the black Crown Vic that had pulled away from the curb out front not five minutes before. The killer or killers had preceded me to Berryhill's house by just minutes. If only I hadn't stopped for the pronto pup, which was by the way gurgling in my stomach. Still, I went from room to room, upstairs and down, to assure that the killers were not hiding somewhere, ready to pounce on me. But I knew full well they would not have stuck around to admire their handiwork. Pulling out my cell phone, I then called Byrd.

"Boss, you need to send the cops and M.E. to Berryhill's apartment. He's been murdered. It was made to look like a suicide.

"Damn!" he exclaimed, uncharacteristically. "Are you still there?"

"Yes."

"Then you'd better get out of there before someone sees you. You don't in any way need to inadvertently connect the team to this."

"It serves to reinforce your suspicions about the questionable deaths of other members of good old Charlie Company. Somebody's still knocking people off to protect somebody's ass," I said.

"And now *somebody* likely knows we're opening up an investigation. Maybe they found out that Berryhill had bent the Chief's ear," he added.

"If that's the case, then more people besides you, me and the Prez know about this new interest in the village massacre. You're sure no one else has been told about my investigation. Maybe Eagle One blabbed."

"No. That wouldn't happen. I don't think he would have confided in anyone else because of who this man is. He said he would not even involve the Bureau or the Company."

"Then he needs to know about this murder before the cops get here. Maybe he has clean-up people that will take care of this matter besides the cops."

"Will see. Now get out of there pronto."

"I'm already at the back door."

I hadn't touched anything in the house except Berryhill's neck which I wiped with my handkerchief just in case a super-slick CSI team was able to lift prints from flesh. I wondered as I walked between the houses to my car if anyone next door had seen me. Perhaps someone had even heard the commotion in the house when Berryhill was murdered, if he in fact put up a fight. After entering the Suburban and starting up the engine, I checked the yards, porches and windows next door to the house and across the street. There were no faces peeking from the blinds nor was there any activity around and about the area. Either most people were at work or if at home, they did not make it a practice to be nosy.

As I drove out of Falls Church and made my way toward I-66 and the Shenandoah Valley, I was wondering more than ever who Charlie Company's company commander was back in the early '70s…and who he is now. He would have to be in his upper fifties. And it was either he or those loyal to him over the past thirty-two years who had been systematically and sometimes creatively ridding themselves of the people who were considered threats to expose the particulars of the Dak Trang massacre.

While I was making verbal notes into the recorder feature on my cell phone halfway down I-81, the phone rang. Birdman.

"Yes, boss."

"Before I had Virginia send an anonymous tip to the locals that there was a disturbance in the house on Fontaine, I sent Candellera and Marshall there to go through the place. Berryhill was indeed murdered as you suspected. The perps also took his P.C. All that remained were the monitor and keyboard. There wasn't a piece of paper left in any of the drawers and an empty briefcase was standing open. It was obvious they were looking to void the apartment of all documents and memorabilia associated with his Vietnam cohorts. But it was a sloppy murder. Berryhill's death may have been haphazardly intended to look like a suicide, but his bloodied fingernails containing his killer's skin coupled with the missing computer will tell the real story to the CSI team."

"Maybe in retrospect they weren't intending to fool *anyone*," I commented. "Maybe they just hanged the man to make a statement to anyone else who might be thinking of taking the story to the press or the authorities. So tell me, Condor, why wasn't this former Army captain investigated and questioned after Eagle One learned about him? Why send me to the other side of the world when somebody can put this guy in a room and hook up his testicles to a twelve volt battery?"

I heard Byrd exhale a long breath before replying. "It's a very sensitive matter, Bruce. And I pledged to Eagle One I would get you to complete your investigation ASAP, then he would move on the suspect."

"Okay, now you do have to tell me. Who *is* he, boss? Obviously, somebody important."

"Again, I can't, Bruce. Let it go at that for now."

"And again, no one at Army CID or the FBI could be trusted on this?"

"It's…complicated, Bruce."

"You know my investigation would go a lot quicker if I had the guy's name."

"And again, it would taint your objectivity, Bruce."

"But I'm am bound to find out his name from the

Vietnamese witness."

"Not necessarily. You may not be able to make the connection to who the man is now."

"Hmm. Now I'm confused. Does he not have the same name?"

"Give it up, Bruce. Just do as instructed and the information we need."

"Can we talk about a raise when I get back?"

"You elected to be a contractor, Bruce. You get paid by the job now."

"And not very well I might add."

"Spare me the whining. Few people in the Sneaky Pete business make what you do."

"Okay then. Up my Christmas bonus from $25 to $30."

"Done."

"You're too easy. I should have asked for $50."

"Goodbye, Bruce. Call me over there if anything goes haywire."

"What could go hay…" I then heard his disconnect.

*　　*　　*　　*

It had been an emotionally exhausting day what with digesting all the requirements and instructions of the fact-finding mission, not to mention finding the primary witness in the matter deader than four o'clock. I pulled into my driveway at Wolf Laurel about six that evening still dealing with the thousand thoughts flitting through my brain like a swarm of mad bees and which prompted me to sit in the Suburban for a few minutes longer. I was also putting off going inside to the little woman who with her naturally inquisitive nature would immediately bombard me with questions about where, what, when and how come, bless her heart. I wasn't sure she would quite understand this deal since I couldn't tell her any particulars about it, but it would make her mighty apprehensive, even fearful about it all. I figured it also may be just enough of a mystery to her to finally put the squelch on my part-time duty with CTT once and for all.

As she had obviously heard my tires crunching on the gravel driveway moments before, Adrianna came out to meet me on the veranda. She then held her arms out from her sides with an expression that said, "Well, are you just going to sit out there all evening?"

I turned off the engine and stepped out just as she trotted down the three steps to greet me with a much needed kiss.

"Missed you," she said.

"I've only been gone since the morning," I replied, laughing.

"I miss you even when you're away from me for an hour," she said sweetly. And it was words like *that* that melted my heart into molten honey.

"Come on inside and let's talk," I said.

"Uh oh. What is it and where are you going?"

I didn't respond until we were inside the inn and had plopped our derrieres on the leather sofa in the sitting room.

"Want a beer?" she asked.

"Not right now. Maybe later. Hey, I see two new cars in the parking lot. Who are our guests?"

"Well, the couple we were expecting from Ohio is here for four days and then there are two ladies from California who are on kind of a road trip together, staying in B&Bs along the way until they get to Maine. Nice girls."

"Girls, huh? What do they look like?"

"And that's supposed to matter? I suppose if they're cute, you want to play the role of Mr. Innkeeper, take them on a garden tour and serve them their breakfast in bed."

"And *are* they?"

"Are they what?"

"You know…cute."

"Let's say a lecherous old so-and-so like you would definitely approve. So just leave it at that."

"Can't wait to meet them," I sparkled.

Adrianna slapped me playfully on the thigh and then asked, "Okay, where is it that you are off to this time?"

So, how was I to answer this? Her face broadcast her impatience to hear about it while I tried to remember the words I had rehearsed much of the way home.

"Oh, just a small country in Asia."

"Which is?"

I didn't really think it would matter to Birdman if I just told her *where* I was going; so I said, "Vietnam."

"Vietnam?" she echoed. "What's the deal? Are you planning to start up another little war over there?"

The very question I posed to Byrd.

"Just getting some information from some people for the State Department, that's all."

"Don't they have other people like consultants and attaches to do that?"

"Normally, yes. But this is a different kind of mission."

"Mission, huh," she said. "Which sounds like you may be in danger."

"No, no. Nothing like that. It's mostly just a fact-finding mission.

"Which you are not at liberty to tell your wife about."

"Pretty much."

"How long will it take you to do this?"

"I'm not sure." Of course, I knew these questions would be coming. "I guess until I have all the information I need. Could be a few days or even a week or two."

"Two weeks?" she exclaimed.

"I don't know, Adrianna. I just can't say." I didn't respond to her last question in a really pleasing tone of voice, which put a frown on her face. She was quiet for a while and looked away, out through the window and into the blossoms of a pink dogwood across the parking lot.

"So, tell me, Skip. When will these days be over? When will you get tired of playing with the boys and settle down to a full-time marriage?"

And did that get my blood boiling. I'm sure she noticed that my tanned face had turned beet red. "You could have put that a different way, you know. I don't consider the work I do...doing my small part to help my country be safe...as 'playing' with the boys." I then stood up and turned away before I said something I would regret. She didn't say anything more for a while, but then finally came up to me and placed her small hand into mine.

"I didn't mean to go off on you, Skip. I'm sorry. I know what you do and what you've done for this country is priceless. And I'm proud of you. It's just that I love you and worry about you. I need you here with me to live out the rest of our lives without me thinking when it will be that somebody puts another bullet in you…or worse, that you won't come back to me. Can you not see that from my perspective? How would you feel if the scenario was reversed?"

I took her in my arms and pulled her tender body into my chest, then kissed her left ear. I said in a soft voice, "I do understand how you must feel. But I will always come back to you. And I will also promise you that when I return, I will continue to re-evaluate my future with CTT. Okay?"

She then placed her moist, velvet lips onto mine and held them there for a moment. Her breath was sweet and warm. "Okay, then, Superspy, I'll be holding you to it."

Passionate adrenaline shot through my arteries and veins like a hot flood. And it set me to thinking…why the hell *was* I gadding-about on CTT assignments when I could spend every glorious day of my life with this woman? Funny how the little brain can get the best of the big brain…which served to take our conversation upstairs to our apartment for a little late afternoon dee-light.

*   *   *   *

It was Thursday morning and I still had a full day to throw together both a light ditty bag and some penetrating thoughts about the mission before I flew out on Friday. When I turned on the network news, Susan McGinnis was saying 'Good Morning,' and then she commenced to telling everyone why it *wasn't*. A child was missing somewhere in North Carolina and foul play was suspected; there was an earthquake in Argentina and over two hundred people were feared dead; and another pro baseball hero to our nation's youth had just admitted to using steroids. After ten minutes of bad news I clicked Susan off and found a replaying of the

1999 *Sports Illustrated* Swimsuit programming. "Now that's more like it." I said to myself. Adrianna must have heard my voice coming out of my head because she quickly picked up the remote and changed the channel to a syndicated episode of *Designing Women*. "There," she said. "*These* ladies have their clothes on." A guy has to give up an awful lot of his hobbies and interests sometimes, not to mention his freedom, when he gets married.

As Adrianna began busying herself in the downstairs kitchen preparing sweet buns, melon and cereal for the guests, I went out for a morning run. The air was fresh and sweet and the sun rained upon my face like an ever warming oven. It was nearly eight as I sailed past old Mr. Van Meter's pasture where his prize bull, Biff, King of the Meadow, eyed me menacingly. The cranky old side of beef would have just loved for me to cross over the rail fence so that he could ram one of his bone-white horns up my backside. He had done that to one of Van Meter's farm hands a couple of years ago who to this day still walks like a prissy fourteen year old girl.

After a couple of miles my knee began to stiffen on me…the one that still had a small hunk of shrapnel in it, which took my brain back to my *last* vacation in good old Vietnam. Speaking of which, I intended to sit for a good part of the remainder of my day at the computer brushing up on the *new* Vietnam. Although the country showed signs of normalizing relations with the American government, it was still being run and policed by the Red Army…the same regime that shoved our collective butts out of the country in 1975.

I pulled up to a halt just as I remembered that I forgot to bring my sippy cup filled with clear, sparkling Greenbrier tap water. So, I stopped at a small roadside store for a $2.00 bottle of *Evian*, which is of course *Naïve* spelled backwards. I always shove a twenty in my running shorts along with my driver's license just in case one of my Nikes has a blowout and I need a taxi or I'm found dead in a ditch from cardiac arrest. People generally want to know where to send the carcass.

I also carry my cell phone in the other pocket of my shorts just in case Mrs. McGowan needs me for something. I can't imagine whatever for. I don't contribute much around the inn. But as my FBI agent daughter, Caroline, would certainly be up and on her way to the Denver Bureau office by now, I decided to give her a call. It may be days on end before I had another chance to talk with her.

"Glad you called, Dad. I was going to call you a little later. Guess what?"

"Okay…you're quitting the Bureau and moving back to Virginia to be close to your dear old dad."

She laughed. "No, silly. I'll be out here for a good while…that is, unless I get transferred." She then paused as though she was trying to find the best way to put it. "I'm getting married."

"You're what? I'll kill him, whoever he is."

She laughed again. "His name is Troy, Dad. He's twenty-nine, already a successful lawyer, and oh, did I mention he's a great looking guy?"

"A lawyer? A leech on society?"

"He's not an ambulance chaser, Dad. He's a corporate defense lawyer."

"He's still a lawyer and you know what I think of *those* people."

"I want you to meet him and that's the other good news. We're going to Virginia this weekend and I want you and Adrianna to come meet us in Fredericksburg."

"Oh, I'm sorry, Caroline," I lamented with a very audible groan. "I've got to fly out of country on a case tomorrow and will likely be gone a week or more."

And then *she* groaned. "I hate that, Dad. Are you sure you can't postpone your trip a few days?"

"Not this trip, Caroline. I wish I could."

We were both then silent for a moment.

"How did you meet this guy Troy?"

"I was working on a case that involved a company he represents. My eyes fell on him and his on me, and well, it just happened."

"And how long have you known him?"

"About two months. We haven't set a date yet, though."

"Two months!" I exclaimed. "I've taken longer than that to decide on a car to buy. Did you not want to take a deep breath and think about it for five or six years before accepting his proposal?"

"*His* proposal? I asked *him*, Dad."

"You can do that? That's legal out there?"

"We live in a different world than when you were young. Romance is a whole different ball game these days. Those old ideals held by traditional men and women are a thing of the past."

"And I don't like it one bit. But I guess I'm just an *old* fart when it comes to this new society."

"You just want what's best for me, that's all. And I love you for it."

"I wish you all the happiness, sweetheart. But you have

to allow me to meet this guy before you set a date. By the way, ask this Troy how you can tell the difference between a dead skunk and a dead attorney lying in the road."

"Okay, somehow I knew this was coming. How do you tell the difference?"

"The vultures aren't gagging over the skunk." And then I yukked it up big time.

"Very funny, Dad. I'm sure that's one he hasn't heard." Of course she was being facetious.

But I wasn't through yet. "And then what's the difference between a lawyer and a catfish?"

"Okay, I know this one," she said. "Only because you've told it to me not less than fifty times. Let's see…one is a slimy, bottom dwelling scum sucker and the other is a fish. Now are these all out of your system?"

"Yeah, yeah. The problem is, little daughter, you used to laugh at all of them…that is, before you decided to *marry* a lawyer."

"Well, anyway, let's talk about this case you're traveling on. Is it hairy? I worry about you mixing it up with danger."

"Not to worry this time, my dear. No terrorists or other bad guys involved. It's merely a fact-finding mission."

"That's good. You need to quit the business one day, you know. Cold turkey. You've got a great life back there with Adrianna. You have served your country well all these years and now it's time to go to pasture."

"Like an old nag ready for the glue factory, eh?"

"I didn't mean it that way."

"I'll quit if you quit. This thing works both ways. When you get married, will you turn in your badge and gun and let

Mr. High Dollar Lawyer support you?"

"No man, no matter how good looking or rich he is, will *ever* support *me*, Dad," she replied emphatically. She was almost indignant when she said that.

"Sorry. Forget what I just said. I just wondered if someday it will cause you to think about doing something else."

"I won't rule that out. Maybe one day I'll have kids, but we haven't talked about that yet. If I do, then I probably will quit the Bureau. But I'll always have some kind of profession."

"Grandkids. Ah, nothing would please me more."

"We'll see, Dad."

"Well, I'm at the halfway point in my morning run, so I'd better restart my ticker and get back to the inn."

"Give Adrianna my love."

"I will."

"And be careful, Dad."

"Always. Tell Troy or whatever his name is that your very sinister and crazed father is looking forward to meeting him."

She giggled. "I will. Bye now."

While jogging back to the B&B, I felt like I had a new kick in my stride. I smiled just to think that I would soon have a son-in-law, perhaps even someone I could call 'son,' that is if I liked him. And a grandkid or two? My life would become all the more perfect. But of course I would have to bone-up on my repertoire of lawyer jokes.

CHAPTER FOUR

My brother Joey who runs the family mortuary business, McGowan and Sons, is one of the county's most respected citizens, yet is avoided like the plague…for obvious reasons. If they *ever* have to do business with him, as old Mr. Cheever from down the street would say, "somebody done got his self-dead."

Adrianna and I met Joey and his wife Cora at *Food and Friends*, a favorite restaurant on Washington Street in town, for some burgers and cheese fries…except my wife's burger was a combination of turkey and tofu, I think, and she didn't touch even one of the fries. In the two wonderful years of our marriage she hadn't gained an ounce on that hundred-ten pound frame. I wish I could say that. But, at fifty-seven, a hundred-seventy and six feet one, I can still go one-on-one with the best of them. I can still bring it.

We engaged in a bit of small talk about people around town to include old Miss Haymaker, Joey's and my fourth grade teacher who at eighty-two had just passed on, and how uncomfortable it must have been for Joey to be draining the woman's blood. He said it actually wasn't, because over the years he had seen quite a few county icons laid out in their birthday suits and had gotten used to it. But the idea of seeing Miss Haymaker in the raw? I had to choke down several swallows of my Heineken to void that image from my brain.

Joey was leaving for Charleston at first light on Friday to pick up the carcass of a fifty-three year old fellow named Grayson from Ronceverte who expired while watching cartoons with his granddaughter in Kanawha City. He had checked out about the time Elmer Fudd was poised to blow away that wascally wabbit. Joey said I could catch a ride with him instead of having Adrianna take me the two hours to the airport. He would be out in front of the inn at 6:30. I said that would be fine.

*   *   *   *

As always, whenever I am about to embark on a team mission for a few days, Adrianna puts on her solemn face the night before. This night was no exception. And as a post script to her earlier foreboding feeling, she appeared to be even more apprehensive about my leaving her this time.

"It's just an investigation, sweetheart," I reassured her. "No gun play…no bad guys. I should be able to wrap up this deal to include travel in about a week."

"Will I hear from you while you're gone?"

"Absolutely. I'll call you every couple of days." It set me to remembering the times I called my folks back in 1970 on the Army's communication system called MARS, the Mobile Army Receiving Station. To Mom and Dad it sounded like I was actually *talking* from Mars. One had to go through the mobile operator in San Francisco who would relay the message, "I love you, over." Then the response would be, "I love you, too, over." The mushy dialogue sounded not only garbled but came out rather impersonal as well.

"Will I be able to get hold of you if I need you?" she asked.

48

"I doubt it. I'll be staying at the Hotel Beaufain in Saigon (I still refuse to call the old capital city of South Vietnam 'Ho Chi Minh City'), and will be traveling north into the Central Highlands. I have no idea what the cell coverage is over there anywhere."

"I just don't like this, Skip. This trip seems to have a lot of uncertainties about it. I know you never tell me much about what you're doing, but I just have a bad feeling about this one. Especially since you're going alone. Maybe it's that the whole idea of Vietnam is stuck in a dark part of my brain. My dad's brother died there and so did my next door neighbor."

"Well, it's different now. That was war. A whole generation has come and gone; and the U.S. and Vietnam are well on the way to normalizing relations. A lot of GIs go back there to visit…not only to reminisce, but to see again the beautiful land of the orient they couldn't enjoy before. *I* plan to do a little of that as well."

She shook her head. "I can't say that I would ever be interested in going there myself…maybe another Asian country like Thailand or Japan…"

"Then, one day we shall go to one of them…maybe both."

*   *   *   *

That Thursday night was another night of thunder and lightning, both outside and inside our bedroom. A late evening spring storm had brewed up over the Alleghenies and swept through around eight, then circled back to pound us again around nine-thirty. And in the small bedroom in the turret at Wolf Laurel, a love storm had also brewed. It was as though our own sweet duet being played together in carnal harmony was brought to a crescendo along with the metaphoric flashes of cymbals and climactic thunder of

49

drums outside our window.

After the storm had died away and my beautiful wife had knocked the stuffings out of a man twice her size, I retreated to the fridge for a brew and sat at my computer pulling out any information I could find on village massacres in Vietnam. Of course, the My Lai massacre was number one on Google with more than 10,000 sites. There was a smattering of other stories here and there about questionable raids on the villages of Phu Bai and Dung Vao which allegedly were under VC control; however, most of the information was speculative and unproven. A couple of former Vietnam vets who were obviously into conspiracy theories and tabloid sensationalism had some nutso ideas about the Phoenix Program. As *Phoenix* was a military intelligence effort engaging our Special Forces, of which I had been a part, designed to weed out the Vietcong and NVA infrastructures in the villages, these two loons knew that our government had used the program to wreak onto the hamlet systems its own version of terrorism in a vicious response to the terrorist atrocities of the enemy. They believed it was an attempt to evoke fear into the people rather than a pacification of the people. Funny, but I didn't remember it that way.

I then clicked onto whatever I could find on the Montagnard villages and whether there was any traffic on the internet about American soldiers raiding, killing and razing. I remember reading a couple of books on the Degar (Montagnard) people that had been plighted by the North Vietnamese Army when it swept into Kontum province in 1972, two years after I had left there, killing most and scattering the rest. Some migrated into Laos and Cambodia to escape and others sought refuge in Special Forces camps. Our Green Berets protected them as best they could and helped resettle many in North Carolina down in the Charlotte and Greensboro areas. We had been their best friends. I knew that if I was ever in one of their villages or out performing a search and sweep with them, I was well protected. Any Montagnard soldier would gladly have given his life for mine.

For the most part, the 'Yards, as we called them, were despised by the Vietnamese. Primitive, tribal, rounder-eyed with darker complexion, they were considered non-citizens. The Vietnamese soldiers (ARVNS) also resented our association with and the training of the Montagnards. After all, we were there to defend *them*, not unwelcomed invaders and squatters of the ethnic persuasion. And so from that time forward to present day, a campaign of systematic ethnic cleansing had ensued.

I also recall the day in March, 2001, when the Degar immigrants in *this* country called for a Million Montagnard March on Washington, D.C. to protest present day Vietnam's repression and persecution of their people and their religion. The Montagnards openly accepted Christianity when the French and later the American missionaries moved in, at first in the form of Catholicism, and later Protestantism. I was there that day in the nation's capital. As these proud, beautiful people walked with dignity down Pennsylvania Avenue carrying American, Vietnamese and Montagnard flags, they wanted nothing more than to be given back their freedom, their land and their religion, all of which had been taken away by the communists.

As I sat in my 'big easy,' the plush leather recliner that Mrs. McGowan had allowed me to bring into our marriage, I closed my eyes to dust off the cobwebs from my brain and to pull from my mental attic the picture of *my* days with the Montagnards…particularly the Jarai and Rongao tribes. My area of operation in the Dak To District was about fifteen kilometers long and six kilometers deep that extended from well east of the village of Tan Canh to the tri-border area of

Laos and Cambodia where we operated out of the Special Forces camps of Ben Het and Dak Seang. Yes, I was part of the Phoenix Program, and yes, we caused a number of known VC hamlet chiefs and elders, both Vietnamese and Montagnard, to disappear. But it was neither terrorism nor counter-terrorism. It was what we called psychological operations (PSYOPS). We were good to the people…even benevolent. We issued them uniforms and M-16s, paid them and gave them rice allowances, laughed and prayed with them, and bounced their babies on our knees. We gained their confidence just as they gained ours. However, if we found there was a communist-controlled leader element working against us that threatened the peace and good life enjoyed by the villages, we took care of the problem. Permanently. One might ask…was that any different from what Calley did at My Lai or this mystery Captain did at Dak Trang? You bet your ass. It kept a hell of a lot of friendlies from getting whacked.

I diverted my eyes for a moment from the computer screen to allow an old memory to invade my brain. It was the village of Dong Tom Ri that became the subject of the one nightmare that has haunted me more than a hundred times in the past thirty odd years. Dong Tom Ri was the only known purely Vietcong village in my A.O. Village enemy propaganda teams also operated in and around the hamlet. And from this village were sent patrols to ambush not only U.S. convoys and elements of our own Special Ops teams, but innocent civilians working the rice and coffee fields. It was the Vietcong's terrorist acts against their own people that prompted our aerial combat assault on their village.

When we had swept our weapons over the village and killed most of the enemy, we landed. The last act of hostility was committed by me alone against the occupants of a thatched-roof hooch where a glint through a window had caught my eye. I popped from my M-79 a 40 mm grenade that entered the open window and exploded, blowing out the reverse wall. A child and her mother died. Upon entering the hooch, I found that the glint was where a ray of smoke-filtered sun had caught the shiny ladle of a sauce pan hanging on an inside board. The faces of the girl and her mother have haunted my dreams incessantly.

In a few days my contact at the Hotel Beaufain would be briefing me on the massacre of the village of Dak Trang and subsequently accompany me to the razed site where the mass graves of its people were discovered. Here's the double standard. If the village had been purged by the NVA in its advance into the area in 1972 or by the current communist-controlled government, there would have been an investigation of some degree by the U.N. or some global life advocacy group that might end in sanctions, heaven forbid, or a verbal outrage that would last about two weeks, then forgotten. But if this recent information was correct…that a U.S. infantry commander had ordered the annihilation of a village of perhaps eighty to one hundred innocent men, women and children, and there was a cover-up, the story would then reverberate throughout the world and be considered a hundred-fold more atrocious than My Lai.

At eleven fifteen I closed down the computer, brushed my teeth, drained the lizard and hit the sack. Five-thirty would arrive all too soon.

And it did. The alarm on my watch went off at five-thirty three, and as because everything was exact about me, the obsessive compulsive nut that I was, I figured I had inadvertently made myself late.

At half-past six as the dark was gradually changing to dawn's early light, Adrianna was back in the downstairs kitchen putting her wonderful self-rising hoe cake in the oven. She knew how I loved those enormous pan biscuits with a slab of butter on a hefty wedge swimming in sorghum molasses. She wasn't playing fair, tempting me to stay and eat, and to hell with Lionel Byrd, CTT and Vietnam. It would be fifteen minutes before her masterpiece would come out of the oven right about the time Joey would be at our doorstep. So, he would just have to come in and have a slice with some country ham.

Adrianna smiled and tossed me a kiss as I approached the kitchen. I could see that her eyes had been a bit weepy, but her smile was like sunshine that had come out in all its glory to dry up the rain. A young couple was already lounging on the leather sofa in the sitting room with coffee and a copy of the *Gazette* in hand, waiting patiently for their 'breakfast' half of the B&B. While I was waiting for Joey I struck up a conversation.

"Hi, I'm Bruce…the 'mister' part of our little inn. Are you having a good time?"

"Yes, thank you," piped the cute twenty-something blonde vixen in the shorty pajamas with the hearts on them, bare feet tucked up under her. All the time I was standing there, for some reason I never got a good look at the guy.

"You're from Ohio, I understand. Where 'bouts?"

"Columbus. We both just graduated from Ohio State and got married. I'm Mindy," she said, "and this is…"

"Mork, right?" I jested.

She didn't get it, seeing as how she wasn't even born when Robin Williams made *nanoo-nanoo* a household word.

"No, Rich," she replied. "This is the first stop on our honeymoon."

I had wondered what all the racket downstairs last night

was all about. I could have sworn I heard a man's voice pleading for his life.

"Well," I said. "I hope the accommodations here are worthy enough. Congratulations. We feel honored you chose Wolf Laurel."

"It's beautiful here with all the flowers and spring blossoms. And we love the poster bed."

I'll bet you do.

"Say," began Rich. "We're outdoors people. I understand there are a lot of caves around here. We thought we might do some exploring today. Can you recommend one of them?"

My eyes were still having breakfast on the blonde. I'm married, not dead.

"Sir?" he followed up.

"I'm sorry…*Rich* is it? You said something?"

At that moment Adrianna popped into the room and tugged on my shirt. "Is this guy bothering you two? He's sort of a vagrant around these parts and just stops in from time to time for a handout."

"No, not at all," Mindy giggled. "He's being a very nice host, Mrs. McGowan."

"Call me Adrianna. I'll have breakfast out here in a few minutes. And you, vagabond, I need your help in the kitchen."

"Yes, dear. Well, gotta go. Nice talking with you. Enjoy the day."

Once in the kitchen, she handed me a plate of ham and gave me a bit of a smirk. "I saw the way you were flirting in there. Cute isn't she."

"Do you really think so?" I replied. "I guess she is, if you like that kind of look. But I go for the more mature, Jane Seymour look in a woman, like the woman who lives upstairs with me."

"Uh huh. Flattery will get you everywhere. You sure you don't want to stay another day and play house with me?"

"As much as I'd love to, Mrs. McGowan, I can't. Guess I need to be on my way. I just heard Joey's meat wagon roll up."

"You're not staying for breakfast? I made your favorite…good old West Virginia hoe cake."

"It's like this…I'd have one piece, then another, and before I know it, I'd miss my plane."

"That was the idea. But suit yourself, husband dear." She walked me to the door where I set down my bag. The couple was watching us.

"See you in a few days," I said, sweeping her into me.

She teased my lips with hers, unashamedly, and smiled. "You come back to me in one piece, McGowan. And don't dally." She then stuck her tender lips on the tip of my nose and onto my chin before settling back on my lips. I heard Mindy say, "Ooooweee."

I must have flushed, then turned to the young lass and said, "We're kind of still on *our* honeymoon as well. Twenty years from now, I hope you feel the same way about one another."

I then heard Joey's foot hit the steps, so I pushed out the screen door to go meet him.

"Ready?" he said.

"Yep." I squeezed Adrianna's hand and kissed her again.

"Bye, babe. Be back before you know it."

I tossed my bag behind the front seat, then opened the passenger door to see that Adrianna was still standing on the porch. We waved to one another and she turned to snap an errant Bougainvillea vine that had found its way onto the banister. She didn't look back as we drove away.

CHAPTER FIVE

I bid Brother Joey adieu, then went into the terminal through security where I passed with flying colors…no metal objects, no guns, box cutters or bombs in my shoes. All I had with me was my knapsack with three changes of shirts and jeans, nicely folded, and my shaving kit, minus the razor and aerosol cream. I could pick up the latter two items when I arrived in Saigon. I also had my valise which contained my passport, visa, a couple of pens, notepad and a micro-cassette recorder.

After blowing out of Charley West, I arrived at O'Hare an hour later at ten-forty five finding that I had an unplanned lay-over for two hours. Finally, after a three hour ten minute flight to LAX, gaining hours along the way, I landed just after two-thirty. It was kind of deja vu after that…the flight to Honolulu on an American 777, another eleven hours across the Pacific and into the Philippines, then into Tan Son Nhut. It was like flying back into time for me, back into history, back into the war zone. I would enter Vietnam about midday tomorrow which was still today. I always became confused coming and going across the International Date Line as to what day it was and especially when coming back if I would experience the same things I did the day before. So, I didn't know if I was a day younger or a day older than I was yesterday in West Virginia or had actually missed an entire day of my life. I figured if I stayed in the air traveling west forever or was it east, it wouldn't take me long and I'd be thirty again. Either that or ninety. Trying to figure all that out, being the mathematical moron that I was at reading problems in school, it would give me a headache. That's why when I saw the coast of Vietnam come into view off the left wing of the 777, I asked the flight attendant for a couple of Advils.

Or was it the reality of actually being back *In Country* again.

There are specific smells and odors that we associate with people and sometimes places we have been. It's a kind of olfactory memory our brain has. When I smell hot coffee brewing and bacon sizzling on the stove, it takes me back to my childhood and mornings at the McGowan homestead. And I remembered all too well the smells of Vietnam, especially out in the boonies. Back home when I would smell wood fires or cow dung in the meadows, my brain returned to the Montagnard villages and hamlets in the Vietnam highlands. There were also the smells of certain perfumes I picked up from passersby in the Virginia malls that reminded me of the street girls up and down Tu Do Street in Saigon who propositioned every GI for a thousand piasters (ten bucks American). The goods they sold came with free Saigon Tea and something else one didn't wish to take home to his wife.

The last time I disembarked from the aircraft at Tan Son Nhut, I set foot on the concrete where other green American soldiers in spanking new, jungle fatigues and unscuffed canvass boots stood looking scared and lost in a strange and ravaged land. Now, I was back and it felt like *I* was lost...lost somewhere in time. In a faintly familiar but different land.

Once inside the terminal, I was herded with others to customs where military types carried AK-47s and wore red stars on their caps and shiny helmets. It seemed all too wrong, considering the last time I went through, they were American GIs with MP armbands and M-16s. After handing a rather impudent-looking soldier my passport and visa, he put the evil eye on me, comparing my mug with the photo in his hand.

"What your business here?"

I started to reply "What business is it of yours?", but thought the better of it. I didn't need to spend my first hour in a Socialist Republic of Vietnam interrogation room.

"I'm in the clothing business and will be meeting a representative of my company here. But I also intend to do a little sight-seeing," I lied. Well, the last part of that was not a lie. I did intend to do some touring and was anxious to see what the commies had done to Saigon.

He gave me a shit-eating grin like I was just another ex-GI who wanted to reminisce his days in 'Nam and get all teary-eyed about his comrades that his predecessors had killed…just before the last of us were booted in disgrace in 1975. With a flick of his hand he shoved my papers back to me and jerked his head to his right for me to move on. My first encounter with a commie snot. I was sure it wouldn't be my last.

After I had cleared customs, I exited the terminal to hail a cab. And that's when the odors of Southeast Asia hit my nostrils. I was not disappointed; it still smelled as I remembered…dank, fishy, pungent. A kid on a cyclo, which is a three-wheeler bike with a seat for two in back, stopped in front of me, but I motioned for him to move on. And then a white Hyundai taxi quickly replaced him at the curb. I opened the rear passenger's door and tossed in my ruck.

The driver was also straight out of the circuit board of my memory…five feet tall, a hundred pounds, black shaggy hair, pruned face and an ear-to-ear grin that revealed not more than five teeth. As soon as I shut the door, he started on me.

"You ex-GI?" I nodded.

"You come back to see old girlfriend?" The grin widened even more.

I shook my head and scowled at him.

Every bit sixty years of age, he was nosy as hell. Maybe he felt if he became my chum I would slip him an extra five. American money was all I had on me which is like gold in Vietnam. At least it used to be. I had no idea what the exchange rate was now.

"Where you go?"

"Hotel Beaufain, and please don't take me from one end of Saigon to the other to get there."

He slowed the cab to a near stop and turned around. "No say Saigon. They be angry. Other GIs say *Saigon* and police push them around."

"Right," I replied with disgust and turned my head.

"I too Army long time ago. South Vietnamese Army. I sergeant. They put me in jail two years. Wife leave with boy. I not see again ever."

"I'm sorry," I said. "I'm sure it was hard for you." I was now beginning to loosen up on him.

He nodded and I thought I saw him wipe a tear from his cheek. The traffic was as crazy as I remembered, except now there were more cars…mostly Chinese or Korean made. But the bicycles were still there, hundreds of them zipping along inches apart. As well as cyclos and lambrettas. Surprisingly they weren't running into one another. It all seemed like some mechanical, choreographed parade where each knew where the other was and what turns each would be making. The police and commie military were on nearly every corner, watching and waiting, like they expected at any time there would be trouble.

The cabbie spit out his window. "They all pigs. Look. Very important they think. I kill them all if I could."

I was starting to like my driver; but then again I wondered if he was just playing me, thinking I was buying his mush so that I would more readily empty my wallet on him. But there *was* something earnest about him. I've learned through the years to read people and what they're telling me through their non-verbal behaviors as well as their dialogue. And I've learned that whatever their nationality or ethnicity, people are the same. It didn't take me long to determine that he actually was being straight-up.

"I'm sure you're proud of your service, Mr....Nguyen," I said, checking out his name on the dash. "I cung tu hao duoc phuc vu o day."

He grinned like a Cheshire cat. "Ah, you remember Vietnam words. That good."

"Just a few words. If you don't use it, you lose it."

I don't think he understood that saying. He just gave me a blank look and nodded.

"Okay, GI. Hotel Beaufain there."

As he pulled into the curb he just about clipped a bicyclist. The woman on the bike stopped to chew his ass and then moved on. Mr. Nguyen then hopped out to get my door for me.

"How much?" I asked.

He shook his head. "No. No money. My favor. For old days."

"No, Ong Nguyen. You have a living to make. How much?"

He shook his head again and grinned.

I then reached out to shake his hand and enclosed a twenty dollar bill in his grip. He bowed three, maybe four times and said, "Too much. Only ten anyway."

"Go get you some Saigon tea from one of the ladies down the street."

Nguyen just kept grinning and nodding, then said, "Be careful, GI."

"That I will, Mr. Nguyen," I said as I turned to walk toward the hotel entrance.

The lobby of Hotel Beaufain showed its age, but did have a large brass and crystal chandelier, tasteful, but tattered red drapes on the windows and what appeared to be a piss-stained marble floor. A smelly fleabag if I ever saw one. I knew the French word *beau* meant good, but unsure about fain…maybe *god*. As I continued looking around, there were bums sleeping in a couple of the corners and a tot lying in the middle of the floor naked while his mother was changing his diaper. Then she just laid the crappy mess on a table and left. So, maybe Beaufain stood for *Good God!*

A few of the Vietnamese guests moving about were dressed in Westernized garb such as New York Yankees shirts and blouses with *Nike* logos. One buxom young lady was wearing a shirt that said *Guess*, which reminded me of the time I was in San Francisco and saw a chesty gal wearing the same shirt. As I passed her I said "Implants?" Which nearly got my face slapped. So it seemed that the whole world had become logo loco. But I also saw women wearing the traditional ao dai look which is a colorful, sexy-silky look where the dress is slit all the way up to the thigh on either side and flowing with the breeze over the woman's white silken bottoms that go down to her ankles. And then they complete the look with high heels. I stopped to set down my bag a moment to admire a young co (girl) or two for old time's sake.

The desk clerk was an older woman with a hard, ultra-narrow face that looked as if it had been compressed by a Suzanne Somers thigh master and a set of upper teeth that protruded far beyond her lower lip, whether or not her mouth was open or closed. She could eat corn through a picket fence.

I approached the desk and said, "I believe I have a reservation here. The name is McGowan."

She looked at me with frozen black eyes, offering no smile, and said "Magow. I don't see."

"It's McGowan," I said again, spelling it for her this time. *Learn to speak English.*

"Okay. One night, right?"

"Yes."

"Okay. That be one hundred ninety American dollars."

"You're kidding, of course," I replied. "For one night in this place?"

She then looked around the lobby as though it were the Taj Mahal and said, "You no like? Then you try other hotel. They more."

I sighed. Then I began shelling out cash. That left me with just under five hundred. Byrd would hear about this when I got back. *He* sure as hell wouldn't stay in a dump like this one. I thought since this was Eagle One's deal, I'd be in the lap of luxury for the night at the Hotel Rex or the Sofitel I saw on the way in.

"Does a jar of Vaseline come with the room?" I asked, plunking down the cash.

"Vaseline?"

"Never mind." I picked up the money and gave her ten twenties, then held out my hand for the ten spot. She reached out and shook it.

"Don't I have change coming?"

"You want change?" She obviously thought the ten dollars was her tip.

I sighed again. "No, I guess not. Don't spend it all in one place."

"You in 715 on seventh floor. Stairs over there."

"You don't have an elevator?"

"Elevator over there." She pointed in the opposite direction.

"Good," I replied. I then picked up my bag and valise and began walking away.

"Elevator broken," she added, which stopped me in my tracks.

"Broken," I repeated.

"No work for three weeks."

"You're *really* going to hear about this, Birdman," I said under my breath and continued walking toward the stairs.

I was pretty beat anyway from the twenty-some hour trip and had a case of both the red eye and the red ass. After reaching the top step, out of breath and sweating profusely, since the hotel's air conditioning obviously wasn't working as well, I found my room three doors down on the right. As soon as I unlocked and opened the door, the gagging stench of Nuoc Mam hit my nasal passages. The last guest had obviously been cooking with the same nasty fish sauce that I had inhaled in villages for nearly a year, swearing that I would never taste or smell again. That's what I get for swearing. The room itself was adequate and actually had a bathroom. Clean, however, was another story…one that I don't care to describe. The bed was of mobile home quality…like lying on a sway-back camel, but smelling worse. But I didn't care. I set my bag down, crashed onto it and the lights went out in less than fifteen seconds.

It seemed like only five minutes had lapsed when the phone rang…rather rudely I might add. I picked up the receiver and offered a very weak "Hello."

"Mr. McGowan?"

"Y…yes."

"My name is Thanh. I am glad you made it here."

I saw that it was dark outside *and* inside my room. "What…time is it?"

"It is eight o'clock. You have been asleep?"

"Not long." Actually it *had* been three hours.

"Would you meet me downstairs for dinner or a cocktail?" His English was nearly perfect. Maybe better than mine.

"I'll splash some water on my face and be right down," I replied.

The water smelled and tasted foul which reinforced the fact that my opinion of the place was definitely not improving. I sat on the edge of the bed for a moment and went over the questions and notes I had written down on the plane to see if there was anything else I could think of to ask Secret Asian Man. Somewhere in my head I started to hear Johnny Rivers singing. I remember going into a Vietnamese village one day where some kid living in a hooch had somehow acquired a tape recorder and an 8 Track tape of Rivers' song, *Secret Agent Man,* and he played it incessantly. I had thought long and hard about whether to go inside and put a bullet in the machine.

I locked my door and then began meandering down the flight of stairs to the lobby where I found the bar. Seeing as how I was the only man of European descent in the room, the smallish Asian man about my age with a pencil thin mustache and dressed in matching khaki shirt and trousers approached me.

"Mr. McGowan?" He held out his hand.

"That would be me."

We shook hands and as he bowed slightly, so did I.

"I am Thanh. Have you eaten?"

"Actually, I can't remember when I did eat last. Yesterday? What day is this?"

He laughed and said, "It is Saturday night. Perhaps we should get you something."

As my stomach had growled obnoxiously a couple of times while we were standing there, it agreed with the idea.

"Shall we?" I directed my hand toward the dining room and followed him in.

After a couple of small goblets of plum wine, our young server communicated only in Vietnamese and with Mr. Thanh. I assumed that she assumed I only spoke English.

Thanh ordered only a shrimp cocktail and I told the co in the best Vietnamese I remembered, "Hu tieu kho (noodle soup)" She smiled, bowed and turned heel.

"Ah, I didn't realize you speak Vietnamese," Thanh said. "You were here as a soldier?"

"I was. Special Forces in II Corps."

"Then I thank you. And many of our South Vietnamese patriots who remain here under the scrutiny of the Hanoi government thank you."

I nodded my welcome. "You speak English remarkably well, Mr. Thanh. Apparently you didn't pick it up from the GIs."

He took a sip of his wine and nodded. "I was schooled as a young boy in the United States. My father was a chemical engineer and worked for DuPont in Delaware. The language I learned was English, although we spoke Vietnamese at home."

"Then how did you get here?"

"When we saw what was happening in this country in 1968, I begged my father and mother to allow me to come here to join up with the South Vietnamese Army. Father was resistant, but also feeling the same as me, reluctantly agreed to let me go. I was twenty anyway and going to school away at Yale. I could make my own decisions. When I arrived, I was offered a commission as a trung uy (First Lieutenant), but I told the Army I wanted to come in as a Private and work my way up. I was a senior sergeant, trung si, in the Kim Long 11th Infantry Regiment in 1975 when the war ended."

"I know that regiment. My *A Team* worked with its leadership."

"Then you and I served in the same area of operations," Thanh remarked.

"In and around Kontum Province," I added.

As we were talking, I looked around at the other tables to take account of the faces of our fellow patrons. There didn't appear to be anyone that resembled the Vietnamese Gestapo interested in the conversation between a Thanh and American. About three tables over, two scraggily-looking Caucasian men who had just sat down were conversing loudly over their bottles of Ba Mui Ba. They were either contractors or ex-GIs who had fallen off the world and returned to Vietnam for some kind of illicit financial opportunity.

"Are we safe to talk here?" I asked Thanh.

"I believe so, but suggest we keep our voices out of range of our neighbors."

I immediately liked Thanh and as I would probably be spending several days with him, traveling to the highlands, I was very much at ease with him.

"What do you do here, Mr. Thanh?"

"You mean besides being persecuted for my past service with the South Vietnamese Army? My wife and I own a small business…a jewelry store. Each time I travel out of country, I am shaken down when I return. If I have gold or diamonds on me that I have purchased from South Africa or the States, the police confiscate it, making me then go to their headquarters to later retrieve it. And when I do, sometimes half of it is missing."

"A shame. Then why do you stay in the business? Sounds like you are losing money."

"I still manage a meager living and am allowed to do so

as long as the police get their self-obtained payoff. I still love this country and even though I spent the first twenty years of my life in the U.S., I've always considered Vietnam as my home."

"Do you get back to the States much?"

Occasionally," he said. "Again, that is where I buy some of my jewelry. Both my parents are now dead, but I do manage to get to D.C. every so often to see my old friend, Berryhill."

I winced as Thanh mentioned the sergeant-major's name. "Mr. Thanh, I have some bad news about him. Four days ago Mr. Berryhill was found dead at his home."

Thanh's mouth dropped open and he buried his face in his hands. "How…how did he die?"

"He was murdered, Mr. Thanh. Hanged. His death was made to look like a suicide."

Thanh was visibly shaken and tears glistened in his eyes. "So, they got to him."

"*Somebody* got to him."

"That makes me sad and angry at the same time. He told me that many of his friends from his old company with whom he stayed in touch had died. Some mysteriously. Some murdered. Others of his friends no longer wanted to talk with him, afraid for themselves and their families. Many had been warned."

"I do know that. My boss provided me with the statistics."

"This makes it all the more important that you get what you need on this former commander."

"Do you know his name?"

"Yes, it is Jack Randall."

At last, I thought. At last somebody told me the name of this guy.

"And did Sergeant-major Berryhill ever learn what happened to this Jack Randall?"

Thanh settled back in his chair and chewed on his lower lip. "He only said he *thought* he knew, but I believe he *absolutely* knew. He said the least he talked about this man, the better. I could see the fear in his face when he did speak about him."

Our food came rather quickly. The young server placed my bowl in front of me and the aroma of the noodle soup delighted my nostrils. I waited for my dinner companion to begin tasting his shrimp, but he didn't seem interested in his food. The news of Berryhill's death had apparently killed his appetite.

"Please," he said. "Begin. Don't wait for me."

I took a few bites with my chopsticks, finding it a bit difficult to eat the slippery noodles and soup without a spoon. But other patrons in the restaurant eating the same soup seemed to be doing okay. Even a child perhaps six at the table next to ours. It set me to wondering about something. American mothers feed their babies with tiny little forks. Do Asian mothers feed their babies with toothpicks?" However, this wasn't the time for such frivolous thoughts.

"Tell me what you know about Dak Trang, Mr. Thanh," I said in a low voice.

He took another sip and picked out one of the shrimp from his goblet. "I was an intelligence sergeant in the G2 section of my regiment. I had met with Sergeant Berryhill several times at Regimental Headquarters to compare notes on the current enemy situation. He was a G2 sergeant as well attached from his brigade to Charlie Company. And so we became friends. Sometimes we got together in the evenings to have a few beers and a cigarette and talk about what was happening in the States.

"One morning in the fall of 1972, I went out on an operation with the regiment and we heard on our section radio that a VC Montagnard village had been attacked by an American infantry company the evening before and all the people in the village had been killed…maybe eighty or ninety. Our unit then met up with that unit, Charlie Company, outside the village and I saw my major and the American captain off in a tree line laughing and shaking hands. That's when I saw Sergeant Berryhill standing alone, wiping his eyes. And that is when he told me his company had swept the village, firing at everything living with their automatic weapons and grenade launchers. There was no reason for it, he said. No one had fired a shot from the village. As a matter of fact, when the chief and others saw the Americans coming, they came out to greet the soldiers with open arms and smiles. Sergeant Berryhill then heard from another sergeant that the village was not VC after all.

"It was a week later he found out that my major had paid Captain Randall the equivalent of ten thousand dollars in piasters to destroy the village and all the people in it. The major had fabricated the intelligence information about the village being Vietcong, because years before, the Degar people had migrated in and built the village on a parcel of what used to be his land. It had rich fields and the major's family had grown rice and cane there. When the major's father died at Dien Bien Phu in 1954, his mother then died soon after of tuberculosis. The land fell vacant and the house lay in ruins after the major went into the army. It was not long until the Montagnard tribes came in and took over much of the land east of Dak To District. Not long after that, Major Bao was promoted to Colonel."

I shook my head and took a deep breath, then laid down my chopsticks. Suddenly, I was no longer hungry. "Why didn't Bao just order his own troops to attack the village? He would have saved himself some money."

"It would have raised suspicion, considering that someone would know that Bao had owned the land. He was afraid it would be traced back to him."

I re-settled deeply into my chair, laid my head back and closed my eyes. "What inhumane atrocities we human beings will commit for mere gain of wealth and power."

"That is not all," Thanh continued. "In that village was a small Catholic church and hospital. A French priest lived there, teaching the people about God, Jesus and Mary. Three Swedish nuns took in and nursed those in the village who had tuberculosis. They were killed as well. Their remains were among those found in separate graves."

"And the young girl I learned about, whose mother hid her?" I asked.

"When we travel north, we will meet with her. Her name is Siu Ramhan. She has become an advocate for her people. I will take you to her and to the site of the destroyed village. We will start out tomorrow and should be there the next day."

"Good. I'll need your handwritten statement on what you just told me, and hers as well. Can she write?"

"She can not only write, but can write and speak four languages: her tribal dialect, French, Vietnamese and English. All very fluently. I have met her twice and found her to be a most impressive young lady. Sadly, she is frequently persecuted. She has been imprisoned, beaten, raped and received death threats from the area police. She also must keep up her guard as some of the colonel's men have made unsuccessful attempts on her life. Did I mention that the colonel lives just a few kilometers away from her adopted village in his old house?"

"I see. So, how do we get up there?"

"My car. We will leave at first light."

"Okay." I then stood and shook his hand. "Your information will be extremely important to the people back in Washington, D.C. It may also serve to save others' lives. Have you written your statement about what you know?"

"I have. Perhaps tomorrow when we are traveling to the north, you will have an opportunity to read it. I hope it will contain everything you need."

"You seem like a very thorough man, Mr. Thanh." I paused and then added, "I'm sorry about your friend, Sergeant Berryhill."

Thanh nodded and I thought I caught a tear forming in one of his eyes. "Tomorrow, then, Mr. McGowan."

I reached for my wallet to pay the bill, but he said, "I have already told the young woman to see me about payment."

"Thank you, Mr. Thanh, and I hope you have a good evening." I then felt rather badly for not having eaten even half of the noodle soup.

CHAPTER SIX

By the time I hit the top stair on the seventh floor it was after ten. And when I stopped in front of my door to put the key in the lock, I found it ajar. Instinctively, I reached under my left arm pit for my Glock, of course finding it was not there. I was going to feel naked without it. Slowly, I pushed open the door and switched on the light. The first thing I saw was my travel bag lying on the bed, its contents completely emptied out. But my valise was gone. The only things I had of value in it were my tape recorder and a nice, antique fountain pen my mom gave me when I went off to the university. I was pissed about that. I still had my tablet in hand containing the aforementioned notes. And thank goodness I also still had my new-fangled Nikon mini-digital camera in my pocket. I had paid over $400 for that. I had also kept my passport and visa with me. Either somebody knew I had arrived or some scum-bucket burglar who was looking for money and valuables decided to break into my room. Maybe the lady behind the desk with the fangs was in cahoots with a burglary gang and the rich American that I was, I could be a profitable target.

I thought I would be wasting my time by going downstairs to complain and demand a house detective, if there was one. Anyway, I didn't want to climb back up those stairs again. So, if all they got was the $50 valise and my sentimental pen, so be it. I decided to just fortify the room a bit more while I slept by shoving a straight-back chair up under the doorknob. I also made sure the window was locked just in case a cat burglar tried walking along the eight inch ledge and getting in that way. I further snapped the handle of a broom in half and wedged a two foot piece of it between the top and lower window casing. The added security would help me sleep a little sounder.

I must have slept hard because it felt like I had been injected with anesthesia before an operation and the next thing I knew I was opening my eyes a second later. Actually seven hours had lapsed. I guess I didn't realize how wasted I was. Checking the chair against the door and the window, I then knew I had not been murdered in my sleep.

What came out of the spigot in the bath tub looked like what went into the commode. I decided to forego brushing my teeth and instead, stuck nearly a whole pack of Dentine in my mouth. From my travel bag I pulled a fresh pair of jeans and what used to be a starched, neatly-folded khaki shirt with shoulder epaulets…that is until some inconsiderate burglar dumped it out in a wad on the bed.

Around seven I received a call from Thanh on my room phone and he said he would be out on the street in fifteen minutes. Not wanting to spend another moment in a room that still reeked of nuoc mam and was crawling with roaches, I closed the door and began my trek down the long flight of stairs. When I got to the landing at the third floor, I passed a kid about twenty who had on sunglasses and dark, green matching shirt and pants. Lo and behold, sticking out of his chest pocket was the gold fountain pen my mom and given me. As he was coming up while I was descending, I quickly stepped in front of him.

"You speak English, boy?"

"I speak. What it to you, asshole."

"Well, sonny boy, that's my pen you have in your shirt."

"You full of shit, man. Move out of way!"

When he attempted to side-step me and continue on, I grabbed a handful of thick, black hair and slammed his head into the stairwell wall. He then tried to take a swing at me; but I stunned him with a karate-style chop from my left hand just below his left ear, following in a split second with the same kind of chop from my right onto the bridge of his nose. Chop! Chop! He crashed immediately onto the steps out cold, after which I pulled the pen from his pocket.

Oops.

Well, when it was in his pocket, it *looked* like my pen. Unfortunately, it wasn't. Unfortunate for the both of us. *He* had fallen victim to a McGowan hand job…and *I* was still missing my pen. As his lights were still out, I didn't want to wake him to apologize…so I patted him on the head. "Sorry, fella. Sleep it off."

Drats. As I had quickly jumped to the wrong conclusion and cracked the guy's head, I had also just cracked my visage of infallibility. I can be wrong *once* in a while, can't I?

Quickly, I approached the lobby desk, tossed my key on the counter and took off. When I passed through the front door and into the street I saw that Thanh was already waiting behind a couple of taxi cabs, thank goodness. I didn't need to be around when the kid woke up and called the cops. I wasn't sure how much time I'd do for assault and didn't need to find out.

I tossed my bag in the back seat of Thanh's Kia and he immediately pulled away from the curb. Thirty some years ago, Saigon was a war-torn city decorated with sandbags and concertina wire and where the streets were jumping with

American and South Vietnamese soldiers in jungle and tiger fatigues, respectively, driving jeeps and deuce-and-a-halves. Now the street scene still had its hectic and chaotic pace what with the cyclos, bikes and automobiles, but I can actually say the city became beautiful. There were now high-rise office buildings, some of which were fifteen or more stories up, and modern street lights, signs and neon marquees over colorful shops and restaurants that broadcast a Westernized influence. The city actually exuded, paradoxically so, an aura of capitalism and materialism. I supposed what I was seeing was mostly just a façade where it came to the communist ideal, to tell the world this is *who* we are on paper, not what we *actually* are in practice.

For the first hour or so we conversed a bit about his years in the United States and that he had thought many times about returning there for good. But Thanh said he remained in Vietnam as an activist, besides a husband and father, as part of a political underground that was growing in strength and numbers day by day. Perhaps one day his covert group would win over enough converts, which were now in the hundreds, to oust the communists and begin free elections. His cohorts met in secret in backrooms of stores, barbershops and restaurants in small groups in and around Ho Chi Minh City in different locations each time, discussing how best to make that happen. But the government knew who he was and had been watching not only his house, but tailed him every place he went…which made me wonder if they were on *our* tail. He had been hauled in for questioning on numerous occasions and several times received threats against his family. However, as he was both careful *and* sly, the police had been unable to put a case of conspiracy together to lock him away for good. He was surprised they hadn't, considering some of his friends had been caught in unlawful assembly. But none had squealed.

"One thing we need, like every organization does, is money. We are getting some from groups within the United States, Canada and Australia who want to see democracy return to this country. But we need more than just money. We need the support of freedom-loving people all over. If a major communist empire like the Soviet Union can go down and cease to exist, it can happen in a tiny country like Vietnam."

I noticed that Thanh had been continuously checking his rear view mirror and supposed that this was a daily ritual with him. "I am sure someone has been watching me...watching us both...since we left the hotel," he said. "I have not seen anyone as yet because of the heavy traffic, but they are there, believe me. I ask that you also look in your mirror as we go along."

And so it was just north of Phan Thiet that I spotted the jeep that had been following us. It tracked us for about twenty minutes and then moved in on our rear bumper. After we heard two quick blasts of the siren, Thanh pulled off at a roadside market where there were scores of people who would be witnesses to any unjust treatment by the police.

"Another day of harassment," he said, watching in his side mirror as two military types approached from the rear. "I was not speeding so there will be nothing they can arrest me for."

The men overtook our car on either side and stood with their hands on their guns. The thin, cocky-looking cop who resembled an Asian Barney Fife shouted something at Thanh which I couldn't understand. Thanh answered him and I was able to make out a couple of his words which translated to "my friend" and "trip."

Then the little bastard looked past Thanh and turned his

attention to me. "So, you American, huh?"

"That's what my birth certificate says, Ho Chi Minh."

"You try to be funny, yes? Like Bob Hope."

"Funny, yes. But I'll never be a Bob Hope. Maybe a Robin Williams."

"Don't know Robin Williams," he said.

"Yeah, you remember. He was here some time back. Used to say, *Good morning, Vee-et-nam*!!!"

"What you do here?" he barked.

"Are you asking me what I am doing here in Vietnam, bozo?"

"What is *bozo*?"

"That is English for *sir*," I replied.

"I think you should be in shame coming to this country. You look like ex-GI American. We kick your ass out in 1975. Defeat great American Army." And then he laughed, which prompted his sidekick who had a face resembling a frog to laugh as well.

I knew he was trying to get me riled up so that he would have a reason to arrest me, but I still had to put the little bastard in his place. It's just something I never can resist. Calmly, I replied, "Well, the reason we left was that we were tired and bored of killing all you pricks. What was it…over a million? I probably even had *your* old man in my sights before I pulled the trigger." Here I was being the Ugly American again.

And then the little asshole got a bit huffy with me and walked around to my side. "You get out of car and show me passport!"

I did as instructed, pulling both my passport and visa

from my knapsack. A gaggle of mama-sons and kids stopped what they were doing at the market and began watching. Barney saw them and then knew that he wouldn't be able to bash the head of an American butt hole with all the witnesses around. But then after looking at my picture, he showed it to his toad partner and they both began laughing like a couple of hyenas who had just corralled the village idiot.

As I stood there in the stinking-hot sun which was now causing me to sweat like a pig, I sought to end our little conversation. "Have you now had all the fun you can stand, moron?"

Barney gave me a puzzled look. "What is moron?"

"Another English word of respect which means I think you are a very smart, like Confucius and Mao Tse-tung."

Thanh turned his head so that Barney could not see the smile breaking out.

Barney grinned and nodded to Kermit. "He think I smart?" And then he laughed.

"Just a tad smarter than a maggot," I replied.

Barney's grin quickly faded to a scowl. Obviously, he knew what a maggot was. He then threw my passport and visa back at me, hitting me in the chest with them. "I think you *not* respect me. You try to be funny again. Why you with this man?" He pointed to Thanh.

"This man is my tour guide," I replied. "I am just here to see the country again."

"No believe you. This man is enemy of government. He not in tour business."

"Then think what you want. I'm traveling to the Annam Highlands to see the place where I was based thirty years ago."

"Where my people run you out."

I sighed. "Whatever, genius. Can we go now?"

Barney looked at the toad and then back at me. "You go now, but we watch. We have police in all places."

"Good. I'll be sure to give them a finger when I see them." Which I demonstrated to him.

He didn't respond, but gave me a parting glare as he turned toward his jeep. I think he understood the international 'up yours' symbol.

Thanh allowed the cops to pull away and then he merged onto the road behind them. "Okay, Bob Hope," he said. "You could've handled that a little better without the antagonism."

"I was actually being nice compared to how I usually am. So, obviously, you're well known by the police everywhere."

"Yes. Not just in Ho Chi Minh City. The police and military show pictures of me and my fellow dissidents all over. It will be no surprise when one day we all disappear without a trace."

"I'm sure your family stays worried."

"My wife and sons understand and stand behind me. My oldest son is very active in our group."

"You must be proud."

"I am proud of both of my sons."

I nodded. "How much further up to Qui Nhon?"

"About two hundred miles further along Highway 1. We will stay the night with an old friend."

"Good. I remember how beautiful the beaches were with the black mountains in the background. Hopefully, your friend will provide us better lodging than I had last night."

He smiled. "Not to worry."

*   *   *   *

At just after seven, we pulled off of 1 A onto a nicely-maintained dirt road that traveled parallel with the sea alongside a host of picturesque palms flanked by lovely slipper orchids, sugar cane and banana grass. Momentarily, a white villa of French design with a red, tiled roof that over-looked the Bai Dai Beach on the Pacific came into view. Not only did I realize Thanh's friend had some money, but true to his word, I was sure to have a comfortable bed for the night. But then I saw a small house at the rear that appeared to be servant quarters and it suddenly appeared to me that the friend could be the caretaker and I may be sleeping in the stable.

"If your friend lived in a place like this on Malibu Beach, I'd say it would be something close to a ten million dollar estate," I commented.

"This was built with my friend's family money. Mr. Huynh was a senator during the fifties and sixties. In 1975 when the North took over, they tried to take the place from him. But he was spared by a high-raking general from Hanoi who happened to be his cousin."

"Kind of the same thing as when during our Civil War General Sherman took Atlanta and Savannah. He knew a couple of ministers here and there in Georgia towns…even had some relatives in the south, and was selective about the places he burned and razed. If Mr. Huynh communicates with his cousin and others, is he also aligned with you and

83

your organization?"

"He is sympathetic to us, but does not participate in our work."

"But you are considered a dissident. Does he not then risk persecution and losing his property?"

"I have been careful not to let anyone know…even my friends in the underground…that we are associated. I have also been watching behind me to see if I have been followed each time I come here."

"Yeah," I replied. "I noticed the jack rabbit turns you made that last mile on the highway. I didn't see anyone on your tail."

Thanh entered through a gate over which were written the words *Nha Cua Hy Vong*, which means House of Hope, and pulled up in front of the house. Did I mention that it was a magnificent estate with manicured landscaping complete with sculptured evergreens and a gigantic fountain of swans with water shooting out of their mouths?

Two children dressed in loose, white linen clothing, who had heard our car approaching, ran from the wide porch toward us. Behind them at the double front door stood a man with white hair and chin whiskers looking ironically like Uncle Ho. He then followed the children to the car and put out his hand.

"Ah, chao mung ban," he said to Thanh. He had a kind face with a smile to match.

"My friend, Huynh," Thanh responded. "This is my friend Bruce McGowan from America."

I walked over to Mr. Huynh, bowed and shook his extended hand. He dropped his head and bowed in return.

"Hello, Mr. McGowan," he greeted me in sparkling

English. "My grandchildren." He then waved his hand in their direction. The boy and girl, perhaps five and eight, came to us and also bowed their little heads. Lots of bowing going on.

"Welcome to my house. Would you come in for some food and wine?"

"Yes, thank you. Seems that we last ate some banh bao at a roadside café around noon. Needless to say, it didn't go very far."

He laughed. "You Americans with healthy appetites are not used to our small portions. I have tasted your hamburgers and pizza, though, and I must say they are filling…but good."

Suddenly, I was having a Big Mac attack just at the mention of the word *hamburger*.

The children watched me curiously, and as I towered over Thanh and Huynh who stood no more than five-three, I knew they didn't see many men my size. The boy stood up close to my left leg and measured off his head with his hand to my waist. Mr. Huynh eyed him sternly and motioned him away.

"My son and his wife left the children with me for two days. They are in Ho Chi Minh City on business."

"They are very lovely children, Mr. Huynh. I have no grandchildren as yet, but look forward to the day my daughter will drop her children at *my* doorstep."

He nodded, smiled and held out his hand toward the door. "Please come in."

We all shed our shoes just inside the door and continued on into the foyer in our stocking feet. I found the house very warm, but certainly not as hot as it still was out of doors. However, there were ceiling fans throughout that at least kept the air moving.

The interior of the house was elegant as I had expected. The stucco walls were dressed with several original oils and numbered prints, mostly from China and Japan. The floors, a combination of rich hardwoods and marble, glistened royally. I also took account of several colorful vases along with statues of Asian figures including a large Buddha with a well-rubbed belly. Paradoxically, however, modern furniture and appliances gave the house a Westernized look.

As we walked further into the house, Mr. Huynh pointed out to me the room in which I would be staying and then we moved to the dining room.

"I was not sure when to expect you, but held dinner for all of us until you arrived. You may wash your hands in the toilet room at the end of the hall and I will have my servant set a place for you at the table."

It was the first bathroom I had been in anywhere in the country of Vietnam, including my last tour there, that was nicer than most any in which I had done my business in America. It even had a marble bidet for washing one's behind. After scouring my hands with the lavender soap and running my pocket comb through my salt and pepper hair, becoming ever more salt, I thought myself presentable enough for the dinner table.

As soon as I took my seat, a lovely young woman cascading about the room with blithesome grace immediately set a bowl of rich, steamy broth containing won tons in front of me. As was the custom, I kept both hands in my lap on my napkin until the host nodded and took the first sip of his soup. Then the children began to sip theirs.

Dinner in Mr. Huynh's house was an elegant, even religious experience complete with piped in, traditional

Vietnamese music played on a moon lute, a conch trumpet and bamboo pipes. A woman singer's own beautiful pipes accompanied the instruments with a variety of sweet runs. Mr. Huynh smiled and nodded a few times without speaking, glancing often at his grandchildren. He had a generous, God-like spirit about him…a kind of royal caste.

I learned that Mr. Huynh's family had obtained its wealth from the coal business of all things which was an education for me. I think of coal country as Pennsylvania and West Virginia, and the nations of South Africa and Poland. He spoke fondly about his ancestors, how they had worked hard and were self-made. He had been fortunate to have inherited what he had and was afraid that one day when his Hanoi cousin died that the communists would come in and take his place away, claiming that he and his family were dissidents and traitors.

His wife had died a few years back and the only person who lived there with him was his servant, Co Dong, the aforementioned nymph. She prepared his meals and kept the house in exchange for a modest salary and board. He assured us with a wink that these were the only services she rendered.

As I sat at the table, sipping my wine and savoring the succulent quail (trung cut lon),I had to reach far back into my memory to pull out deeply-stored information regarding Asian customs and protocol at the dinner table to assure I committed no faux pas. Like inhaling my food since I was so damned hungry and failing to breathe between bites. I kept my feet flat on the floor so that the bottoms did not point toward anyone at the table. I made sure that my left hand remained in my lap, never on the table and never taken to my mouth. Neither would I touch anyone with it. In their culture, the left hand is used only for wiping one's self after one's business is done in one's privy. And speaking of the dinner table, no matter how good or bad the food was, one must leave a single helping of each item in the serving dish. If I took the last piece of meat, it told the host that he didn't have enough to feed me. If I left two or more pieces or didn't eat every morsel on my plate, I insulted the host by insinuating that the food was not good.

The children were delightful and stayed close to me the remainder of the evening, grinning and chattering in Vietnamese, much of which I didn't understand. I came close to committing a major faux pas that I remembered just in time. I had taken out some Dentine to give to them, but in their country, one must first ask the father, in this case the grandfather, if it was okay for them to have the gum. Then on the sly, I would give *him* the gum to give to them, which I did. And they were delighted with the gum. It was something to chew which actually had flavor.

My room was just as classy as the rest of the house, but as there was no air conditioning, the place was cooled in the evening by opening the windows, allowing the fresh sea breeze to flow in. But with the night air, the mosquitoes came. Over my poster bed was a mosquito net which would keep the little vampire bastards from sucking out my blood. It *is* one thing I intend to speak with God about. Why didn't he allow Noah to be a humanitarian and swat those two damn mosquitoes?

At ten everyone was in bed. But even as weary as I was, I didn't get right off to sleep. I thought about Adrianna and remembered that I hadn't called her as promised. I closed my eyes and her face appeared in my brain, smiling, inviting. Her beautiful eyes danced and I heard her voice in my head, soft and musical...like a lilting sonata. And I thought I caught a hint of her perfume...the kind she always dabbed behind her ears before she went to bed, on the possibility that I would be enticed. Like that would really never happen without it. She was never out of my head very long, but especially on those occasions when I was away from home. I would be sure to call her tomorrow in the early morning hours when it would be tonight there. I think I got that right.

CHAPTER SEVEN

At daybreak a rooster woke me and I thought for a moment that I was back home as a boy on our old farm in Greenbrier County. Mom was making bacon and flapjacks and Dad was stumbling around in the bathroom on the other side of my wall. But then I remembered where I was, went down the hall, took a bath and performed other bathroom chores before putting back on my jeans and khaki shirt to go to breakfast.

Mr. Huynh's maidservant had prepared porridge and some fruit which were on the table by the soy milk. But where was the coffee? I found out soon enough that our host did not drink coffee and had none in the cupboards. And there was no McDonalds or Dunkin Donuts down the street. I was going to have an awful migraine. But he did offer me some hot tea, of which I gladly partook. At least it contained some caffeine.

At eight something we bid Mr. Huynh adieu. I thanked him for his kindness and hospitality and almost committed another grave error. I started to pat the kids on the head, but quickly remembered that one never touches another's head with his hands. There was more bowing and I thought if I stayed there much longer, my back would go out. I would then walk around for three days or more looking like a human question mark.

As soon as we were in the car, I hit speed dial # 1 on my cell phone, immediately seeing there was no service. "What?" I exclaimed.

Thanh saw my exasperation and said, "There is no cell phone service up here, Mr. McGowan. If we were further south in Ho Chi Minh City, you would be within the cell tower's range and connected to an operator who would dispatch you through to the states."

"Drats! My wife will be sick with worry if she doesn't hear from me in a couple of days."

"Perhaps then we can take care of our business in no more than two or three days and have you back in Ho Chi Minh City on Wednesday."

"One would hope. So, what is the name of the village where we will meet the Degar girl?"

"We will meet her in the Montagnard church in the village at Kon Pia, east of Tan Cahn," Thanh replied.

"Is it supposed to be on a certain day and time?"

"As I understand it, she is always there unless she is out petitioning somewhere for Degar rights. But she does expect us this week and will remain close by. We will be in Pleiku by three o'clock and Tan Cahn by six. We should be at the village within another hour depending on the condition of the road."

*   *   *   *

As Thanh zipped along Highway 14, I took the time to read his statement which had been typed out and printed on three sheets of paper at the end of which he signed his name. Everything he had told me at the table in the Hotel

Beaufain was there in black and white to include the particulars of several conversations that occurred between Sergeant First Class Berryhill and him just after the massacre at Dak Trang. Thanh was both precise and succinct in his account. Captain Jack Randall and Thanh's commander, Major, now Colonel, Hung Bao, had schemed to destroy the village that sat on the Colonel's land and Sergeant Berryhill had, to his immense regret, taken part in the raid. Although it would now be hearsay without Berryhill's own testimony, Thanh's statement along with that of the Degar woman would hopefully be enough to bring Jack Randall, whoever he was and however important he was, to justice. Once he and his conspirators went down, then perhaps those remaining company members with consciences and who no longer feared for their lives would come forward. As many had also feared they would go to jail for their part in the massacre, they would be given immunity from prosecution in exchange for their testimony. At least it *should* go down that way. The Feds would be after the *big* cheese.

I folded the statement and placed it in my knapsack. Thanh nodded and told me he had another copy of the statement in a safety deposit box in case something happened to the original. I told him it would be placed directly in the hands of the man at the top. He didn't know it would be *the* man at the top.

Thanh was pretty much on target with the time. We made it to Pleiku at five minutes till five, filled up the tank, and had a bowl of rice along with some nasty meat on a stick, which could have at one time been named Rover or Miss Kitty for all I knew. I knew it wasn't beef, pork or chicken.

As we continued on out of town, I saw off to our right where I thought the 71st Evac M.A.S.H unit, the air strip and the MACV compound used to be. It was now nothing but rubble; however, a few Quonset huts remained standing. Pleiku's buildings had been beautifully refurbished. The last time I saw the French colonial masterpieces, most of them bore the horrible scars of direct fire weapons and artillery. Some had crumbled beyond repair. The city, often defended by American and Vietnamese forces, had been under siege by the North Vietnamese Army numerous times. If any good at all came out of the war, it was the massive restoration process that was undertaken to bring this colonial city and others like it back to their pre-war states.

We whizzed through Kontum in another hour and Tan Canh just as the sun began to set. Just off a road that led deeper into the highlands, peasants lined the edge of the pavement drying casaba root. And then a few hundred feet further along, we picked up the one-lane road we found to be little more than a dirt path under triple canopy jungle, much of which looked like the stuff my *A Team* hacked through with machetes from village to village. My head was rocking back and forth so hard, I banged it twice on the door frame.

"Damn!" I exclaimed. "You're sure this is the way to her village?"

"Yes. I have been there twice before. But don't worry; we have yet to go through the roughest part."

And he was right. I let out a low whistle when the roof of his Kia caught a low-hanging branch.

"I hate your having to bring your sedan into this back-country. A lot of *jeeps* would have trouble negotiating *this* terrain."

"No matter," he said. "This car has seen its better days, but it just keeps on going. I am not worried about the body…just that we don't bottom-out and put a hole in the oil pan or transmission case."

A couple of times we had to blow our horn to move a few Montagnard people off the road along with the water buffalos they were prodding with sticks. They grinned and waved as we went by. A few of the men wore old and frayed Army fatigue shirts, loose-fitting pants or loin cloths and sandals. I did see an elderly man with long, white hair wearing a pair of U.S. issued canvas jungle boots. I would have thought they had rotted off the man's feet by now. He must have only worn them on special occasions like when he was visiting his girl friend in an adjacent village.

I saw that some things didn't change. The man still made the woman trail along behind him, carrying baskets of collected firewood on their backs or crops in smaller baskets on their heads. After all, the man was *king* in his family. The woman was the work horse who carted, cooked and laid with the man at night so that he could manufacture as many babies as he could, hoping half of them would survive the scourges of tuberculosis, malaria and diphtheria. I remember going into a Montagnard village the Christmas of '69 when my *A Team* brought candy, cookies and balloons for the kids. Of course we would first give them to the village chief so that he would get all the credit. However, this time four women intercepted me before I got to the chief and grabbed the balloons, nearly ripping the skin off my hands. I could imagine the mama-son telling her old man that night, "Here's your rubber, mister. We aren't having any more brats, you hear?" And then I thought about what an 'abrasive' scenario *that* would be...for the both of them.

We did bottom out a couple of times on the ruts in the road, but thank God there was no damage. I would have hated riding a water buffalo out of those woods back to Ho Chi Minh City. Not too far along, however, the jungle seemed to go away when we came to a wide, sweeping valley. What was amazing was that even thirty plus years later I could see large bowls and depressions now covered with grass where 500 pound bombs had been dropped in B-52 Arc Light strikes. In 1970 when I flew over much of the Central Highlands, especially toward the tri-border area of Laos, Cambodia and Vietnam, the heart of the Ho Chi Minh trail, the entire landscape resembled the moon. Agent Orange had defoliated the area and hundreds of bomb craters gave the naked terrain a lunar look. What we had done to this beautiful land was tragic. I was glad to see that the area had recovered.

"It is not far now, Mr. McGowan…another three to four kilometers."

"Don't you think it's about time you called me *Bruce*, Mr. Thanh? And if you're good with that, what do I call you?"

"*Thanh* is fine. That is how most refer to me. More formally I would be Ong Thanh, but I prefer just Thanh."

"Okay, then. *Thanh* it is."

I knew we were approaching the village when a dozen or so children, mostly dressed in tank tops and shorts, began running barefooted alongside, placing their hands on the car. I'm sure they did not see many vehicles, especially automobiles, and then there was this strange white gentleman riding shotgun. In a few moments, several men appeared in the roadway ahead of us, looking much like a reception party. They appeared neither fearful nor unfriendly. Some were smiling. I thought perhaps they recognized Thanh's car since he had been there before.

In my days in the jungle that year and a half, I had never lived in or visited a Montagnard village where the people were not affable, smiling and inviting. When I was out operating with Degar soldiers, I always felt safe. Down to the man, they would give their lives for us American Special Forces soldiers. We were professional soldiers who respected them and thought enough of them to train them, fight with them and live with them, even though they were primitive non-citizens. When I was out on night missions with the 'Yard soldiers and needed to catch a couple of winks, one would be sitting vigilantly on either side of me, listening for the slightest snap of a twig. Many times I placed my life and the lives of my team in their hands. It was good to see these people again.

The men who greeted us motioned for Thanh to pull his vehicle through the bamboo gate. I wondered if they had any idea who we were, but we were welcome just the same.

"I guess since you were here before, obviously they recognize your Kia."

"It has been more than a year since I was here," he said. "But I came here with a friend in his truck." He then pointed to the northwest quadrant of the village. "The Degar woman will be in that building there. It is the church where she stays."

We dismounted the Kia and the men and children came to greet us like we were royalty. The village was thick with wood smoke where the people were cooking their evening meals of rice and fish heads. From one of the thatch-roofed hooches, all of which stood on stilts to keep the family dry during the monsoon season, I caught a whiff of the ever pungent, stomach-curdling nuc mam sauce. It was an odor that my olfactory memory never forgot and hoped would never experience again.

From the gaggle of greeters, out stepped an older man with a full head of white hair and brown skin resembling tough rawhide that had been baked for over sixty years by the merciless Vietnam sun. He said something that neither of us understood and motioned us in the direction of the Happy House, a tall centerpiece of a structure made of bamboo that towered over every other hooch in the hamlet. It was a place where the people congregated for meetings and celebrations, and where gallons of rice wine disappeared nightly. How they worked the fields all day and drank most of the night, then were out again at first light doing it all over again without missing a beat, was beyond me.

"He's inviting us in there to drink wine with them," Thanh said.

"For some kerosene, you mean. Will we not see Siu this evening?"

"It would be better to get a fresh start with her tomorrow morning. She will probably have retired by now."

Well, it *was* nearly dark and time for some serious drinking, of which if I partook, would likely leave me seriously dead.

"We must do it, you know," Thanh said. "If we didn't, it would be insulting to them."

"At the peril of being poisoned?"

He smiled. "I am sure you have poured worse than this into your stomach. Come on, my friend."

The hamlet chief, six of his elders, and Thanh and I sat cross-legged on the bamboo floor of the Longhouse around the 55 gallon drum of the rocket fuel, waiting for the man on the left of me to finish sipping through the long, plastic hose until the wine dropped below the notch on the stick. When he was done, someone would then fill the vat to the top and the next guy would have to guzzle until the notch appeared again. It was finally my turn and after I had sucked down about three minutes of the rot gut, I nearly passed out. You see, JP4 tends to cause the brain to boil after a few minutes of exposure. I quickly became *dinky dau*, or crazy in the head, and started swaying back and forth like a hypnotized cobra. I tried to steady myself with my hands, but crashed into the floor a couple of times. My antics evoked laughter among the tribesmen. But I could tell it wasn't the kind of laughter where they were making fun of me…they were laughing *with* me. It wasn't long until I was guffawing out of control. Knew it, but couldn't stop it. I attributed it to our having had no supper.

After a while, Thanh, who seemed to be in perfect control of his faculties, picked me up by the shoulders and said, "Come on, Tiger. Let's get you back to the car. Can't control your liquor, huh?"

And that's where we slept that night…me curled up in the fetal position in the tiny back seat, and Thanh, reclined in the front passenger's seat.

*   *   *   *

The morning sun pierced through the side glass about six-thirty like a laser beam, rudely penetrating my eyelids. Somehow I managed to pull myself up to where I could see that the passenger side door was standing open and Thanh was about four feet from the car heaving his guts out. When I see someone retching like that and then catch a whiff of the vomitus, it causes *me* to gag. So, I turned my head and covered my nose with my sleeve to be sure *my* stomach didn't end up in the back seat. However, I was also sure that a rat had somehow crawled into my mouth during the night and died, and the smell and taste of it was more than I could stand. From my pocket I pulled the Dentyne and shoved three sticks in.

"So, friend Thanh, the shit last night didn't affect you at all, huh?"

Still on all fours, with a sweep of his hand he waved me off. I'm pretty sure his middle finger was extended. After a few moments, he slowly raised himself to his feet and allowed his body to crash into the side of the car. "In the glove compartment, Bruce, is a .38 Special. Would you kindly get it out and shoot me?"

I laughed which nearly caused me to swallow my gum, further gagging me, but my cookies managed to stay in my gut. Crawling out of the back seat, I then pulled my travel bag out and began rifling through it until I found my toothpaste and brush. The gum had quickly gotten old, so I spit it out. As we had no water on us and I thought perhaps any water in the village could be polluted, I substituted a small bottle of Listerine to brush my teeth. My mouth now feeling refreshed, I grabbed some TP from my bag and stumbled out of the front gate to the woods for nature's call. I definitely was not going to use the village latrine which was an open pit oozing with urine and feces and covered with flies. When I got to the woods, a wave of nausea swept over me so intensely, I think I remember calling out for my mommy. Ultimately, however, it was a successful constitutional, but what I left behind would likely be seen on the horizon at night as some strange atomic glow.

Feeling now about 60% better, I fought off the urge to eat or drink anything. When I returned to the inside of the village, I found Thanh still wearing the pale green face, but otherwise functional.

"That will not happen again tonight," he said. "I don't care how impolite it is." I thought I caught a slight smile of embarrassment.

The village was almost completely void of men, women and older children. Obviously, they had departed for the fields and streams. A few older, more feeble villagers sat around watching the children who were too young to work. Some of the women were washing clothing in large pails, subsequently beating them with rocks so they would not shrink when they were laid out to dry in the sun.

Thanh and I, now quasi-presentable, made our way from the car to the small Catholic church. Inside, we found a young girl about nine lighting candles at the altar and a woman about thirty-eight or forty dressed in a long, white linen garment and wearing a crucifix.

"Chao, Sue," greeted Thanh.

So, the woman with whom I would meet was a nun. Thanh had told me that she preferred the name Sue rather than Siu (see-you) when other than her tribesmen spoke to her.

"Chao, Ong Thanh. Ban nhur the nao?"

"Very well, Sue. You may speak English for the benefit of Mr. McGowan."

"Good morning, Sue. I'm Bruce McGowan. Please call me Bruce."

"Ah, Bruce. You are a friend of Sergeant Berryhill."

"Well, not exactly. You see, I never did get to meet him."

"You speak in the past tense as though something has happened to him."

"Yes," I replied. "He died just a few days ago."

Thanh interjected. "He was murdered, Sue. Just as I told you about the others."

Sue placed her hand over her breasts and sat down on a stool. "I am saddened about that. I met with him and he sent me many letters, telling me how sorry he was of what happened to my village. I always answered his letters and told him not to dwell on it. God has long forgiven him and the others."

"I suspect the very people who did not want the story about the village to get out did finally kill him," I said.

She shook her head and crossed herself. "The tragedy continues even to this day."

"That is why it is ever more important that you write down what you remember about the raid on your village by the American troops. I would also like you to take me to the village site and where the bodies were found."

She gave me a puzzled look. "But the village was burned to the ground. There's nothing left there and the bodies were buried in a mass grave outside of the village."

"I know, but I have to get a feel for the area to appreciate what happened. Sometimes it helps to go to a place and envision the killing and the suffering, like when I have visited some of our American battlefields. I know it sounds morbid, but that's what I need to do."

"Then I can take you there, Bruce. When do you want to go?"

"As soon as possible. Today, if you will. How far is it from here?"

"Just three kilometers east along that trail that travels off the road where you came in." She pointed toward the path that led to some very dense jungle. "I can take you in about an hour." She then approached me and placed her hand onto my forehead. "You look very pale. Are you ill?"

"Poisoned I think is a better word."

Thanh laughed. "When we arrived last night, your chief took us directly to the village center to drink rice wine with him."

"Oh, I am most sorry," she said. "It is a very bad drink."

I chuckled. "I think you're telling us something we already know."

"Then would you have some rice and fruit with me? My altar girl, Pham, and I were about to eat." The child's bright brown eyes sparkled in anticipation of joining us.

"Maybe a little starch *would* take care of my queasiness. Yes, thank you."

I looked at Thanh who still didn't look well. He shook his head. "Nothing for me."

We sat on small benches across from one another while Pham brought us plates filled with the steaming rice from the pot, banana slices and some mangos. She also neatly laid a set of chopsticks down by our plates, left and returned with another glass pot of hot tea.

Sue smiled and nodded. "There is more when you are done."

"Thank you, Sue. I'm sure this will be enough."

She then dropped to her knees and began to pray over the food in her tribal tongue. I bowed my head and listened, although I understood not a word. After she had blessed the food, she crossed herself and I followed with an *amen*.

As I ate, I cranked up a dialogue. "I don't know if you were told, but thirty plus years ago I was about forty kilometers west of here leading a Special Forces *A Team*. We served with the Montagnard people of the Bahnar tribe."

She smiled. "I suspected that you were military at one time. I am glad you were not with the American unit that murdered my people."

"That was tragic, Sue. I'm sorry for your village. There are evil people everywhere...even in our American government. You said you met Sergeant–major Berryhill. Did he come here?"

"Yes. About twenty-five years ago the first time when Americans were first allowed to travel to this country. He was with another American and he came by the place where my village stood. He heard from some people in this village that I was the only one who had survived and that I was living in an orphanage. It was where the people you call AmerAsians lived."

Thanh nodded. "Children fathered by American GIs. Once the soldiers left their duty here, the mothers usually gave the babies up for adoption. The woman who had the baby would be scorned if she did not."

Sue continued. "When Sergeant Berryhill came the first time, he was sad. He fell onto his knees before me and cried. He asked for my forgiveness for himself and those who killed my people. He wanted to adopt me, but ran into problems with the Vietnam government. When he returned, he wrote me many times and sent me money. I did not spend one dollar of it. There must be over two thousand dollars buried in a box under my church. I did take the rest and gave it to the orphanage. It would be difficult for me to spend it anyway. It has no value here…maybe in Ho Chi Minh City."

The more I listened to her, the more enamored I became with her. Beneath the unflattering habit, I could tell that she was a blithe, shapely woman who moved with captivating poise and grace. Her voice, soothing and prayer-like, had a melodious, rhythmic quality about it, revealing only the slightest of accent. But I somehow knew that she could also be fiery and animated if riled. As she spoke, her eyes glistened like black diamonds showcasing a fervid determination that transcended an otherwise gentle spirit.

"I was surprised to see that you are a nun. How long have you been *Sister* Sue?"

"Since 1988. I went from the orphanage to a convent where I took my vows to follow the Lord. I hope I have been a good religious teacher to my people."

"I understand you have also been an advocate for your people and continue to protest their persecution by the Vietnam government."

"It became very bad about three years ago when I led about twenty thousand of our people in a march on Pleiku and Buon Ma Thuot. The police had arrested two of our leaders, Rahlan Pon and Jimhan Djan. The government brought in the military with tanks to put us down. Four of my people were killed. As journalists and tourists had been banned from traveling into these highlands, this action was not publicized internationally."

"It seems that you have become the Degar people's Joan of Arc," I said.

She smiled and shook her head. "I do not think of myself as anything like that. Anyway, I do not wish to end up burning at the stake as she did." She took a sip of her tea. "Our resistance group is called FULRO, which stands for the United Front for Liberation of Oppressed Races. Its history goes well back into the 1950s. You see, Bruce, the Hanoi government and the Cong An Nhan Dan or People's Police have continued to harass our people at will and have even forced our women to become sterilized, to which they openly admit. They also enter our villages and burn our churches, both Protestant and Catholic, killing several of our priests. Last month, because the American government took in 800 of our refugees and re-settled them in North Carolina, the communists retaliated by capturing several of our leaders, cutting their Achilles tendons and severing women's breasts. They have cut the ears off of several of our younger men at random. Over fifty of our people were found west of here in the Dak To River, brutally massacred. Unfortunately, the world has not been given the opportunity to learn of this persecution."

Thanh added, "I have seen evidence of this as well, Bruce, in my travels to the highlands. My resistance group and the Bajaraka people have been aligned over the past few years to form a kind of Underground Railroad like the enslaved Black people in your country formed in the Nineteenth Century. And when it is learned that people of both our races have been smuggled out of the country, members of our organizations have been jailed, killed or have just disappeared. The government calls what we do *human trafficking*."

"What is the Bajaraka?" I asked.

"It is the name of a group that combines our four most powerful Montagnard tribes: the Bahnar, Jarai, Rhade and Koho people," Sue replied. Then I saw the ire in her eyes as she clinched her fists. "I know that you are here to learn about the Dak Trang massacre, and I will gladly give you your statement, but there is something else you should know. The former ARVN Colonel named Bao, who paid the American commander to raid my people, lives on many acres close to our village. The burial ground for my slain people is on his property. He continues to work with the Hanoi government to persecute *all* tribes, driving them from their land which they own…land that was granted to them by President Nguyen Van Thieu in 1968."

"So, Bao *is* still alive. I wondered."

"It will not be easy to go onto his property as he has roving guards all over."

I glanced at Thanh. "Then we will see about them."

Sue continued. "It is that our rights as indigenous hill people continue to be violated. The communists say they want to live with us in peace and punish those who violate our rights, yet they themselves have placed over one million of us in prisons and labor camps, killing thousands more since 1975. We have lost over thirty of our more vocal leaders in the past two years. The number of Degars has gone from three million in 1975 to about seven hundred thousand. There is a systematic genocide of my people, tribe by tribe. The sad thing is that the world and even the United States government have turned a blind eye to our people. Only organizations like your Special Forces groups have been supportive. When we are all dead and gone, who will hear our cry?"

"Who indeed?" I replied. I sat and listened to her plea for the better part of an hour, getting an education that brought back my early morning nausea. It especially affected me because here I was, former Special Forces myself, failing to stay in touch with any of my brothers so as to be cognizant of the plight of these same tribal hill people that fought alongside us. We betrayed them just as our government betrayed every American soldier who died on this soil. We gave up on Vietnam; but worst of all, we gave up on the Montagnard people.

CHAPTER EIGHT

We moved into a smoking hamlet at the break of day. The hooches lay in dying embers. Gone their roots of clay. The cattle lay in bloody pools awaiting their decay. The only sound, the crackling embers gorging down their prey.

LT Richard A. (Dick) Morris
Smoking Hamlet (Together We Can Empty the South China Sea)

After we had eaten and the girl, Pham, had cleared away the cups and bowls, Sue turned and knelt at the altar above which the image of Jesus on the cross hung on a rafter. She then said a few words beneath her breath, bowed her head once and crossed herself. The sun now streaming brilliantly through an open window cast its rays upon her head. Suddenly, I felt a holy presence that had not come to me in years. As Sue communed with God, I had the impression that I was watching a young Madonna, a woman so deeply spiritual and with a heart as pure and virgin as a fresh snowfall. It was during that brief, seraphic moment of worship that both Thanh and I felt compelled to kneel as well until such time that Sue rose and bowed once more, hands folded in praise.

"It is time for us to go," she said. "I must take you to the Garden of Souls and be back here for our evening prayer service."

"What is the Garden of Souls?" I asked.

"It is the holy ground near where eighty six of my people departed for Heaven. We should be there by noon."

After I had stopped by the Kia to retrieve my knapsack and several granola bars for the day, Sue gave us each a canteen of water which had been sterilized by boiling. And from the trunk of his car, Thanh pulled out a vintage U.S. Army entrenching tool which is a small shovel that folds neatly into an eighteen inch long utensil. He then opened the glove compartment and handed me the snub-nose Smith and Wesson .38 that he had earlier spoken about in jest. And from a cargo pocket in his tan pants he pulled a .45 automatic which I had no idea he had been carrying. He then allowed the clip to fall into his left hand to see if it was fully loaded and returned it with a smack of his palm into the grip.

Sue gave him us both a stern look. "I pray those will not be necessary."

I nodded and quickly shoved the .38 between the small of my backside and my jeans.

It was already probably ninety degrees with 90% humidity. As we began to trek onto the narrow path, the sun all but disappeared through the canopy above us. Unfortunately, however, the mosquitoes had already begun their feast on the back of my neck. My brain suddenly began experiencing a kind of déjà vu, throwing me back into a thirty year old war zone where at any time we could come under enemy fire from a sniper. And as ironic as that was, we suddenly heard the god-awfullest screeching followed by some kind of flying brown mush, one pellet of which struck me in my left shoulder. I quickly found the .38 in my hand.

"What the hell?" I exclaimed.

"Duck!" Sue yelled out. "Howler monkeys."

And then I remembered. When these crappy little bastards are surprised by humans or other intruders, they get scared, start screeching, poop into their hands and then bombard their invaders.

"I can't believe I came all the way back here just to get shit on by a stupid monkey," I lamented.

Sue laughed. "I am afraid so. Do not worry, though. If you can live with the smell on your shirt for a while, we will soon come to a stream where you can wash it off."

"Fine, but if it happens again, I'll plug the nasty little sons-of-bitches."

Thanh who had somehow avoided getting nailed could not contain his laughter. "A shitty day already, eh Bruce?"

We did soon arrive at the stream she mentioned where Sue and I washed the poo-poo off our clothes. I then scooped up a handful of cool water to smear onto my sweaty face.

"Do not drink the water," she warned. "To the north of here is where water buffalos are washed and there is feces in the water."

More shit, I groaned beneath my breath. "*Now* you tell me," I said, spitting out what little water had drained into my mouth.

Sue then rose from the stream and began leading us further along the jungle path up and down small hills at a fairly lively clip. As she had spent all of her life in the mountains, this little jaunt was a piece of cake for her.

Thanh was doing quite well immediately behind her, entrenching tool cocked on his shoulder, but I was puffing a little while bringing up the rear. Just a little. Being an avid runner helped me negotiate the terrain, but in humping the steep inclines, I was using different muscles. Thirty years ago it was nothing.

In another hour Sue announced that we had arrived at the village site. I wasn't sure what I was expecting, but she was right…there was no evidence that a village had once stood there. Not a stick of bamboo or piece of pottery. What had at one time been a clearing was now grown over by weeds, trees and banana grass. She stopped at the point where she said the gate had been, dropped to her knees and folded her hands in front of her. Thanh and I stood respectfully off to the side as she crossed herself, whispered a few words and completed her spiritual moment with "In the name of the Father, the Son and the Holy Ghost."

She rose and then pointed, saying "The village went beyond those trees. Around our village the men had built a double bamboo fence with pungi stakes in between, that in principle protected us from the enemy soldiers. The American unit came through here," she motioned in front of her, "and advanced so quickly upon us that it was all over within ten minutes when the last person was killed.

"My mother whisked me up and ran out of the gate when she saw the first of the soldiers. Somehow she knew what would happen. One soldier went after us, but we hid in the bushes just over there." She pointed to where a thick mass of bamboo had grown over.

"And then I saw them descend upon the village, firing their M-16s and throwing fiery grenades into our houses. They swept upon us like the wind. A hateful wind. I heard the screams of our women and children. When the firing finally diminished, so did the screams. I heard some of the soldiers yelling at one another. Two men came out of the gate and I saw that they were crying. Another threw down his weapon and placed his hands upon his face, spinning around this way and that way. And then yet another soldier spotted my mother and began running after her. She cradled me in her arms as she ran toward the river. She then hid me in the thick bushes and held her finger to her lips. When she stood up and began running across the river, I heard a single shot. Then I saw her body drop into the water. The water where she lay quickly turned red and I knew she was dead. I was six at the time, but it was like yesterday that it happened."

For once, I was without words. I could see through my own clouded eyes that Thanh's were glistening as well. He said, "I came here the next day with my unit and helped carry the bodies of those innocent people away in wagons pulled by the village's own water buffalo." He wiped his eyes on his sleeve. "I will take you to where we buried them."

Before we moved on, I took out my digital Nikon and snapped three shots of where the village had stood, although the generic pictures of banana grass and trees would not tell the story. The mass gravesite Suc called the Garden of Souls was about five hundred feet to the west.

Again, one would not realize we were standing over a cemetery since it was covered with thick weeds about thirty by fifty feet. I could see that the ground was sunken in somewhat and a portion of the site showed signs of recent digging, most probably where the tribal farmers had unearthed the remains of the priest and nuns. Realizing that it was holy ground, Sue said that the farmers who were from another hamlet did not dig any further.

We had scarcely been at the burial ground for two minutes when I caught sight of a figure emerging from the tree line to the south. A young Vietnamese man in a ball cap and olive drab green shirt with an AK-47 pointed in our direction quickly advanced on us.

"Dung lai! Ban muon go o day?" (Stop! What do you want here?)

Sue replied in Vietnamese, "I am Sister Sue from the village of Kon Mia. These are my friends."

"Ban khong tra loi toi! (You did not answer me!), the intruder said to Thanh and me.

Thanh then responded. His English interpretation was, "We are geologists for the coal company and are assessing the land."

The guard responded, "Day la tai san ca nhan!" (This is private property. No coal here!)

I turned to Thanh and told him to ask the guard if he wanted to see our papers authorizing us to be here. Maybe he wouldn't call our bluff. Thanh nodded and did as I instructed. The man then approached us and held out his left hand. "Cho thay toi." (Show me.)

As I removed my bag from my shoulders and started digging out my passport and a notebook, the guard thought perhaps I was reaching for a weapon. He shouted "Dung lai!" (Stop!) and drew down on me with the AK.

I threw up my right hand and slowly pulled my passport out first and then the notebook with my left. Feigning a fumble, I allowed the passport to drop to the ground between us. When the roving guard took his eyes off me to look down, I quickly snatched the AK away from him by the front hand guard all in one swift movement. I then gave the man a horizontal butt stroke on the chin with the stock of the rifle and he went down like a rock.

"Sweet dreams," I said. "He won't wake up for a couple of hours and then won't even remember who he is." I then pulled his limp body off into some weeds so that he would not be seen sleeping on the job.

Sue bore down on me with biting eyes. "Was that necessary?"

"I suspect he's one of Bao's guards. Yes, it was necessary. He might have killed us on the spot."

"It *is* his land, or so he says. If you will look through those trees to the west, you will see his house."

As I peered through the hardwoods, I saw what resembled a large, white Tuscany-style estate sitting majestically on a sector of high ground about a half kilometer away. Since we were that close to the house, it was pretty much a slam dunk that there would be other guards roving about as well on the large tract of land.

Sue went back to the large depression beneath which lay the Garden of Souls. "The bones of my mother lie here, but even if all the bones of my people were removed and buried in separate graves, I would not know which of the remains would be hers." She wiped away a tear with her handkerchief. "At least the soldiers had enough respect for the religious people to bury them in separate graves. But they were shallow graves."

"I wonder if it was the American or South Vietnamese soldiers who did so," I said.

Thanh replied, "It was *our* soldiers who did so. I watched them."

"Whatever. They were all in this together. And it was all about the land."

Sue lifted her head and looked at me, black eyes

piercing. "More than that, Bruce. It was about hate. My people have been treated despicably through the years…even worse so now. It is just like your American Indians and the Black people in your country were treated at one time…like they were below human."

I nodded. She was right. "I do know that the animals came and desecrated the individual graves," she added. "Within days they began digging out the bodies to eat them. The first time I came back here was when I was thirteen. Two sisters from the convent came by the orphanage to get me at my request. That is when we saw the scattered bones of the priest and three nuns. They had just been left lying there. Their garments were scattered about and we couldn't tell what bones belonged to who." She then pulled from the deep pocket of her habit three objects and held them up to me. Crucifixes. "We found these on the necks of what was left of the bones and clothing. They are always on my person."

I held them in my palm, allowing their chains to drape along my forearm. They were in remarkably good shape, having been buried and then surviving the animals' feast. I squatted to the ground above where Sue said the bones were re-buried and sifted through the soil with my fingers. Soil that had been saturated with the blood of four of God's emissaries. It all must have broken the Almighty's heart. After giving the crosses back to Sue, I snapped off several pictures of the site, again which would not reveal much. But at least it was proof that I had been there and had seen what had been wreaked by the massacre that Sue called *a hateful wind.*

"I have to tell you," I said to Thanh and her. "Even though I was not here when it happened, I can *feel* it. I can feel the horror of this massacre. Much the same as I have experienced time and again in my own personal nightmares.

This makes what haunts I have endured about the war all too real. You see, I too have the blood of the innocent on my hands."

They both looked at me with bewildered eyes, but I let it go at that. This was not about me, my own horrific experience or my nightmares.

I then stood up and saw that tears had formed in Sue's eyes. Within a few moments she was weeping bitterly into her handkerchief and I drew her into my chest. She was releasing three decades of sorrow into my now soaked khaki shirt.

Suddenly, like a roaring beast springing from the jungle, a large red truck appeared on the road, quickly descending on us. After it slid to a stop within a dozen feet of us, the driver jumped out and pointed his AK-47 in our direction. Another much older man with white hair remained in the passenger's seat.

"Nhung gi ban muon o day?" (What you want here?)

"Here we go again," I said to Thanh. "Tell him the same thing you told the other man. We're geologists and Sue here is our guide."

Thanh did not answer the guy. He just kept staring at the man still in the truck. Finally, he said in a low, but chafing voice, "Colonel Bao."

"That's him in the truck?" I asked.

"Yes."

The driver shouted out his question again.

Thanh then told the driver in Vietnamese he wanted to speak to Bao. The man stalled at first and then motioned to his boss to dismount. Slowly, the door opened and Bao stepped out. He was frail-looking with his thin white hair and eighty-something year old face that resembled a white prune. The guard then turned to meet him and to help him negotiate the uneven terrain.

I looked at Sue who was in turn glaring at the old man. Though she was a devout Christian, her eyes were contemptuous and unforgiving. Bao returned her stare with a look of disdain. He knew full well who she was.

"Ban trespassing. Nhan duoc off dat cua toi!" (You are trespassing. Get off my land!)

Thanh finally replied, "I want you to speak English, Colonel Bao, as I know you can. I want my American friend here to hear what you have to say."

Bao opened his mouth and stammered. I thought perhaps he was trying to remember the words of English as he probably had little opportunity to speak them in years.

"Who are you and who is the man with you?" Bao replied.

"This man is here to gather information about a murderer," Thanh shot back.

Bao shook his head. "I do not understand."

"You do not recognize me, Colonel Bao? I was in your command when you paid the American captain to attack the village of Dak Trang and murder its people. The ghosts of the men, women and children whose bones lie beneath us are in my dreams. I know they meant nothing to you, but they were human beings…not animals."

Bao did not immediately respond, but stood digesting the three sets of accusatory eyes affixed to his face. I perceived that it was all slowly coming back to him. Finally, he said to Thanh, "I do not remember you and I do not know what you speak about."

"You know very well, Colonel Bao. You are a murderer…a despicable, greedy man. And you represent the very communist dogs that continue to persecute me and my friends…freedom loving people."

Bao then turned to his guard and said, "Nguoi dan ong nay disrespected toi. Giet ong. Giet tat ca chung." (This man has disrespected me. Kill him. Kill them all)

And that I did understand. When the guard brought up the AK, Thanh's .45 was already in his hand and aimed at the man's heart. The pop was deafening and sent the birds nesting in nearby trees scurrying and screeching. The man fell backwards against the truck's grille and then plopped face down into the clay.

Colonel Bao nearly fell backwards himself, but then steadied himself against a tree. I was stunned and so was Sue.

"What have you done?" exclaimed Bao.

"Ong Bao, I want you to get to your knees and beg this woman for your life," Thanh ordered.

"I do not understand. Who is this woman?"

"You know her. She is the only survivor of Dak Trang. Now, enough talk. Do as I told you."

Bao stood obstinately at the position of attention and tightened his jaw. "Khong bao gio." (Never)

"Then you will go to Hell without hearing her words of forgiveness." Thanh fired two rounds into Bao's chest, spinning the old man backwards. His already-dead body then dropped quickly to the ground.

Sue screamed and grabbed Thanh by the shoulders. "Why? Why did you do this, Thanh? This man's death does not pay for what he has done. You have committed murder just the same as he did."

"No, Sue. Today I was only his judge, jury and executioner. He deserved to die. Your Bible teaches an eye for an eye. It is too bad that he had only one life to atone for the lives of eighty of your people, to include the life of your mother. His heart was never true to South Vietnam as he quickly became one of the Hanoi puppets. It is men like him who have persecuted your people as well as mine. I have now rid your people of only one of its enemy."

She shook her head. "We may both be activists for our people against the communists, but we do not have the same heart."

"You should feel vindicated as do I," he said.

"No, Thanh. I feel sickened. I must ask…why you? Why would you do this when it was about *my* people? Why should you risk certain arrest for killing a man when he did nothing to you?"

"Because by serving with him and carrying out his orders to bury your dead, he made me a part of it. Maybe I could have done something about it before it happened. I could have reported him and see that he was brought up on charges."

I then jumped in. "As powerful as Bao was at the time, you would have lost. Maybe they would have brought conspiracy charges against you and you could even have lost *your* life. You two quit beating yourselves up. Sue, our own lives were at stake here. Our bodies could have been added to the Garden of Souls today."

"He is correct, Sue," Thanh added. Now it is our task to get rid of the bodies and the truck, or we will be connected to their deaths."

Sue sighed and said softly, "There is an abandoned

quarry near here where they used to mine alluvial deposits. It is largely grown over. You can take them there." And in suggesting this, Sue had just become a co-conspirator whether she had to this point or not.

Thanh and I placed the corpses of Bao and his man in the bed of their truck. He then walked to where I had dragged the first guard into the brush and I heard a single shot.

Sue cried out and fell to her knees upon the Garden of Souls. She then laid her face in the soil as Thanh placed the third body in the truck bed beside the others. The war, his cause…all of it…had made him ruthless. Thanh returned and placed his hand gently upon the back of Sue's neck as she prayed.

"Sue, this man would have told the police and brought them down on us. They would find you and then be down on Bruce and me before we reached Kontum. They would also kill you. You *know* that. I am sorry you had to witness this."

"More killing," she whispered back to him. "Will it never end? Will these killings lead to more?"

He didn't answer her, but stood and walked away. When he joined me at the truck, he said, "It matters little what she thinks of me, Bruce. I will have a clear conscience about this day."

I nodded in response. "And so will I. *I* didn't pull the trigger."

He gave me a wry smile. "We had better go."

I asked Sue if she would be all right where she was until we returned. She replied that she would and then told me that the quarry was two kilometers west just off the road and to the left. We should be returning within the hour.

En route to the quarry, I noticed that Thanh had become quiet. I thought perhaps it was because he had never pulled a trigger to kill anyone, even in combat. He had only been an Intel sergeant and worked out of his headquarters. Looking straight ahead while he was driving, he said, "It did not give me pleasure to kill these men, Bruce…but it was necessary. I knew we were about to be killed. But more than that, Colonel Bao needed to die."

"Death was to be with him soon, anyway, Thanh, given his advanced age and feebleness."

"It was important that he die this way, though, Bruce. I am not as ruthless a man as you may think, but I have been hardened through the years. Perhaps because he had fallen in with the Hanoi regime and represented everything I and my fellow dissidents detest, it made it easier to pull the trigger."

I didn't respond with anything but a nod. Anyway, we caught sight of the quarry a couple hundred meters off to the left. Thanh turned onto a broken trail and after negotiating some serious brush on either side, the huge pit loomed ahead. Thanh set the gearshift to neutral and we dismounted the truck. The two of us then pushed the Dodge to the quarry's edge and watched it drop into the pit at a spot where it disappeared among fifteen foot trees that had sprung up over the last ten years or so. The vehicle should not be readily spotted from the air or ground. It then took about a half hour to hoof it back to the Garden of Souls where we found Sue pacing. She still appeared rather vexed, but I figured that after she had galvanized the day's events in her mind over the next few weeks, maybe she would then begin to realize some degree of vindication. And maybe in time, she would even forgive Thanh as well.

CHAPTER NINE

Sue spared us from the village elders and their standing invitation for another night of camaraderie around the rice wine barrel. She explained to them that as we appreciated the offer, we had to leave in our car very early the next morning and didn't want to leave pickled or worse…without a stomach. They probably didn't understand what the concern was all about.

After a plate of rice, fish and bread, the crusty kind with baked-in flies, we thanked Sue for guiding us, feeding us and ministering to us. Thanh said he wished she had not witnessed the killings at the Garden of Souls and begged her forgiveness.

"It is for God to forgive, Thanh. You must however show your remorse and ask for His forgiveness. He will hear you if you are sincere."

Of course, he knew her God was not the same deity that he worshipped in his Buddhist faith. But he nodded anyway and vowed that he would pray.

Before Sue turned in she wrote her statement by candlelight. I was still up writing notes of my own in the passenger's side seat of the Kia via the vanity light on the visor. Around nine Sue came to the car to give me her seven page account of the massacre, penned beautifully in English. Upon scanning the statement, I found it vivid, comprehensive and articulately written. Everything she had told us was there in compelling detail. She also used the last page of the document as a sounding board for the benefit of whoever in the American government would read it, asking for the support of the U.S. as well as the U.N. to help her people gain their rights and liberties as promised through the years. She signed it *Sister Siu Ramhan*."

I smiled and thanked her. "I am sure it will be read by those at the highest level of our government, Sue."

"What will happen from this letter? Will the American commander be found and punished?"

"I promise you that he will," I said.

"I am not sure why you wanted this statement. I would not be able to identify the man or any of the soldiers. How could these papers be of value?"

"The statement will serve to attest that the village massacre actually took place. Thanh's statement will provide the actual details including eye witness accounts of meetings between Bao and the American captain. Sergeant Berryhill had already given his verbal statement to someone very high in our government. All three versions together will place the nails in Captain Randall's coffin."

"Randall. That is his name? As I neither put a face or a name to the man that murdered my people, somehow this gives me a degree of closure. And when he is finally brought to justice in your country, I hope you will inform me. Then I will be content.

Having slept again in the back seat of the Kia, I woke up just before dawn with a hell of a stiff neck. I downed a couple of Advil with the rest of yesterday's canteen water and then hit the woods to kill some weeds. Thanh had still not stirred and I wondered if his conscience had kept waking him up during the night. Killing people is a bit troubling to people who aren't used to it.

A number of the villagers were now moving around, cooking their morning grub and smoking their rancid tobacco. An elderly woman with a deeply-weathered face and no teeth squatted outside her hooch and chewed betel root (beetlenut). Her mouth was blood red from the narcotic. Nearby, a naked two year old with a swollen belly was giving chase to a swayback pig through a mud hole.

Finally, Thanh was on his feet and moving slowly through the village to where I stood at the steps to the primitive Catholic church. Sue greeted us and asked that we come in and kneel with her at the altar before we departed. We did so and then, touching us on our heads, she blessed us in her native tongue, in Vietnamese and then in English. When she had finished, I rose and gave her a hug.

"Thank you, Sue. When I return to the States, I will contact the Special Forces groups that are working with your people in North Carolina. Perhaps they will challenge our government to stand with your leaders against the Vietnam socialists and compel them to stop their persecution. I also pledge to help you and your cause by writing letters and donating money whenever I can. And…I will personally see to it that this Captain Jack Randall is punished for what he did to your people. You have my word on that."

She bowed and thanked me. Thanh stood erectly and snapped his head in a bow, which she returned. Her eyes still reflected the ire that had apparently not diminished at all. She had seen Thanh kill three men in cold blood, and that horrific scene would forever be etched in her mind…as clearly as her memory of the Dak Trang massacre thirty-two years before.

When we walked from the church into the center of the village near the Happy House, the village chief approached us along with five of the tribal elders. His wide toothless grin even more so accentuated the mass of cavernous wrinkles on his elastic face. In the chief's brown, rugged hands were two Degar bracelets that appeared to have been at one time ammunition brass, flattened and shaped. After passing off the bracelets to Thanh and me, one of the elders then shoved into my hands a mason jar of the Montagnard moonshine that had gone down like Drano the night before last, cleaning out all my pipes. I bowed and said *thank you.* They may not have understood the words, but my smile reflected my gratitude. I would wear the bracelet with pride, but the antifreeze inside the jar would fly out the window as soon as we were out of shouting range of the village.

I felt badly about having nothing in return to give the chief, but then suddenly remembered I always kept in my pocket my Special Forces challenge coin for good luck whenever I traveled, although I've never been the superstitious type. It was shiny and colorful and I hoped it did not *one up* his gift to me. He eagerly accepted it as though it were treasure and bowed three or four times. I knew I would be able to secure another one at Ft. Bragg, especially if I lived up to my promise to take up Sue's impassioned plea of support with my Special Forces brothers.

A steady rain began tattooing our windshield as we back-tracked along the heavily-rutted and otherwise eroded road. The Kia, with its light body and rear wheel drive, slipped and slid on the orange clay that had become as slick as snail snot. The mud was starting to collect between the tires and fenders, not only slowing us down, but putting a bit of strain on the engine and transmission. It would take us twice as long to negotiate the trail as it did coming in and we would likely not make the asphalt of Highway 14 until late afternoon. This would put us in Pleiku somewhere around six, well behind schedule…that is if we actually had one. But Thanh was anxious to get back to his family and I could see his frustration the further we trekked.

Once we had cleared Tan Canh and were halfway to Kontum, we passed a trail that led to Rocket Ridge which was barely visible through the fog and mist. Back in the war, U.S. and ARVN artillery batteries were positioned on a number of fire bases in those mountains to provide indirect fire support along corridors approaching both Kontum and Tan Canh where the 42nd ARVN Division was based. It brought back a memory from 1970 when my team was working with ruff-puff Montagnard soldiers in the village of Dak Tang Ri and we were over-run by an NVA sapper company. We pulled the people out of the village and retreated with them to Firebase Six. No sooner had we entered the firebase, it was hit by a flurry of .122 rockets, a daily target for the enemy. Ergo, how Rocket Ridge got its name. Now, Rocket Ridge was just a heavily-wooded, unoccupied mountain range which I'm sure contained scores if not hundreds of unexploded artillery rounds which would continue to kill or maim hunters, children or any other creature that happened upon the area. More lives would be lost in Vietnam any given year from stepping on mines or from picking up still armed rocket and artillery rounds than would die in traffic accidents in Hanoi, Hue and Ho Chi Minh City combined. And that was a statistic that was hard for me to believe, considering how I saw people drive.

Just south of Kontum I tried to reach Adrianna several times on my international cell, but each time I tried, I got an annoying rapid busy signal. I knew she couldn't be on her cell phone the entire time. I also heard the same signal when I tried calling our home phone. The problem was obviously on my end or somewhere twelve thousand miles in between.

I could imagine that after four or five days in not hearing from me, she was either getting pretty worried or pretty pissed.

About four-thirty, it had stopped raining and the sun was starting to peek through the clouds in the western sky. Thanh and I then stopped to find lodging and something to eat. The only thing I had had since breakfast was my last protein bar which I wolfed down with some water. I had offered Thanh half of it, but he respectfully declined. As we did not see any golden arches or a Pizza Hut, we settled on a place just off the highway called Quan Cung Dien or Mandarin Palace. I had certainly had enough rice the previous few days to last a couple of months. I remember when I returned to the States after my tour and a half, I didn't want to look another bowl of rice in the face for five years. But some Kung Pao chicken and a couple of egg rolls might be good.

As fate would have it, and fate had *had* me a hell of a lot more times than I deserved, just before we left our vehicle for the restaurant, two cops in a jeep, wearing green uniforms and red stars on their caps pulled around us and stopped abruptly to our front. Thanh jammed on his brakes to avoided rearending the jeep. What *was* it with cops and why did they think a Caucasian man traveling with a Vietnamese man warranted checking out? Of course, there was no such thing as *probable cause* in Vietnam. Maybe they just needed directions. And I could certainly tell them where to go.

Both cops jumped out of the jeep and made their ways toward the Kia. The driver was a beady-eyed little guy with a cocky swagger and an inch long mustache under his nose that made him look like Adolph Hitler. He practically ignored Thanh and came around to the passenger side of the Kia to get in *my* face.

"Cho toi xem giay to cua ban!" (Show me your documents!)

Thanh spoke up. "He wants you to show your papers, Bruce."

I reached into my travel bag and pulled out both my visa and passport. "Here," I said, practically shoving them in his face.

Adolph looked at them like he was studying for an exam. "You think I speak no English?"

"Sounds like you speak it a little…but not very well, trung si."

"I am a *dai ui*," he replied impudently.

"Okay then, Captain. What do you want with us?"

"Get out of car and bring me bag." He pointed to the back seat.

I did as instructed, but Thanh remained behind the wheel while the second cop stood by his door. I then exited the Kia, pulled open the back door and pulled out my knapsack.

"You do know that I have rights under international law. You have to tell me why you're detaining and searching us."

The captain didn't reply, but kept his eyes on me as he snatched the bag from my hand. He then dumped its contents onto the asphalt parking lot and rummaged through my underwear. Just to be a prick I presumed.

"If you're interested, homo, you see that I wear boxer shorts. Is that what you're looking for?"

Adolph glared at me and then jerked his head in the direction of the second cop. "Tim kiem chiec xe!" (Search the car!)

Uh oh.

Sure enough, the cop went immediately to the glove compartment and found the .38 Special. "Choi oi!" he exclaimed as he pulled it out to show his captain.

"Gun yours?"

"Day la mo (It is mine)," Thanh said.

Adolph then drew his revolver from its holster. "You. Get out," he said to Thanh. "Get on knees. You too, American. Put hands on head."

We both dropped down and I said, "What are going to do now? Put bullets in our heads?" I wasn't sure why I was being such a smart-ass, considering I was in the international execution position.

"Tim kiem chung!"

The second cop pat me down first, finding nothing but my hard abs, tight buns and my cell phone. But when he put his hands on Thanh, he immediately found the .45 jammed into his belt.

The captain then ordered his sergeant to handcuff us. "You break law, American. No one allowed to carry gun. You have two."

"I told you they are mine, Captain," Thanh interjected.

"This man did not know about them."

Adolph then went to his jeep, lifted the mike from the radio and carried on a conversation with someone. Then he returned cockier than ever.

"Look, dai ui," I said. "I really have to get home. It's getting late and you don't know my wife. She…"

"Silence!" he shouted. "No time for joke. I call truck to take you to headquarters."

"If I am not in Ho Chi Minh City by tomorrow, the American Consulate will be knocking on your commie president's door up in Hanoi."

"You not make Ho Chi Minh City tomorrow. You be in jail."

"You're taking us to jail? Look, Mac. I'm in your country on important business. Don't get your ass in a crack by delaying us any longer."

Thanh then spoke in English to the captain so that I would know what he was saying. "Mr. McGowan is a very important man, dai ui. What he says is true. Let him go and keep me. *I'm* the owner of the guns."

"We deal with you about that." He then turned to me. "How you important man?"

"I'm here to negotiate an agriculture deal between your government and mine."

"You have other papers to prove?"

"Back in my hotel room in Ho Chi Minh City," I lied.

"Who you meet here?"

"Your Secretary of Agriculture of course."

"All government people in Hanoi…not here…not in Ho Chi Minh City. Why you lie?"

"What makes you think I am?"

"You not answer question. Who is agri…agri…secretary?"

"Agricultural. I think his name is Phuc Yu or something like that. Say, can I get up? I have a bad left knee."

Adolph motioned for his sidekick to help me up. "You back up to car. Not try anything."

People coming in and going out of the restaurant rubbernecked to see what was going on, careful not to get too close. In less than two minutes, the paddy wagon came for the bad men. The captain's man scraped up my few belongings and tossed them back into the bag. He then threw the bag into the back of the truck along with Thanh and me. They kept the pistols.

As the police van negotiated the narrow streets of Pleiku for what seemed to be a half hour at a clip of forty-five or fifty, the driver sounded the horn to clear pedestrians and cyclos from the road. Thanh and I both ricocheted off the inside walls a couple of times. Either the captain was in a hurry to get us somewhere to beat us with rubber hoses or there was a donut with his name on it. Cops are cops; I don't care *where* they are.

Finally, the van screeched to a halt in some gravel and a few seconds later the rear doors were flung open. When I stepped down, I could see there was no more Pleiku…no city lights, no nothing but countryside. I wondered if we had been brought out to the boonies to be executed. After being prodded a couple of times in my back with a Type 77 Chinese pistol, the first thing I saw was the red-orange rays of the sun fading over a mountain range. It reminded me of terrain somewhere in the Shenandoah Valley of Virginia, which is where I wished to hell I was right about that time.

There were only two buildings within what seemed to be a half-mile, a cement block building over which was a sign that read *Tram Canh Sat* (Police Station), and a second, similar building of equal size about fifty feet behind it with bars on open windows. Probably our hotel for the night unless there were plans that we would be planted in a field behind it.

"Di! Di!" the dai ui ordered. He motioned us toward the first building.

"Wait, dai ui. I'll say again. I have rights under international law. I demand you contact the American Consulate…"

"You have no rights. Go!"

It was futile to argue with him any longer. I could see that he was neither a man of reason or ultimate authority. After the driver of the paddy wagon saluted the captain and pulled away from the station. Thanh and I were then moved on into the building.

The police station was a dump and stank from B.O., cigarettes and what smelled like Raid. A rather over-weight third policeman who was smoking an obnoxiously pungent Vietnamese weed and who had obviously had a tad too many of the afore-mentioned donuts jumped up to the position of attention as the dai ui and I passed by him.

"Be at ease, Porko," I said. "Don't get up on *my* account."

Adolph pushed me further on and into a room on our right where an older policemen sat at a table opposite a vacant folding chair. The dai ui then went behind me, pushed on my shoulders and sat me down hard in the chair. His sergeant took a position in a corner of the room.

"Hey, Dai ui. How about taking the cuffs off me?"

He looked at the older man who was also puffing on a cigarette and the man nodded. Apparently, the senior man also spoke English. The cuffs came off.

When the captain left out, I could see Thanh through

the open door being shackled to a metal pipe that came out of the wall. It appeared that I would be grilled first and given the opportunity to rat out my new Vietnamese friend for the gun-toting, ex-ARVN, subversive dissident that he was…then I could go home.

I sat at the table for what seemed like two or three minutes waiting for the police interrogator to say something. He was a small man about five-two, perhaps sixty or more, with an uncharacteristic receding hairline and two squinty little eyes. Hard eyes. He had been reviewing my passport and visa.

Finally, I broke the ice. "Nice evening, huh? The rain cooled things down and the Good Lord sent us that neat sunset."

He then looked up at me and said in a low voice, "Do not speak."

Well, par-don *me*, Mr. Sunshine.

The old guy had a serious, no-nonsense face which had probably not worn a smile in years. Irritable Bowel Syndrome perhaps? He seemed to be intrigued with my passport.

"State your name."

I didn't respond.

His eyes then started to singe into mine and his mouth formed a scowl. "You will answer!" he said sharply.

"I'm sorry. You now want me to talk? A moment ago you told me *not* to. Which is it?"

"You will not be impudent with me, American. Now tell me your name."

"You didn't find my name somewhere on that passport?"

He brought his fist down hard on the table. "Silence!"

"Well now you *are* confusing me. Since you now want me to be silent, should I *write* my name down for you?"

Seeing that he was going to have just a bit of trouble from his smart-ass American prisoner, he looked over at his sergeant in the corner and shook his head. But then he took a deep breath to compose himself and leaned back in his chair. "You may answer my question now and tell me your name. Only answer what I ask you."

"All right. My name is Bruce McGowan, just like it reads on my passport."

"Good," he replied. "Now. What are you doing in this country?" His English was very good which set me to wonder if he was former ARVN.

"Doing a little business and a little sight-seeing along with it."

"What business?"

"Well, like I told Wyatt Earp out there, I'm putting together some agricultural deals between your government and mine."

"If that is the case, what are you doing riding with a man who claims to be in the jewelry business, but conspires against our government?" I saw that he also had Thanh's ID in front of him.

"Mr. Thanh is a friend from thirty years ago."

His eyes were unwavering. "Then you were an American soldier here."

"Yes."

"And that is how you know him…through military association."

"Yes."

"You kept in touch with him for thirty years, then."

"Has it really been that long?"

"So, why were you in the Montagnard area?"

Which told me that we *were* followed…maybe not on into Sue's village, but far enough. And the police obviously had some serious Intel floating around about Thanh.

"The Montagnard area? What makes you think we were there?"

"We are not stupid people, Mr. McGowan. Our police network may not be as sophisticated as it is in your country, but we are resourceful and have very good methods."

I studied him a moment and was set to wonder why a man with such obvious intelligence and the ability to speak nearly perfect English was at his age stuck in a small police outpost far from the city lights. Had he screwed up somehow or if he *was* a former South Vietnamese officer, was this the best position he would ever see?

"May I ask your name, sir?"

"I am Major Chanh Trong Vann, if it matters."

"It does. I like to know who my enemy is."

"Why do you think I am your enemy? I am only interrogating a man who accompanies an armed dissident against the government and who is not telling the truth as to why he is here."

I nodded, not in agreement, but because my suspicions about the man were becoming more real as we talked. "You were a former military officer as well, weren't you, Tut ta? And not NVA, but ARVN. I think that after the war, your intellect and experience were recognized and you were re-indoctrinated to become a policeman."

Did *that* ever press his button. *"You will not speak about such things!"* he shouted. His black eyes widened and bore down on me like lasers.

I continued. "And you have worked your way up all these years to become a major, a tu ta, which is not very high. You resent this communist government and they still resent you. Am I on to something here?"

"You must now keep your mouth shut!"

"Maybe you were educated as a young man in an American-run school or university or heavily associated with our troops. That's how you speak English so well."

Again, I had hit a nerve. Vann stood and his chair fell over behind him. Hearing the clatter, Captain Adolph entered the room with pistol in hand. But Major Vann held up his hand and said, "Do la tat ca cal guyen" (It is all right) He waved the captain from the room.

Vann continued. "You have spoken too much. I told you to only answer my questions. My life is not your concern, but *your* life is." He then sat back down. "You have tried to embarrass me. If you continue, I will tape your mouth shut."

As we were getting nowhere fast, mainly because I was intentionally trying to be antagonizing, I decided to let him have his way. "All right, Tu ta, let's have a civil conversation and get this over with."

He nodded once. "What was your job here when you were a soldier?"

"I was with the Special Forces."

"The elite force," he commented.

"You probably heard our slogan: *Join Special Forces. Visit exotic lands, do exciting things, meet interesting people…and kill them.*"

He was not amused, so said his face. His eyes still lay on my passport.

"I came across your people from time to time. They mostly worked with the Degar people." He then looked up at me. "Was that where you were today…with the Degars?"

"I told you I was also touring the countryside, Major. I wanted to see the people again."

"But the people you were with would all be gone by now. What did you expect to find?"

"I'm not sure. I just wanted to experience the area again."

For the first time, there was a half-smile on his face. More of a smirk than a smile, however.

"A nostalgic feeling that you GIs have within you. I don't understand it, Mr. McGowan. Most of you hated to be here, fighting the NVA and VC, fighting the hot weather and the boredom when you were not fighting, fighting to get home to your families. Then you come back here to walk the land, take pictures, eat Vietnamese food, which you never liked."

I smiled. "When we are young, we'd rather be doing other things, like being back home cruising around in our cars with our girlfriends. Then I guess when we get older we tend to think more about our days in the military and value our experiences." I leaned into him and locked eyes. "Do you think about your time as a younger man with the South Vietnamese army?"

Vann was again irritated. "I did not tell you I was with

the ARVNs."

"And you didn't deny it either."

He didn't reply which in essence told me my suspicions about him were correct.

"Where are we going with this interview, Major Vann?"

"You appear a little apprehensive, Mr. McGowan."

"And what gives you that impression?"

"You seem to be anxious to leave this station and we are nowhere done with the questioning. You are also being evasive."

"Well, I'll tell you what, Tu ta. We're just going in circles. Your men have stopped Mr. Thanh and me for no reason and you are delaying my return to the United States. So, we're done here." I started to get up, but the cop in the corner moved toward me and touched his sidearm.

"Sit down, Mr. McGowan. You will not leave here until you tell me the truth about why you are in this country."

"I told you I was here on business and am taking the time to see the country I couldn't enjoy before."

"Then again, what is your association with Mr. Thanh, other than contacting him once more after thirty years?"

"How many times can I say this? He is a friend and volunteered to be my guide. Can I be any clearer?"

"I am afraid I cannot believe you."

"Then you, sir, have a problem."

He actually smiled at my insolence.

"No. It is *you* who has the problem. You were found in the company of a man who commits treason against the state. That makes you just as guilty."

I pushed out my index finger only inches from his nose. "Then prove it. The American Consulate will have a field day with you."

"What is this *field day*," he replied.

"It means, Major, that after he is through with your government, you will be out of a job. You will merely go back to being just another former ARVN soldier begging for food on the street."

The scowl was back on his face. "You are trying to disrespect me, Mr. McGowan. I am loyal to the Socialist Government of Vietnam. I am treated well and with great respect. I have a good position here. Do not threaten me again or I will see to it that you *never* go home."

I looked around the grungy room with the cracked plaster and rotted wooden floor. "This is what you call *good*, eh? You're only being appeased by your government, Major."

Vann placed his hands on the table and pushed himself to his feet. "Dai ui!" he called to the next room. "Toi day!"

The door opened and Captain Adolf re-appeared, gun in hand. Vann nodded to him.

"Mr. McGowan, you will not need to spend money on a hotel room tonight. You will be our guest and will remain here until such time that you decide to cooperate."

"And again, I protest and demand that you release me immediately," I shot back.

Vann didn't respond and idly shuffled my documents around as Adolf prodded me to my feet. The second cop then stepped in and pulled my arms behind me to cuff my wrists. They were wisely being cautious with me, since they instinctively knew I could take all three of them out in mere seconds if not for the gun in my face.

As they shoved me back through the doorway, I looked at Thanh who was still shackled to the metal pipe. I shook my head which was my indication to him that I didn't rat him out. I hoped he in turn would follow suit. Adolf and the lard-ass cop then pushed me into a back room and out through a rear door of the station toward the concrete block hoosgal.

CHAPTER TEN

Well this was certainly a fine mess, sitting in a mostly dark cell on a bench with a large rat in one corner licking his chops. The varmint was as big as a cat. I hoped it wouldn't come down to either one of us having the other for supper. When I awoke this morning, I had no goddamn idea I would be a guest of Pleiku's version of the Hanoi Hilton. Son of *a* bitch! As bad as this predicament was, however, I only had an inkling of what John McCain and his fellow POWs must have gone through. I couldn't fathom those years of abuse and isolation they experienced. But this was a quite different scenario. And hopefully a temporary one.

I checked my Timex, which lit up in the dark. One hour had passed, after which it became totally dark in the cell; then another went by. It was ten-thirty. I wondered where my sharp-toothed cellmate was. He could see me, but I couldn't see him. I heard him scampering a couple of times after I clapped my hands loudly and stomped my feet every ten minutes or so. I wanted him to know for sure that I was not dead.

At a quarter till eleven, I heard the cell door next to mine open along with several voices. Momentarily, the door then slammed and I heard groaning.

"Thanh, is that you over there? I'm in the cell next to you!"

At first there was only more groaning and I wondered if my neighbor wasn't just a drunk the cops had thrown in. But then I heard a very feeble, "Y…yes."

"What did they do to you?" I yelled back.

"They…kicked me many times in the chest and stomach. I think…my ribs are broken and I feel very sick. My…my teeth are loose and there is blood…" I heard him gasp and knew he couldn't finish.

I rammed my fist into the cement wall, which was not the smartest thing I'd ever done. Lucky I didn't break my hand. "Why did they beat you, Thanh?"

"Because…" He sounded weaker with every word. "…I would not sign a confession about conspiring against the government."

"But all they had on you was a weapons possession," I said.

"It was…a reason to arrest me. The police have been waiting for a chance to do so for many years. And…they have my written statement which they took from your bag. They know about Sue and saw Colonel Bao's name on the statement."

"I'm sorry I got you into this, Thanh."

He did not immediately respond, but groaned again. About a half minute later, he replied, "It is no matter. They would get to me…sooner or later, and…" He didn't finish.

"I want you to try staying conscious, Thanh. You can't go into shock." I suspected he may have had more than broken ribs…perhaps serious internal injuries. *Do you hear me?*"

"Yes."

I could barely hear him now.

"We have to find a way to get out of here. But it appears these walls and bars are pretty solid."

"Yes…I must sleep now."

"No, Thanh! Stay awake!"

There was no response and I suspected he had passed out.

"Thanh!"

No answer.

For a half hour or so I stayed seated on the wooden bench which would also serve as my bed…that is if I ever decided to sleep during the night. I heard the rat again a couple of times and yelled out to Thanh so that not only would the rodent stay away from me, but perhaps I could wake my friend. I didn't hear either one of them again.

About eleven-fifteen I heard footsteps outside my cell door. Suddenly, it opened and something clamored on the concrete floor. The door then quickly closed. Thanh's door then opened and I heard the same noise before it closed again. Although I wasn't able to see what was thrown into my cell, I suspected it was food in a tray or bowl. I *was* very hungry and needed to be quick about getting to the grub ahead of the rat. But then I thought that if I did manage to get to it first, the rodent would get a case of the red-ass and bite the hell out of me. However, it wouldn't be the *first* time a rat had bitten me in this God-forsaken country.

Anyway, I made a lot of noise in going for the bowl and picked it up. It was a simple bowl of rice. Did I really expect anything else? In the faintest of light, I could see that there was another item on the floor and as I wanted to be sure it wasn't the rat, I kicked it. It was a tumbler of water. Although it fell over from the kick, I managed to salvage half of it. But all I had to do was smell it and I knew it was foul. It smelled like raw sewage. So, if the rat wanted it, he could have it.

I scooped the rice from the bowl with my fingers and in about thirty seconds, it was gone. I hoped the water to mix with it had been boiled enough. But I'd still probably get dysentery.

Midnight. I knew I probably wasn't going to sleep for a couple of reasons: first, my brain would never turn off, no matter how tired I was; and then, I was taking no chances on the rat having the feast of its life, leaving nothing but my skeleton for the guards to find in the morning.

I paced a bit and continued wondering about Thanh. After calling his name several times each hour, he never responded. I also wondered about my lovely Adrianna. Was she also pacing the floor, having not heard from me for now five or six days? I was sure she had called the Birdman many times, who was probably also wondering about me. I could almost smell her perfume and the clean, crisp sheets she had likely just pulled from the dryer. And I could almost taste her wonderful spaghetti and meatballs, my favorite…a recipe that had been handed down through the generations of her family. And then there was the ice cold beer that went down with it.

I tried pulling at the bars on the window, hoping that the mortar would start to work loose and the frame would separate from the wall. But it was solid. I gave up on that idea.

Having to go number one, I groped around the wall until I found the nasty honey pot on the floor that likely had never been cleaned after other prisoners had done their business in it. I relieved myself and then wondered, 'where *were* the other prisoners? Were we the only ones? Surely, there were thieves and murderers just like me somewhere out there in Pleiku.'

Even though I thought I never would, I must have dozed off sometime after five in the fetal position on the bench. It seemed only like two minutes until a shard of sun hit me in the eyes. During the time I must have been in la-la land, I thought I had heard voices in Thanh's cell, but I could have been dreaming. Through blurred eyes, I checked my watch which read six-forty. I also checked around the room to look for my cell mate, the creature of the night, but he was nowhere to be seen. I then checked all my body parts to assure he had not nibbled anything off.

After filling the pot again, which was damned near full, I yelled out for Thanh. There was still no answer. I was then set to wonder if he ever woke up.

My mouth felt and tasted like cotton as I was thirstier than I ever remembered. I think it had been since two-something the previous afternoon that I had had a sip of water from my canteen. The rice was also long gone and I was starved. I then realized that the mosquitoes had not gone hungry. There must have been a hundred welts on my face, neck and hands. Hopefully, none of them were of the female anopheles type. I missed getting malaria the first time around and I'd be mighty pissed off if I got it thirty-two years later.

The morning had come and gone and I had not gotten Thanh to respond. Neither had I heard from the innkeeper. What kind of B&B was this? No bed, no breakfast, no service. I would be compelled to take the matter up with the management. I tried yelling several times for someone inside of the station to come and get my ass out of there, but no one came. Until one-thirty that afternoon.

Upon hearing the footsteps, I positioned myself to one side of the cell door so that when it swung open, I could jump the guard. But when it was flung open, no one came in. They were smarter than I gave them credit for. I then heard Captain Adolf's voice.

"McGowan, show self at door!"

Hesitating a moment, thinking he may just unload on me at any second when I did, I carefully peeked around the door. He was standing back about five feet with his T-77 trained on the cell.

"Okay, so I come out and you shoot me. Is that the plan?"

"Not shoot. Tu ta want to see you."

Slowly and with a great deal of apprehension I presented myself in the doorway. I then saw that his large set deputy was standing further back bearing down on me with an AK-47. I could probably have made a move on the captain as we walked the fifty or sixty steps to the station, but I wouldn't escape the spray of automatic weapons fire.

"Di di mau!" shouted Adolf.

"All right, I'm coming out." Passing through the doorway into the bright sun, I squinted a bit. I also had my hands up even with my shoulders.

After parading down the dirt path to the rear door of the station, I felt the muzzle of the AK in my back, coaxing me through the open doorway.

"Back in room!" he ordered, which meant I was to return to the interrogation room where Major Vann sat smoking one of his nasty cigarettes. The pungent reek of the smoke coupled with the fact I was both parched and ravenous turned my stomach.

"Sit, Mr. McGowan," he said.

I did as ordered in the chair opposite him. Immediately, I saw that he had in front of him both Thanh's and Sue's handwritten statements of the Dak Trang massacre.

"I…"

Vann held up his hand. "Do not speak."

"I would like some water, Major Vann."

He looked up at me with his beady little eyes and said a few words to his man who had taken his position in a corner. The guard then left the room, returning in about twenty seconds with a tin cup of the water. It smelled all right, which told me it was probably the same water that *they* drank.

Vann continued to smoke and read the documents that lay before him for a good five minutes as I drummed my fingers on the table. I knew it was annoying him as he looked up from the documents a couple of times at my hand. Finally, he spoke.

"This is interesting reading, Mr. McGowan. So, is this why you went into the Montagnard country?"

I ignored his question and laid into him with a barrage of demands. "I would also like something to eat, Major. You have no right to keep food from your prisoners and you damn sure have no right to put your prisoners in that pig sty you call a jail. I have a right under international law to be treated humanely. Now I demand that you contact the American Consulate."

Vann put his icy eyes on me and smiled, but didn't respond. It was his own little version of cat-and-mouse. A game I was not going to play.

"What did you do to Thanh?" I barked. "I know you

people beat him within an inch of his life."

Vann's smile quickly erased. "I'm afraid I have some bad news about Mr. Thanh. Unfortunately, he died during the night."

I slammed my fist hard down on the table and shouted, "You bastards! You murdering bastards!"

The guard then moved out of his corner and approached me. Vann held up his hand to stop his advance. He then motioned his man back into position with a nod of his head.

"We did not think he was hurt that badly when we took him to his cell. I checked on him early this morning and found that he had died. I am sorry it happened."

I put my index finger in his face and said, "You murdered him, Vann. You beat him to death. Why don't you tell Captain Hitler out there to come in here and try his shit with me? I won't allow *him* to suffer as long as he allowed Thanh to do before I break his goddam neck."

"I am afraid Captain Ngoc went too far with his interrogation. I will see that he is reprimanded."

"Reprimanded, huh? Like a letter of condemnation in his file? Before I leave here, I swear to God I will give him a reprimand of the *fatal* kind."

He smiled again and crushed out the butt of his cigarette on the concrete floor. "I am afraid you will never get that opportunity, Mr. McGowan. Now we will get off of the subject of Captain Ngoc and talk about how much trouble you are in. I have read the content of these statements with much interest. It appears they have been written and signed by conspirators against the Government of Vietnam. Mentioned in these documents is the name of my friend, Colonel Hung Bao."

"Hung Bao? Isn't that the Vietnamese word for constipation?"

Vann ignored the quip. "It seems that your *business* you speak of must have been to come here to kill Colonel Bao for the alleged crimes against the woman's village during the American war."

"I did not come here to murder *anyone*, Major Vann. Nor *did* I murder anyone. Obviously, there *is* a murderer in this building, however."

Vann again ignored my accusation. "I took the liberty this morning to dispatch a helicopter to Colonel Bao's home. He and his guards are missing. Colonel Bao's wife has not seen him in two days…and I know you were in the Montagnard village near his home two days ago." He held Sue's statement close to my face. "You see the date, Mr. McGowan?"

"And you think I had something to do with him being missing. If that's the case, prove it."

"I have the proof right here in my hand. I am sure we will find the Colonel's body soon and you can make it easier on yourself by giving me a statement of confession."

It was now *my* turn for the sarcastic smile. "I'm not giving you *shit*, Major Vann. Now I demand at once to be taken to Saigon where the American Consulate will address the entire matter."

Vann settled back in his chair and lit another cigarette. After blowing out a long stream of blue-gray smoke, he folded his arms and stared at me.

"So, the American government sent the CIA here to kill a very respected Vietnamese citizen, a man who is both a friend of the state and a former senator. You must realize that we have good evidence against you, do you not?"

With the statements in hand and the fact that they would ultimately find the bodies of Bao and his two guards, I was in deep ca-ca. And he knew that *I* knew it. I was all he had now that Thanh was dead.

"I'm not CIA, Major. Don't associate me with those prima donnas. But I'm not saying another word until you submit to my demand."

"I am afraid, Mr. McGowan, that you will not be seeing anyone from the American Consulate. Criminals, whether domestic *or* foreign, do not have rights."

"On *that* you are dead wrong, Major. I do have a right as an American citizen with a visa to contact my government. Am I automatically considered a criminal before I am tried and convicted?"

"Our justice system is much different from yours, Mr. McGowan. Our system makes for what you call a *deterrent* to those who will commit crimes. Your system is very liberal and that's why the United States has so many criminals in its streets."

Well, he had me there.

"And you know that how?" I said.

He took another drag. "Yes, you were correct. I was educated in an American school, but not here in this country. I was an exchange student in the early 1960s and went to the University of Southern California."

"Aha. So you became indoctrinated into the American way of life and then you actually came *back* to this hell hole. Now you sit here in a broken-down police station rotting away. And I was also correct when I speculated that you served as an ARVN soldier."

Vann appeared irritated, if not embarrassed. "I have

always loved this country, Mr. McGowan. There is no way I would not have returned. Yes, I was in the Army of South Vietnam and became a trung ui, a lieutenant. I did fight for the former government. But as you Americans say, that was then and this is now."

"And your loyalty ended when the commies took over."

"I do not consider myself communist or anything else. Yes, there is a red star on my cap. But I am Vietnamese, first and foremost, whatever government is in power. And I am a police officer sworn to uphold the law."

"You must have gained *something* from your experience in America."

"Yes. I learned to respect the law. And that is what I am doing now. I am upholding the law of our land by seeing that a foreign conspirator and probable murderer is brought to justice."

"I didn't kill anyone, Major. I don't have anyone's death on my conscience." I then paused. "So where do we go from here?"

He took another long drag from his half-smoked cigarette and stamped it out. "I will bring Captain Ngoc in here to get your confession."

"And when I don't give him one, will he commence to kicking the crap out of me?"

"I will assure that you are not harmed. However, if you do not write out a statement and sign it, you will go back into the hole and stay there until you do."

He then stood, dropped his head sharply in a kind of bow and left the room. It surprised me that he would stoop to bow to a murderer and conspirator. But, whatever I was, CIA, renegade, killer or molester, he knew we had some things in common, one of which was a mutual understanding.

A few minutes later, Captain Ngoc and his itty-bitty mustache entered the room with a legal pad in hand along with a micro-pointed ink pen. His deputy remained in his spot in the corner of the room behind me, eyeing me with hand on holster. Ngoc then slapped the pad down on the table and shoved it and the ink pen in my direction.

"Now you write confession."

I folded my arms and leaned back in my chair in defiance. "Why don't you take off that gun, send your monkey out of the room and then you try to take me down like you did Thanh, asshole?"

"You shut mouth and write…now!"

"Or what? Are you going to come across that table and *make* me do it? You're a big man with that pistol, aren't you?"

"You not threaten me, McGowan!" He looked in the direction of his deputy who took two or three steps in my direction.

"I don't make threats that I can't back up, Ngoc."

"You write confession or you end up like friend. We bury him this morning."

I stood and my flimsy chair fell backwards and clanged against the floor. "Go ahead, asshole. Try to make me sign that confession."

Slowly he got to his feet and then pulled out his pistol. Placing the muzzle against my forehead, he said, "Sit, McGowan. I shoot you *now* if you do not."

So as not to argue with the automatic, I up-righted the

chair and sat down. He sat as well on his side of the table, but the gun remained fixed to my head.

"You write confession now or I put bullet in your head."

"Relax, Dai ui. Put the gun away and I'll consider it."

"If you do not sign in one minute, you die. No threat." He shot a glance at the guard who had moved in behind me.

I then knew that Major Vann understood that Ngoc would ultimately kill me, whether I signed a confession or not. That's why he was not in the room with us. It made me wonder which one of them was actually in charge. It was obvious to me that Vann still held his old life in South Vietnam in great esteem, but the younger Ngoc was part of the new order, and *his* allegiance was with the Socialist Party of Vietnam. And I knew that if I did not make a play soon, I would only leave the room feet first. The headlines would read, *American Murderer Confesses to Crime. Dies While Escaping.*

I then began to look for a window of opportunity. It would be difficult with two guns in the room, especially when one was still against my head.

"Holster your gun, Ngoc, or you'll have to go ahead and kill me without the signed confession."

Ngoc took a moment and looked again at his deputy, then eased the gun back into its leather container.

I pulled the pad toward me and placed the fine point of the pen to the paper. If I signed it, I knew I would be admitting guilt of crimes against the Government of Vietnam and of course, murder, or at least accessory to murder. I would also cower under pressure when I didn't so much as put up a fight. And that definitely wasn't me. Furthermore, I had no intention of signing any goddamned confession. I was only continuing to stall in order to look for an opportunity to make some kind of move.

"*Sign!*" Ngoc barked. He took from a sheath on his belt what looked like a seven inch dagger and pointed it at me.

Defiantly, I laid down the pen, crossed my arms and leaned back in the chair. "Why don't I instead rip your head off and piss down your neck."

Ngoc lifted the dagger and pointed it over the table to within an inch of my nose. "You sign or I put blade up your nose and cut off."

I looked back at the deputy who was nodding and smiling. The sparkle in his eyes said he was definitely looking forward to seeing how I would look without a nose. I stared back at Ngoc without blinking.

Ngoc then took the dragon-carved handle of the dagger and banged it sharply down onto the table. "*Sign!*" he shouted again. The blade stood rigidly upright at twelve o'clock. And therein lay my window of opportunity. I glanced behind me again to where the deputy was standing. The grin on his face had changed into a yawn. Apparently, as he likely didn't get much sleep last night either, I was sure he was not his best self. Suddenly and swiftly, I reached out and grabbed a handful of Ngoc's thick, black hair, slamming his forehead onto the blade, driving it through the bone and into his brain up to the dagger's handle. He had to be dead instantly. I then sprang onto the deputy who was fumbling with the snap on his holster and gave him a rabbit chop to the Adam's apple. I thought about killing him with my next punch, thinking that he likely had a hand in Thanh's death as well, but I had seen too many people die the past few days. While the deputy was still gagging, I brought up my fist at light speed and planted it squarely into his chops. A number of teeth immediately fell out of his mouth like Chicklets from a ruptured piñata. A rush of bright red blood followed suit. I then dropped him to his knees with a kick to the groin and put him out with a crushing chop to the back of his neck. I heard it snap. Not stopping to see if he was still alive, I pulled his pistol from its holster, checked the magazine and shoved the gun into my jeans. I then took out Captain Adolf's T-77 and charged through the door. Only the fat cop was in the room, sitting behind the desk eating a pastry of some sort. When he reached for *his* sidearm, I put a bead on his forehead with my pistol and shook my head. Quickly, he raised his hands. He wasn't going to challenge me.

"Tu ta Vann?" I asked.

He motioned toward the door and I looked out of the window. Vann was smoking a cigarette in front of the building. I then went around the desk and pulled fat boy's pistol from his holster. He looked up at me pitifully, hands still raised. There was glaze around his mouth from the sugar-crusted pastry. If I was convinced he wouldn't try anything, I would just usher him in the back room and lock the door. But then he might raise a ruckus and bring Vann through the door, pistol in hand. So I clubbed him hard on the top of his head with the butt of the pistol which evoked a groan. His body fell out of the chair and plastered the concrete floor like a slab of lard.

"Sorry, tubby. You can finish the donut when you wake up."

I stood at the window and waited for Vann to finish his cigarette and come back in. I didn't want a scene outside in broad daylight where some passerby would see it. Within two minutes he took a final drag, dropped the cigarette to the soil and ground it with the sole of his shoe. As soon as he opened the door, the pistol in my right hand was aimed at his chest. Showing colossal surprise, his eyes widened as he made a move for his pistol.

"Don't do it, Major Vann. You can live or you can die. Your choice."

"I will be killed anyway if you escape, Mr. McGowan. The Vietnam government already knows about you. You are connected with the disappearance of a very esteemed man." He then looked at his deputy. "Did you kill him?"

"He's just sleeping for a couple of hours. But he *will* have a headache when he wakes up."

"And the others?"

"The same…except Captain Ngoc will not wake up."

"You killed him then."

"He *needed* killing."

His hand remained on his holster. "I cannot let you leave here, Mr. McGowan."

"Look, I'll tie you to a chair and leave a note that none of this was your idea. I like you, Major, and don't want to be the one to have to kill you."

He smiled. "Tam biet, McGowan." (Goodbye).

When Vann groped into his holster for his pistol, I fired a round that went through his hand and into the butt of the gun. He screamed and then dropped to his knees in pain, holding his right hand with his left. Blood flowed profusely.

I then pulled his pistol from the holster, tossed it across the room and helped him to a chair.

"Why did you not kill me, McGowan?" His face was full of venom.

"Mrs. Vann would not have liked that."

"My wife is dead. I have no family. It would have been a release for me."

"Like I said, I only kill the people that need killing. I have to believe you had nothing to do with Thanh's death. You looked genuinely sorry that Ngoc murdered him."

"It was unnecessary. There were other ways to deal with Thanh."

"No more talk, Major Vann. Let me dress that wound. Where are your bandages?"

He motioned to an overhead cabinet. In it I found a bottle of alcohol, some gauze and tape. I applied the alcohol which caused him to wince and then I held the compress firmly against his hand to slow down the bleeding. Finally, I bound the hand tightly with the surgical tape.

"What shall I do with you now, Major Vann?"

"You can hand me my pistol."

"You still want to kill me, then," I said.

"Not *you.*"

I shook my head and went around behind him. "Then this is the only way." I placed my forearm around his neck and locked my hand onto the opposite shoulder. The choke hold would put him to sleep for a few hours. What his superiors did to him when they found him was not my problem. His head eventually dropped onto his chest.

I found my knapsack on a shelf and checked to see if my cell phone was still in it. It was. I then went to the interrogation room and scarped up the two statements, placing them in the bag. The deputy was still out and Ngoc, still dead. Vann would be in la-la land for an hour or two.

I was surprised that there were no other officers or citizens coming in or out of the station, but it *was* a kind of outpost far from the city limits of Pleiku. Checking two other rooms in the station, I found two beds and a few personal belongings. I supposed that two of the officers bunked there on a rotating basis and it set me to wonder how many others were assigned to the small precinct. I knew there was at least one other out there somewhere with the paddy wagon that had delivered us. I did find a gallon of water and after smelling it, took several gulps to replenish my system.

dfgI wasn't exactly sure what my next move would be. It wouldn't be long until someone came into the station…maybe another officer or two or someone reporting a crime. I had an idea. Tubby wasn't needing his uniform and as the smaller dudes' shirts would definitely not fit my frame, his clothes would be the closest fitting. I figured all I would need was his shirt and hat and since I'd be high-tailing it out of there in one of the police jeeps, no one should readily notice I had on jeans.

The shirt was a little baggy, but the sleeves were short. It would do, however. His gun belt would work out since it was one size-fits-all. I did have to gird it up a little to fit my size 34 waist. Being American and six-feet one, I knew I'd still stand out, but I could hunker down in the jeep and pull the cap down over my face. More people would be looking at the police jeep than me, anyway.

After making sure nobody inside of the station was coming back to life, I opened the front door to the station, looked up and down the road and stepped out. I wondered how far I'd get down the road toward Qui Nhon before somebody would discover the mess I created and light out after me.

CHAPTER ELEVEN

I think it was Ngoc's jeep that I stole. There were two in the parking lot and the second one didn't have a canvass top. But both were old American Willys that had obviously been appropriated by the conquering victors along with other abandoned American hardware. Both were black versus the Army green and looked as though they had been painted by a brush. It served to reinforce the fact that Major Vann and troop, who occupied the last outpost of Pleiku, were pretty damn low on the police totem pole. The jeep now wore a red star which had been painted over the white U.S. star. However, it cranked easily and I sped away, throwing gravel behind me.

Seemed like old times, wearing a green uniform and driving the old mule down Highway 19 toward Qui Nhon…like déjà vu. I checked the fuel gauge and saw that Ngoc had been thoughtful enough to fill up the tank before I left, God rest his soul. It would be about dark before I made Mr. Huynh's hacienda…that is if I could remember how to get there. It was for sure I needed his help. Before I clocked ten miles, somebody would be finding Vann and the authorities would be all over me like flies on a shit house.

My trek along the two-lane asphalt which meandered past small townships, groves of bananas and sugar cane, huts and roadside markets was largely uneventful. The cops had absconded with what little money I had and unless I stopped off at one of the markets to beg for food, the fact that I was an unkempt Anglo in a fat cop's uniform and driving a stolen police jeep may arouse just a tad of suspicion. So, I figured I could endure a little more hunger until the night.

I guessed I was half-way to Qui Nhon when I passed an accident scene where a car had just collided with an ox cart, spilling fruits and vegetables all over the highway. When I didn't stop to investigate and help the people, in my rear view mirror I saw them stomping and pumping their fists at me, the commie bastard cop that I was.

A few times I passed other police vehicles approaching from the opposite direction. The driver would throw up his hand and I would do the same in return, scrunching further down in my seat to look as small as I could. However, I knew that *every* Asian male was not five-foot nothing. I had seen a number of them over six-feet like me. And of course there was Yao Ming.

At Quang IIi I picked up Highway 1A and started south. I did begin to remember things from my trip up country and figured Qui Nhon was no more than ten miles south. The sun had set an hour before and I found it necessary to flip on the lights. Hopefully, I would recognize where I needed to turn off the highway to the House of Hope. I knew straight across the highway from the road to Huynh's house was a large rock that resembled a huge mushroom.

Suddenly, in my rear view mirror I saw the red flashing lights of either a military or police vehicle rapidly gaining on my rear bumper. As it closed in, I saw that it was a Corolla sedan and indeed a police unit. My thinking was that Vann had regained consciousness and sent out an APB to look for Ngoc's jeep. A renegade American killer was driving it, so just shoot the bastard and forget about trying to bring him in. And then I felt the bump. Considering it was little more than a jolt, I figured they were just trying to get me to stop, not wreck me. I then saw my opportunity. I swerved to the right, jumped a ditch which propelled me about five feet into the air, landing me into an open field. In my mirror, I saw the Toyota try to follow suit, but as soon as it hit the ditch, it stalled out. They didn't count on this old West Virginia boy's backwoods driving skills and obviously had never watched *The Dukes of Hazzard.*

After clearing the field, I re-jumped the ditch and continued back down 1A toward Qui Nhon. As I was sure the cops were scrambling to get back on the road, I continued on at a fairly good clip toward the lights of the sleepy coastal city. After a half minute, I could again see a quarter mile back the flashing red lights making another run at me. But then there it was…the mushroom rock on the right. I then shut off my lights and made an abrupt left turn into the entrance road to the House of Hope. Using the jeep's blackout lights, I continued on a few hundred feet, then glanced back to see the flashing red lights of the police unit sail on by. I think the *last* time I pulled that stunt, I was seventeen and cruising on old Route 60 at over a hundred miles an hour in my Mustang Cobra evading a State Trooper who even in his Hemi police interceptor couldn't stay with me. Except, he recognized the car a week later parked outside the Court Restaurant and waited for me to appear. I didn't get the keys back from my dad for a month.

Since Mr. Huynh was not expecting me, I was hoping he would not think me an intruder and start shooting. As I had already escaped torture, incarceration and death the past couple of days, I'd have hated like hell to end up six feet under at the hands of a friend of a friend. However, when I zipped through the gate, brought the jeep to a stop in front of Huynh's house and stepped out, I was pleased to find that no flying bullets or Dobermans awaited me.

I knocked twice and within a half-minute the door slowly opened, but not more than six inches. Through the crack I then saw the surprised and wanly face of Mr. Huynh. The light from inside the house enabled him to see me as well. I don't think he recognized me, though, since the cop cap was shielding much of my face. He then looked down at my uniform shirt.

"Dien gi lam ban muon?" I think that meant 'what do you want?'

"Ong Huynh," I replied. "No la toi. It's me, McGowan."

A frown swept over his brow. "Why are you in a police uniform?"

"Would you believe it if I told you I killed a policeman, assaulted three others and stole that jeep sitting behind me?"

He laughed at first and then displayed a look of alarm at the thought I may have really done it, especially when he saw the police unit.

"I…don't understand."

"May I come in to talk with you about it?"

He bowed and swept his hand in the direction of his den. "Yes. Yes of course. Please…this way."

I took off the cap and tossed it back out onto the porch and then shed my shoes at the door. In my stocking feet I followed Mr. Huynh to his sitting room. As filthy and grungy as I was, not having had a bath in three or four days, I'm sure I was smelling up his house. When I started to sit cross-legged on the floor, he said, "No, please sit on the couch."

"I can't, Mr. Huynh. You must see and smell that I am unclean."

He didn't reply to that, which meant that he did. But he did ask, "Where is Thanh?"

I dropped my head without immediately answering. After a moment, I said, "Let me first give you a summary what occurred the past few days and then I will tell you about Thanh."

For the next ten plus minutes I began telling him about going to the Montagnard village, hooking up with Sue, going to the Garden of Souls, encountering Bao and his guards, Thanh killing them, and then on our trip back south, our getting arrested and Thanh getting beaten.

"I am sorry to tell you, Mr. Huynh, that the police beat Thanh so badly that he died in his cell."

"Died? Chet?" (killed)

"Yes."

He then stood and without further word, walked to the room across the hallway and lit a candle at the base of where a statue of Buddha sat on a pedestal above him. After falling forward on his knees, rocking back and forth a few times, praying, he stood back up and returned to the den.

"The police are bastards," he remarked. "The people responsible should all pay with their lives so that he can be vindicated. His soul cries out for it."

"The policeman responsible did pay with his, Mr. Huynh. What I told you when I came into your house was true."

A look of concern then fell onto his face. "They did not follow you here?"

"No. They tried to do so, but I lost them back on Highway 1A." I could understand his apprehension that I would bring them to his door. If they knew that I was there, he would lose everything, go to jail and never see his grandchildren again. My stomach then started gurgling and he laughed.

"You have not eaten today."

"No, I have not, sir."

Mr. Huynh then stood and clapped his hands twice. Within seconds his servant appeared and stood in the doorway of the den. "Please draw Mr. McGowan a bath and prepare him some dinner. He will be our guest again tonight," he said in English so that I would understand.

"You are too kind, Mr. Huynh. I appreciate this very much. But I certainly don't want to inconvenience you or take advantage in any way."

He waved his hand dismissively in my direction and replied, "That is nonsense. I consider you tonight as my guest and Thanh's friend. I now think of you as *my* friend."

"As I do you, sir. Thank you."

"Tomorrow we will have to dispose of the vehicle and find a way to get you back to Ho Chi Minh City. If the police are hunting you, you will need to go immediately to your embassy to arrange travel out of the country. The police will be watching for you at the airport."

I nodded. "Evading them will not be easy."

Momentarily, Co Dong reappeared in the room and gestured for me to follow her. As my other pair of jeans and the two shirts were also soiled and wadded up in my travel bag, I really had nothing to change into. And anything that Mr. Huynh had would be about the size an American twelve year old boy would wear. So, I was stuck with my nasty rags. When we both entered the bath room, she said, "Water ready. Take off clothes."

I began unbuttoning my khaki shirt, but then stopped and looked at her.

"What wrong?" she asked.

"Nothing is wrong; I was just waiting for you to leave."

She shook her head and smiled at my modesty. "Take off clothes. I wash them. Here is robe."

"But…"

She shook her head again and I could see that it didn't matter to her whether or not I stood in front of her wearing only my birthday suit. She was not going to become warm for my form upon seeing me naked as a jaybird. This was merely *service* to her and I suspected she did the same with Mr. Huynh. I had forgotten I was in Asia where every time a woman sees a man with his clothes off does not mean carnal nasty is about to take place. Anyway, I shed my clothes and then quickly slipped into the tub without looking to see if *she* was looking. No sooner than I had set my bottom onto the porcelain, she swept up my clothes and shoes and disappeared from the room.

The water felt immediately therapeutic if not *heaven* to my tired bones. After soaking in the humongous tub for nearly twenty minutes, the largest organ on my body, my skin mind you, was tingling, even sparkling with appreciation. I then dried off with a large, thirsty towel, threw on the robe, which was just a tad tight, and found both some shaving cream and a disposable Bic razor to peel off a four day growth. Co Dong had also laid out some black, pajama-like tops and bottoms for me that reminded me of the type we found on dead Viet Cong after a skirmish.

Although the clothing was short in the legs and sleeves, at least the loose waist band went around my middle.

I'm not sure where she found the time to do so, after washing all my clothes, but when I departed the bath room for the dining area I saw that she had heated up some pork, greens, and yes, rice for me. She had also whipped up a nice crème brulee which was about the best tasting thing I had eaten in years…so said my taste buds. Of course, they were sorely out of practice. All of this made me feel like I had climbed up from the fiery pit of hell into a heavenly resort spa.

Mr. Huynh knew that I was too tired to sit up and socialize, so when I took the last few bites of the dessert, he gestured to Co Dong to prepare my bed. "As the hour is late, Mr. McGowan, perhaps we should all retire and we will determine what to do with you tomorrow."

I checked my watch and actually it wasn't that late at all. Eight-fifteen. "My body thanks you as does my fading brain, Mr. Huynh."

He bowed and left the dining room and I retreated immediately to my bedroom, leaving Co Dong with the dishes. Not thirty seconds after I fell onto the bed, my lights went out and didn't turn back on until dawn's early light opened my eyes a full eleven hours later. I awoke refreshed, but a bit hungry and ready to have a good day for a change.

As I sat at the breakfast table we talked more about Thanh. I had only known him for a few days, but I had developed a kind of kinship with him. "I genuinely liked Thanh," I said. "I wished there had been something I could have done to prevent his death. I made my move on the cops too late."

"You must not blame yourself, Mr. McGowan. It was a matter of time the police would have gotten to him. It was more about his anti-government activities and this was their opportunity to stop him. And you did not know they would beat him as they did."

"His wife and family will be wondering about him soon. They may never even be able to reclaim his body."

Mr. Huynh sighed. "It is all very sad. I will contact her to tell her what happened. She needs to know even if his body is not found. I suspect it will not."

We sat for a few moments without further words. The guilt I was feeling about Thanh was immense. Had I known what we would be facing when we were arrested, I would have taken Ngoc and his deputy down immediately. I had both the skill and opportunity to do so. If not for me, Thanh would be working in his store with his wife this very day. His death may be just one more thing added to my list of personal haunts. Many of the players directly or indirectly involved in the Dak Trang massacre were now dead…Berryhill, Thanh, Bao and a great number of the former soldiers in Company C. But, there was yet one more who needed to die, and although he personally was not on my mission task list, I would take it upon myself to find him. It didn't matter what Byrd and the Prez had further in store for me…or for him. I knew what had to be done.

After breakfast Mr. Huynh's nephew, Lop An, appeared at the door and began engaging in conversation with my host. He nodded to me and then closed the door behind him as he left out.

"Lop will dispose of the police vehicle in a pond two kilometers from here," Mr. Huynh said. "The water is almost black and the jeep should never be found. When he returns, he will take you to Ho Chi Minh City to where your American officials are. Will you be ready to travel within the hour?"

"Yes. I'm ready to go whenever he is."

"Good," he replied. "I will also have Dong pack you some food and water for your trip. To eat again soon will help you restore your strength."

*   *   *   *

At just before ten, Lop pulled Mr. Huynh's vintage 1965 Chrysler Imperial from his stable and tooted the horn once in front of the house.

"Mr. Huynh, I cannot tell you what it meant for you to take me in last night. I think I was operating on my last cylinder. I will never forget your kindness. Maybe someday, somehow, I can repay you."

He smiled. "Nothing to repay, Mr. McGowan. You know I will not see you again for two reasons. I am an old man with not many years left. And then you will never again be allowed to return to this country if you are able to leave it at all."

I nodded. "Well, the second part I agree will likely be the case. But I do wish you a long life with many rich blessings. You are a kind man with a generous heart."

He stood erect and dropped his head sharply. I followed suit. He then extended his hand and I grasped it, shaking it twice per tradition. I followed him to the front door where he bowed again as I passed. If only America could ever again become this socially polite…as it was two or three hundred years ago. I tossed my bag into the back floor of the Chrysler and swung my buns into the front passenger seat. Mr. Huynh was on the front porch with Co Dong, both standing still and straight. From my open passenger side window, I lifted my hand toward them and held it there until we had cleared the driveway. Mr. Huynh was right. I would never see him again, but I would think of him and the

House of Hope from time to time…and often.

I wasn't exactly keeping a low profile riding high and wide in the big, black Imperial. People seeing us would think that the passenger inside the car being chauffeured was one of socialist Vietnam's few wealthy people. But at closer look, the man was American, or at least of the European persuasion. I reached down in the back floor and pulled a floppy bush hat out of my bag, allowing it to drape down over my face.

Finally able to obtain cell coverage after closing in on Ho Chi Minh City three hours later, I found I probably had just enough juice left for one phone call. I was on my last bar. And as much as I wanted to do so, I did not call Adrianna. I pulled out the number I had written days ago on a piece of paper…the American Consulate's office. Just in case the police would be chasing me for some reason…like murder and assault.

"United States General Consulate. Joanna Kitterman speaking."

"Hello, Ms. Kitterman. My name is Bruce McGowan and I work for the U.S. State Department. I'm currently in Vietnam just outside the limits of Ho Chi Minh City. I have to tell you that I'm in a bit of trouble and…"

"Just a moment. You need the Citizen Services Department," she said abruptly. I then heard Muzak. It's everywhere.

After two minutes, another voice came on the line. "Citizen Services, Peggy Nabors. May I help you?"

"Hi, my name is Bruce McGowan, American citizen. I'm here in Vietnam, stranded, and need some help…"

"Just a moment. You need to speak with the Policy and Issues Department." And so I was sent back to Mantovani and *Love is a Many Splendored Thing*. Now my last bar was flashing.

"Good afternoon. Consulate General's Office, Policy and Issues, John Larue speaking."

"Hey, guy," I began. "I don't have much power left in my cell phone and keep getting switched around, can you help me?"

"I'll try, sir. What is your problem?"

"My name is Bruce McGowan, American citizen here in Vietnam on government business, and…" And then my phone powered down. Murphy got me again with his stinking law.

Thank God Mr. Huynh's nephew, Lop, knew a small bit of English and had heard me say the name American Consulate. "Not worry. I know where to go. Consulate in old American Embassy location on Le Duan. We go there."

I didn't exactly remember where it was, but I did remember the building. It was the famous site that was on world-wide television in 1975 where a long line of Vietnamese people were perched on the rooftop trying to board a departing Huey. I wasn't there of course, but I did see the re-enactment in the wonderful Broadway musical, *Miss Saigon*.

CHAPTER TWELVE

At ten minutes past four, Lop pulled the Imperial to the curb in front of the Consulate General's building and deposited me. I thanked him and told him I was sorry I had no money to give him for his taxi services. He said for me to "not worry." His uncle would compensate him well, which again reminded me how much I was in Mr. Huynh's debt. I would have to send the old gentleman a nice gift one day such as a piece of American fine art like a Velvet Elvis painting or one of dogs and cats playing cards. Just kidding, of course. I owed the man my life.

When I entered the building, I was immediately accosted by a large-set American guard wearing a crew cut and a bulldog scowl. A clipboard was in one hand and a walkie-talkie in the other.

"Afternoon, sir," he greeted. "Do you have business here?"

"I hope so," I replied. "I work for the State Department and am in the country on government business. Unfortunately, I've fallen on some misfortune and need help in getting back to the States."

"May I see some identification?"

I fished from my bag my visa and passport. He mulled them over and then said, "And your State Department ID?"

"I don't have it with me. Neither did I bring a wallet. I generally just travel with a money clip with a few hundred dollars in it. But all that is gone."

"How were you proposing to get back to the States?"

"I was confident the Consulate's office would help me with that."

"The Consulate's policy is that we neither provide money nor airfare for displaced Americans."

"But I do know your office is committed to assisting American citizens in emergency situations. I would say my situation is pretty much an emergency."

"You can't go to a Western Union and have money wired to you?"

"Look, Mister…Sanborn," I responded after checking his nametag, "like I said, I'm with the State Department and someone should be getting me home."

"But you have no ID to prove that."

I sighed audibly, making him aware that I was quickly tiring of him. "We're going in circles here, sir. Do I need to have the Secretary of State call the Consulate General to have him address the matter?"

He obviously didn't take kindly to my threat. Placing his walkie-talkie hand on his hip, he retorted, "No need to bust my chops here, sir. I'm just doing my job. And right now, my job is to screen anybody entering this building, American or not."

"Okay, I'm good with that. But I need you to point me to a department where I can talk to someone who can help me with my problem. I at least need access to a phone where I can contact my supervisor, who by the way is connected right at the top…which means somebody important is wondering where the hell I am."

He gave me the kind of look that said he didn't like people who tried pulling rank and throwing their weight around to get what they wanted. But then his face finally took on an expression of resignation and he said, "Alright. Down that hallway at the second door on the right is the American Citizen Services Office. You need to sign in on this clipboard and then go over there through security where that officer is standing. When you leave the building you *will* find me and sign out again." He set the clipboard on a nearby table and then handed me a pen.

When I opened the door to the Services Office, my eyes fell immediately upon a very attractive upper thirties blonde with a voluptuous bosom and a brilliant smile that revealed a set of near perfect choppers.

"Hello," she said with a smile. "How can I help you?"

"Hello," I answered, but not quite in the same musical tone. "I'm in a bit of a pickle here. Name's Bruce McGowan and I'm with the U.S. State Department. Is it possible that I could get you to call my boss's number in Washington, D.C.?"

"I think we can do that. May I see your identification?"

"I don't have my State Department ID with me, but here're my passport and visa."

She took them from me and told me to please have a seat. I liked her much better than the ogre, Sanborn. After making a copy of them, she said, "Okay, Mr. McGowan, if you will give me the number, let's see if we can get your guy on the line."

I borrowed a pencil from a tray on her desk and tore off a sticky to write down the number down for her.

"Thank you," she said gleefully. She then held out her hand across the desk. "By the way, I'm Joy."

I'll bet you are.

"Call me Bruce…and thanks for doing this."

"My pleasure."

And mine.

She dialed the number and in a few moments lifted her eyes to mine, smiled and nodded. It appeared someone answered.

"Oh, hi. My name is Joy Cartwright and I'm with the Consulate General's Office in Ho Chi Minh City, Vietnam. I have a Mr. Bruce McGowan with me and he says he needs to talk with someone at your office."

There was a pause and then she smiled and winked at me.

"Oh, I see…the answering service."

I snapped my fingers. Of course. It was still something like three in the morning in Washington, D.C.

"Well, let me leave you my number." Another pause. "You can see it on your phone? Good. Well, as there will be no one at my number when your office opens, could you then get a message to…" She looked back at me.

"Lionel Byrd," I said.

"…Mr. Lionel Byrd. Have him call here as soon as possible." Pause. "Fine, thank you and goodbye."

I really do like accommodating people…especially vivacious, personable and intelligent accommodating people.

Joy then hung up her phone. "I'm sure you heard. The answering service will get the message to Mr. Byrd. Hopefully, he'll call back before I close out today. May I get you some coffee?"

"Coffee? Something I have not had in a week? Please."

She immediately rose from her chair and sashayed across the room to the coffee pot to pour me a cup. I couldn't help noticing that the well-formed derriere and shapely legs matched the rest of the package. I know what you're thinking. Yes, I'm a 100 % married man. But I'm also a 100 % red-blooded man who appreciates all such of God's creatures.

"I have beignets over here, too. Would you like one?"

"That would be nice."

"They might be a bit stale since they were brought in this morning. I'll throw one in the microwave."

It was about *time* things started going my way. With my luck the past few days, I could have found myself in the presence of a crotchety old crone who only offered me nothing but a bad time.

As we sat in our chairs waiting for the Birdman to call, that is if he drug his bones in to work before six, his time, I noticed that Joy kept looking at me and smiling. I wasn't sure if it was because she was appreciating my healthy tan, looking rather Australian bush-like in my freshly-pressed khaki cargo shirt and tight jeans, also wearing my captivating smile, or that she was just being nice, feeling sorry for the older man sitting in front of her, penniless, displaced and begging for a ride back to the States. But I didn't care; I liked the smile.

"What do you do for the State Department, Mr. McGowan?"

"Call me *Bruce*, okay? Well, I only work for the department part-time. Mostly I profile and investigate people and organizations that have subversive ideas." I didn't mention the termination part.

"Is that why you're here…to investigate someone in Vietnam?"

I was about to think up some big lie when her phone rang.

"This is Joy," she answered. "May I help you?" There was a pause. "Yes, sir. He's right here. It's Mr. Byrd." She then handed me the phone.

"Obviously, the answering service got you out of bed, Lionel. It has to be three or four in the morning there."

"Never mind that. I expected to hear something from you long before now, Bruce."

"Well, it's a long story, boss. I ran into some adversity."

"Why does that not surprise me?"

"At least I got what I came here for and am ready to come back. Just one slight problem."

"Go ahead."

"I'm without cash and am going to need some big time assistance making it through customs and airport security."

"And why is that?"

"It's…complicated. The bottom line is that I'll be recognized and thrown in jail."

Joy's eyes and ears pricked up.

I heard his audible sigh. "What did you do?" he asked.

"It seems I'm probably wanted for a murder of one man and likely three more. Also I assaulted three other cops, stole a police jeep and collaborated with a known conspirator bent on committing subversive acts against the Socialist Republic of Vietnam. And he was murdered as well. It's all a bit sticky."

Joy's mouth fell open and I'm sure Byrd's did as well. There was nothing but silence for a few moments on the other end of the line.

"I have to say, Bruce, when you break something, you do it in a big way."

"Let's just say I acted in self-defense. You knew there may be difficulties."

"Yes, but murder, vehicle theft, assault and conspiracy I hadn't counted on."

"So, how can you help me fix this? It won't be easy getting me out of country."

"You are actually a fugitive from justice? And the police are hunting for you as we speak?"

"That would be correct."

He was silent for a few moments and I could have sworn I heard the cogs and pulleys turning in his head. "All right. I'll send the Department jet for you. It'll drop you at the Greenbrier Airport so that you can first go home to your worried wife. I'll apprise the Consulate General of what's going on. Of course I don't know the particulars of what put you in this predicament. This could in fact have some international ramifications. We will have to get you a whole new set of documents and a new name. Could take a day or so. I will work with the Consulate in getting you a new passport. That's one of their services. In the meantime, find a place to stay. And stay out of sight."

"And money? Can you do something about that?"

"You're a real pain in the ass, you know that? Okay, I'll have five hundred dollars wired to the Consulate's office. I would ask you to explain the particulars of your crimes, but there will be ears on this line."

"You mean my acts of indiscretion."

"Put the young lady back on the line. I will tell her about the money. I will also have dialogue with the Consulate General and arrange for your passage."

"Thanks, boss."

"And Bruce."

"Yes."

"Please refrain from committing any more 'indiscretions' while you're there."

"Will do my very best, sir. I'll now give you back to Ms. Cartwright."

Joy took the receiver and said, "Yes, sir?"

She listened for nearly a minute while scribbling notes on a legal pad. "I'll look for the wire tomorrow. Thank you and have a good morning, sir."

She hung up the phone and stared at me like I was some sort of human disease. No smile this time.

"Tell me you were just kidding with Mr. Byrd when you said you did all those things."

"Okay, I was just kidding."

Well, she asked me to tell her that.

"Whew. You had me going there. You must like to joke around a lot with your boss."

"Oh, believe me. I'm a riot around my office."

"Well, anyway, your money won't be here until tomorrow some time. Maybe in the morning."

"Which presents me with a problem. Looks like I don't eat or sleep in a hotel tonight," I lamented.

"I can take care of the eating part. I'd be happy to buy you some dinner," she said.

I smiled. "I can't let you do that. But if you have an apple or a left-over sandwich in your break area, that would tie me over."

"Nonsense. I've got nothing going tonight. I'd love to hang out with a good looking American guy for a change."

"You mean you haven't been socializing with other Americans here?"

"The guys who work here are either married or very…well, unappealing, if you know what I mean."

Which obviously meant *I* was appealing…but married nonetheless.

She continued. "Other American men in the city are mostly blue collar contractors or boozed up, spaced out Vietnam veterans who like to sit around crying in their beers and telling war stories. I just don't go out with dead beats."

"Well, Joy, I have to tell you…I'm married."

"Oh, I'm sorry. I didn't mean…I saw you weren't wearing a ring…but I…I didn't intend for this to be any kind of date," she stammered. "I just thought I'd help out a very lost American."

"I didn't know I was lost."

"I didn't mean it that way."

"I know," I replied. "And I didn't mean to make you feel uncomfortable by making sure you knew I am married. I will be very pleased to take you up on your offer. For a hamburger today, I will gladly pay you on Tuesday."

"What? A hamburger? I can do better than that."

"No, no. I was just repeating Wimpy's little saying. You know, Popeye? The cartoon?"

"No, I don't think so," she replied thoughtfully.

I forgot that when I was watching Popeye and Olive Oyl, it would be another fifteen years before she was born. Which made me feel down-right ancient.

"Any way, I'm all yours this evening."

"Good," she said gleefully. "We'll leave here at six when we close, go by my apartment, freshen up and then go to Queen Bee's."

"I think I know Queen Bee's. If it's the same place that was around thirty years ago."

"You were here then? You're a Vietnam vet?"

"Yeah, but I'm not one of those old guys you mentioned that sits around crying in my beer and telling war stories."

"Well *that's* a relief. If I hear another one anytime soon, I think I'll commit hari kari."

Joy told me I could hang out in the visitor's lounge until we left and that gave me an opportunity to call Adrianna. I knew she had to be nearly out of her mind with worry and even though it was still early, early morning in West Virginia, she was probably awake pacing the floor. As my cell phone was still as dead as Captain Ngoc, I plugged it in for a few minutes to get it to power up. Fifteen minutes later, when I got back one of my bars, I touched Speed Dial # 1.

"Oh, God, Bruce. I've been so worried. Why haven't

you called?"

"A long story, my dear. There just hasn't been any cell coverage anywhere I've been and when I did get finally get into coverage range, my phone went dead."

"You couldn't use a regular phone somewhere and reverse the charges?"

"Well, for the most part, I have been places where there weren't any phones...like deep in the jungle."

She sighed. It was the kind of sigh that I had heard a few times before, especially where it involved my CTT comings and goings. "Bruce...I can't take this anymore. You've got to come home. I haven't had two nights worth of good sleep since you've been away. I...can't go on like this."

"What do you mean by that?" I replied rather sharply. "You're not going to..."

"Kick you out? No, I'm not getting rid of you, Bruce McGowan, but I want you to know I'm not happy about this whole situation. We really have to talk when you get back." She paused. "Which will be when?"

"A couple of days. Byrd has already sent a jet for me."

"I hope so. Just...be safe. That's all I ask. Just come home to me as quickly as you can. I miss you something awful."

"And I miss you, too, sweetie. Sorry about all this. I'll make it up to you. I promise."

She was silent for a moment and then she whispered, "I know. I love you. And it's when you're gone these long weeks that makes me realize how much."

"Mmm. Hearing you say that makes everything I have endured the last week or more dissipate from my brain."

"What have you had to endure?"

"That's a conversation for when I get home. But don't worry. All that's left is my trip back to you. All downhill from here."

"I'm glad."

"Hey, I guess I'd better get off the line. Now you get some sleep and don't worry."

"Okay. I definitely do need some. Two days, McGowan. No more."

"You can count on it, babe."

And just like on cue, my only bar went away and my phone was dead again. For the remainder of the afternoon, I kicked back on the sofa and recharged both the battery in my phone and in my brain.

*   *   *   *

We left Joy's office about ten minutes after six, passing by the irksome Mr. Sanborn who seeing me leave with her gave me the evil eye. Maybe he had the *hots* for her and had never been able to get out of the batter's box.

"Good night, Miss Cartwright."

"Good night, Mr. Sanborn."

He kept his eyes on us all the way out the door.

We didn't have very far to go as her apartment was three blocks away on Le Duan. It was a nice evening for a walk, anyway. The humidity seemed to have dissipated and the sun was beginning to fall onto the other side of Saigon's beautiful skyline. I was surprised to see that there were actually a few skyscrapers in the distance, giving the city a progressive look, again quite different from what I remember. Who would've thought?

The street that fronted her building was fairly narrow and with all of the pedestrian traffic coming and going, I had to let the lovely Miss Cartwright go ahead of me. In her tight skirt and athletically-shaped legs, she was poetry in motion, gliding along the sidewalk as graceful and poised as a Miss USA contestant, which I was sure she probably was at one time. And just watching her, I was having some immense guilt pangs. I then began to think that accompanying her for a night out on the town not to mention going up to her apartment was a bad idea.

Joy's one bedroom apartment was situated over a dumpy noodle joint which I'm sure sent up to her place an apportioned share of the roach colony. But the apartment itself was pretty nice, mostly as a result of her winsome touch. It was small, about eight hundred square feet, but nicely decorated with a good deal of Asian décor as one might expect. The walls in the living area were wainscoted with white poplar on the bottom and wall papered with deep pink cherry blossoms on the top.

She told me to do what I needed to do first before she got into the bathroom since she would be taking quite a bit longer than me to primp. The room was so small, I had trouble turning around from the toilet to the wash basin without backing out of the room first. I did brush my teeth and ran a comb through my hair, then zipped up my bag and turned the bathroom over to Joy. And she was right. She took three times as long to put on her new face. When she came out, she had on fresh, pink lipstick and was wearing some very delightful perfume…French, she said, when she saw my nose pique up and draw in a deep breath. Whatever it was, my senses appreciated the smell.

Joy did not own a car, so she and I and my knapsack took a two-person cyclo to the Queen Bee which was about ten blocks away on Kwoi, formerly Tu do Street. When the little guy had quit pumping the pedals on the bike, he came to an abrupt stop in front of the restaurant and held out his hand. But when it was Joy who dug the Dong out of her purse, he gave me a shit-eating grin which said "You number one American man. You have woman who pay. Maybe *she* pay also when you sleep with her." He didn't actually say that, but I knew what the little rat was thinking.

The Queen Bee was not exactly a broken down fire trap, but it wasn't a classy place either. The red neon sign over the building showcased the name *Queen Bee Snake Bar and Tea Room* in English and Vietnamese. Joy told me that even though the place wasn't particularly swanky, it had the best steaks and calamari in the city. The beer menu included a long list of international brands and they were always ice cold.

Yeah, I remember when I was out-processing in Saigon to go home hearing the GIs assigned to MACV talking about the Queen Bee. They called it *The Snake Bar* because it was the place where homesick and horny soldiers went to 'snake out' ready-and-willing Vietnamese women. It lay dormant for several years after the fall of Saigon in 1975, but was then reopened by an older woman who inherited some money from her dead ex-ARVN husband. It was a seedy joint during the war years what with the red neon lights over the bar and graffiti written by GIs on every wall.

We found the restaurant so smoky that the new, more modern neon signs throughout were difficult to see. Interestingly enough, the new owner never repainted over the graffiti. I suppose it was to give the dive a degree of character, if not history. We were seated right away in the darker part of the room at a corner table. Next to our table sat three beefy Caucasian men who we quickly found out were American ex-GIs, the very kind of bozos we had earlier talked about. Each was in his upper fifties, had some degree of facial hair and they all looked as though they had just crawled out from under rocks. Occasionally I heard the words 'Nam', Charlie, the World (the USA from which they had obviously divorced themselves) and M-16.

Joy and I hadn't been at our table more than ten minutes putting down our Rolling Rocks, waiting on the calamari, when the largest of the boys wheeled around and said, "Hey, buddy. You wai ki (American)? At first I acted like I didn't hear him and then he cranked up the volume, "I said are you wai ki?!"

I looked at him and nodded, then went on with my conversation with Joy.

"Hey, guy, why don't you and the broad come join us?"

I gave him a sarcastic smile and replied, "No, thanks, *guy*. I'm just content with enjoying the evening as quietly as possible with my dinner companion." I turned my head back to Joy.

But the jerk just wouldn't let it go. "You ex-GI, too?"

I ignored him.

Bubba, dressed in a plaid shirt and an olive drab vest with 1st Cav pins and patches all over it, then placed one of his enormous paws on a piece of blubber that hung over his belt. "You too good to party with the likes of us, *buddy*?"

I could tell this was not going to go well. As I had had about enough of the dolt, I excused myself, went to his table, and placed a hand on his shoulder. "Look, I'm not your *buddy*, and we don't want to join you. We just want to have a nice, quiet dinner alone…the emphasis being on *quiet*."

He looked at my hand on his shoulder as though he were ready to remove it…surgically. I released my grip.

"I had seen her in here a time or two with different guys." He threw a handful of peanuts in his mouth and started grinding away. "You doin' her?"

I gave him a laser-laced glare. "I'm not *doing* anybody except my wife back in the states. But I don't have to explain anything to you, *buddy*. So, adios."

The grunge then looked at his friends and laughed. "Persnickety bastard, isn't he? Got a wife back in the World and over here dickin' this whore. Got it both ways." He laughed again, but his buds only glanced at one another and shook their heads.

I counted to three and took a deep breath. I wasn't going to allow this to escalate to a point where the cops would be called. I heard Byrd's voice rattling around in my head telling me to lay low and refrain from getting myself into more trouble. I was trying to get out of this country and this guy was about to ruin my chances.

"Okay, very funny," I said. "Now that you've had your laugh, I'm going back to my table."

Unfortunately, Joy had heard most of the conversation and fidgeted nervously with her beer. "Is everything okay, Bruce?"

"Yeah, everything's fine. What say we finish our beer, cancel our dinner and go someplace else? I'm not very keen on the atmosphere here. And I definitely don't like the neighbors."

"Excellent idea," she said.

I summoned our server and told him we needed to go and to give us our check. He nodded and returned a couple of minutes later with the bill. The calamari and steak were still on there.

"I wanted to make it clear that I was cancelling our food order."

"Sorry, no can cancel. Being cooked."

Joy touched my hand. "That's okay, Bruce. I'll still pay for it and then we can go."

"That would be a waste. Maybe we can just get it to go."

Bubba, who had made it his business to listen to our discussion then broke in. "What's the matter, Mac; you don't like our company?" And then he laughed again.

"Actually, prick, I don't. Now give us a break here." I then turned away.

Suddenly, he was standing next to me…all six feet four and three hundred pounds of him. "You want a break? Maybe I'll just give you one."

One of his cohorts then interceded. "Come on, Bill, no trouble, okay?"

I stood up and bore down ominously on my antagonizer's face with my baby blues.

"It's okay, Bruce," Joy pleaded. "Please."

"You're right, Joy. This piece of shit is not worth it. I'll just go to the rest room and splash some water on my face." Jerking my head to the right in the direction of the latrine, it was an invitation for the bozo to follow me.

I was standing with my arms folded and butt against one of the two sinks waiting for Mr. Big when he flung the door to the rest room open forcefully, making it bang against the wall. That was supposed to put the fear of God into me I guessed. He then stopped about four feet in front of me with both hands on his meaty hips. "Okay, ass-face," he said. "You want to get it on with me or are you some kind of homo?"

"You don't have to make this happen, you know. You can walk away and not end up in the hospital tonight."

"Ooooo…" he retorted. "Now you got me shaking." As quickly as he reached out to push me and his hands came in contact with my chest, I slammed my hands down onto his and abruptly bent my body forward. I immediately heard both of his wrists snap. He then fell to his knees and cried out in pain.

"You son-of-a-bitch! You broke my wrists!"

Now, not able to use his hands, he stood up and attempted a pitiful karate-style kick which I side-stepped. I then gave him a straight punch between the eyes that knocked him backwards against a stall door. Not through with him yet, I grabbed him by his long hair and rammed his forehead into one of the urinals. The last time I saw him before exiting the latrine, his bearded chin was perched on the bottom of the urinal with the rest of his body lying in a puddle of errant piss on the floor. It wasn't a pretty scene.

I then washed my hands and slipped a comb through my hair. It was apparent that the guy in the mirror, though fifty-seven years old and over the hill by most people's standards, could still bring it.

As I passed by the table where the other two guys sat swigging their beer, I said, "Your friend's in the latrine passed out on the floor. Seems he's had a little too much to drink. Better go check on him."

I sat back down and saw that the server had brought the calamari appetizer. Joy had gathered up her purse and was getting ready to go.

"Are you okay with just staying here to eat now that our food is on the table?" I asked her.

"Yes, I guess. I was a little worried when I saw that guy

follow you into the rest room. Is everything okay?"

"Everything's fine, now," I replied. "We had a nice little talk and he's very sorry for the way he acted."

I then glanced over at the next table and saw that his two friends had indeed gone to see about their mate.

A couple of minutes later, before we had hardly dented the calamari, the steaks and French fries came. It would be the first real American-style food I would have in a week. My appetite *and* taste buds were damn appreciative.

Out of the corner of my eye I then caught sight of three men exiting the toilet room heading for the front door. The taller, beefier guy in the middle was unsteady and bent over, gingerly holding his arms against his chest. None of the men looked back in our direction. Joy took account of my smile and likely thought it was for her. She smiled back and patted my hand.

CHAPTER THIRTEEN

We left the Queen Bee about eight forty-five and then Joy talked me into having a cocktail on the roof of the Hotel Rex, the famous digs of the U.S. military's top brass and civilian muckety-mucks from 1965 to 1975. Not being high up on the Army's food chain, I never got a chance to stay there. But I did see the building on my way to Tan Son Nhut the day I left Vietnam, taking note of the sandbags, concrete barriers and concertina wire all around it. Now, obviously still a pretty fine place to lay your head, I saw that the exterior of the building had been totally refurbished. It was also listed on Vietnam's ten famous historical sites for tourism along with the Reunification Palace, the Cu Chi Tunnel System and the War Crimes Museum, the latter which featured tanks, weapons and other relics captured from or abandoned by the defeated imperialistic giant.

The rooftop gave us a rather stunning view of the city that most of the locals still referred to as Saigon. The government had recently put on an ambitious marketing blitz to attract tourists to give the country a needed financial shot in the arm, coining the slogan, *Pearl of Southeast Asia.* For me it seemed that I was in an entirely different city, perhaps Shanghai or Tokyo, considering the impressive skyscrapers and gleaming lights. It was actually a very nice setting, and the soothing, mood music and lyrics of Sinatra's *Strangers in the Night* put the punctuation mark on what would normally be a perfect romantic evening. Which I *certainly* didn't want or need.

The air was cooler and stirring nicely in the form of a light breeze atop the Rex. Joy had ordered a second Singapore Sling while I was still sipping on my first Vodka Collins. And then she lit up a cigarette which has always been a big turn-off for me…not that I was looking to get turned *on*. In my in-between marriage years I had been with women who tried to hide the fact that they were smokers. But the dead give-away was the stale cigarette breath in my face when a woman was coughing up a lung. Or maybe it was when a dank odor reeked from her hair as her head was being slammed against the headboard. I remember one such gal from about ten years ago who I actually had a thing for. But I should have known she was a puffer the first time I heard her voice. She had a deep throaty laugh that sounded like the noise a dog makes just before it hacks up a bone.

"So, tell me about yourself, Joy. Where are you from and how did you get way over here?"

Before answering me, she spewed out a long plume of smoke and took a sip of her cocktail.

"Well, how about I just give you the Reader's Digest version? I'm from California and went to Pepperdine. I graduated with a degree in PolySci, met a guy named Steve there, got married and we both got jobs in Washington, D.C. He worked for a consulting firm and I took an entry level office job making fifteen grand a year with the CIA in Langley. A dozen years later he had an affair and I divorced him. I then decided I wanted to get away from him and the friends we both had cultivated, who by the way stuck with *him* and not me. So then I saw this job open in Vietnam at the U.S. Consulate's Office. I've been here just over two years. So that's the low-down. Now, how about you?"

The mood music continued with *The Days of Wine and Roses*. I was not going to let my guard down in spite of Henry Mancini.

"I'm West Virginian, born and raised, went to WVU, commissioned ROTC into the Army, joined Special Forces, was over here for 18 months, got married and had a lovely daughter, left the Army, became a Special Agent with the FBI, divorced, served twenty years with the Bureau and retired. About four years ago I took this job with the Department of State. Then a year or so later I met a lovely innkeeper back in my home town and six months later married her. And that's me."

"Happily married?"

"*Oh*, yeah."

She took a final drag from her cigarette and stamped it out in an ash tray. "Just my luck," she said, sighing with a smile. "So, Mr. McGowan, what does your job generally entail?"

"Usually I just gather information about people who present some sort of threat to the people and infrastructure of America."

"Terrorists."

"Yes. Pretty much."

"Sounds exciting."

"Mostly just interesting and enlightening. But sometimes it *does* get exciting."

"Were you looking for terrorists here? I wouldn't think Vietnam would be high on the list as a breeding ground for terrorism."

"I didn't say that was why I was here."

She stirred the remaining booze in her glass with a swizzle stick and kept her eyes fixed to mine. "Then why *are* you here and why have you ended up in a *pickle* as you said earlier? Unless you can't talk about it."

"About all I can tell you is that I was merely on a fact-finding deal for the Department."

"So how did you end up without money and having trouble getting out of country?"

She was an inquisitive little gal.

"I suppose it will somehow come out when your boss gets involved, but I'm in a heap of trouble with the authorities."

"Then you *did* kill somebody."

I needed to side-step the question. "Well, the cops ran my friend and me down while we were traveling back south from the Highlands and took us into custody. They wanted me to confess to something I didn't do. And if I didn't sign a confession, I was either going to jail or mysteriously disappear."

"Pray tell what for?"

"I really can't go into that."

"Classified information, huh?"

"Something like that." I was starting to get annoyed with the twenty questions and I think she sensed it.

"Well, then, what do we do with you tonight?"

"I guess I'll have to find a hotel. Maybe the Rex will put me up."

"With no money, travelers' checks or a credit card? How will you manage that?"

"My good looks?"

"Which might get you a 10% discount with the street girls down on De Voi, but it's cash on the barrel head or credit card at all the hotels."

"And you're sure you don't have a car that I can sleep in."

She smiled. "Sorry. But my *couch* is a convertible."

"Joy, as much as I appreciate the offer, it would neither be proper or prudent for me to stay there. My wife would *definitely* not appreciate it."

"She's thousands of miles away. If you don't tell her, who would know it?"

"I've never kept anything from her or lied to her. I won't start now."

"Well, the offer is open if you want it."

I noted that she didn't offer to front me the money for the hotel until my cash came tomorrow. Maybe she thought Byrd and the State Department were not for real and I just allowed her to talk to some guy who told her he was wiring the money. I would be a scam artist who would hit her up for a meal, a hotel room and some cash, then disappear. But then again, she was allowing me to sleep at her pad and I had just told her I was in trouble with the law.

"Tell you what...I'll just call my boss and get him to arrange a deal with one of the hotels here. The Department can guarantee payment.

It took a few minutes to get through the system to Lionel's cell, but soon the golden voice of the grand old spy answered simply, "Hello."

"Lionel. Bruce. Need your help."

"What? Again? You didn't do anything…"

"No. No trouble. Been a good boy since we've talked." Except for putting an American ex-GI in the clinic to get his wrists set. "I'm…just in need of a place to stay and wondering if you could work your magic through channels to fix me up with a hotel room."

"All right, I'll see what can be done. There won't be anyone at the Consulate's office, but I'll make some calls. I know a guy who knows a guy where you are."

"Can you be a little more specific? I don't relish the idea of sleeping on a park bench with the pigeons."

"Where are you now?"

"At the Hotel Rex."

"Ah, yes. I know it well."

"If you know it so well, why don't you just call the management and square it away?"

"I know it from thirty-five years ago, that's all."

"So," I said, "you were one of the brass that stayed here while I was sleeping in the jungle in monsoon rains."

"Just hang tight there and I'll see about getting it set up. Now, anything else?"

"A suite would be nice. One with a kitchen and a big screen TV."

"Goodbye, Bruce. Check with the desk later. We'll talk tomorrow and I'll give you the particulars on the Department jet. The bird is already in the air."

"Great. Thanks, Boss."

And then he was gone. I hoped he didn't end conversations with the Mrs. that abruptly.

"It sounds like he's getting you set up here," she said.

"If this falls through, is it possible for me to stay somewhere in the Consulate's office? Maybe there's a room with a cot in it there."

"Policy, Bruce. The Consulate is strict about anybody, displaced American or not, staying on the premises. There's also a Federal law that prohibits it. I would love to lend you money until tomorrow for a hotel, but there's also a strict policy against that. I could lose my job if it got out. I didn't tell you this, but I kind of stuck my neck out for dinner."

"If there's policy about Consulate employees personally assisting American visitors, how could you be offering your couch for the night?"

"It's not really about helping out Americans; it's about an employee putting out *money* to help them."

"Okay," I said, nodding. "I *think* I understand the difference. Thanks for the offer of your place, though. I'll just be sticking here until I hear something."

She took that as a sign that we were done for the evening and pulled out her purse. "Well, I had a nice evening with the dinner and conversation, Bruce. You seem like a really great guy, criminal or not." Then she smiled and summoned the server for the bill.

It was about nine-fifteen when we parted company in the lobby. She gave me an innocent hug and then left me at the concierge desk.

I sat in the bar for about a half an hour nursing a glass of Merlot and taking account of my surroundings. There were two TVs on behind the bar. One was playing what appeared to be a Vietnamese cop show and I didn't have to hear the dialogue, which I couldn't anyway, to see that it was pure commie propaganda. Two wimpy-looking heroes in uniform and caps with red stars were rousting a drunken White guy I assumed to be American expatriate like the kind I had just run into at the Queen Bee. In every other scene there just happened to be a Vietnam flag flapping in the breeze either on top of a building or on a billboard the commie cops were passing. But on the other TV was a rerun of Jerry Springer with subtitles. I think it was yet another attempt for the viewer to see the scourge of America airing its dirty linen in front of the world. Two large-set women, probably a wife and girlfriend, were trying to rip each other's face off while the guy involved was shouting obscenities at both of them. Yeah, that's the America I know and love all right. A man and a woman sitting next to me who were watching the melee occasionally glanced over at me. Finally, whether they understood me or not, I shook my head and said to the lady next to me, "How low can people get? Not all of us Americans are like that, and you won't ever find me on a show like that. I take great pains to assure *my* wife and girlfriend will never find out about the other."

The couple looked at me for a moment, turned to look at each other and then moved further down to the other end of the bar to escape the ugly American.

After an hour and the last sip of the vino had gone down, I checked back with the concierge at the front desk to see if someone had called to set up my night's lodging. No one had called about giving Bruce McGowan a room. I piddled for another half an hour and checked again. No message. I then called Byrd's cell. I got his voice mail. Finally, I called Virginia, my trusty and lusty Moneypenny.

"Hi, Bruce. Where are you, darlin'?"

"Still in Vietnam and anxious to get back. Say, have you

seen Byrd?"

"He isn't here today, Bruce. He's tied up in some kind of meeting with the Company."

"The Langley Company?"

"Yes. Kind of unreachable today."

"Did he say anything to you about setting up a room at the Hotel Rex for me?"

"Don't know anything about that, Brucie. Was I supposed to?"

"I guess not. If he calls in, would you have him call my cell?"

"Anything for you, sugar. Can't you get a room on your own?"

"Well…no. Some butt holes ripped off all my money a couple days ago."

"Ripped off 007? I thought you were smarter and tougher than that. What happened?"

"Long story. I'll tell it to you sometime."

"Anxious to see you back. Hope you can work it out."

"You and me both. See you soon. Have him call, okay?"

It was drawing on eleven and the front desk still hadn't heard from anyone. I was pretty darn tired and had no idea when the call would come. The desk captain seemed to also be getting tired…of me checking with him every ten minutes.

"No one call. I let you know," he kept telling me.

"Well, do you mind if I camp out on that couch over there for the night until you do hear something?"

"No lotter."

"I guess you mean you don't want me to loiter. But I'm not loitering…I'm waiting for a call to verify payment for a room tonight."

"No lotter!" he said, now more emphatically.

At that moment a cop came through the door and I saw the guy at the desk look in his direction. All that had to happen was for the cop to approach me ask me for my passport. Knowing that my name would be on every cop's info sheet in the country, I decided it was time for me to hit the street. If the desk guy who knew my name knew the cop, I would be toast. So I slipped away before the cop got anywhere near us.

Now I was in a dilemma. I had no place to go and definitely was not going to end up on a park bench. My dilemma suddenly became a moral one. If I went back to Joy's place to take her up on her offer of the couch, would my conscience allow me to get to sleep? Although I wasn't ever going to do anything to violate my marriage, I *would* be spending the night with another woman who wasn't my wife. And the fact that the woman was drop-dead gorgeous would abrade that conscience like a rock in my shoe I couldn't get out. With no money and risking the police picking up a Western vagrant in the streets, finding out that he was wanted for a cop killing, I felt I had no choice.

My sense of direction being impeccably keen and remembering that the Hotel Rex was evenly halfway between the Queen Bee and Joy's apartment, I found her building in less than twenty minutes. From the street outside of the noodle joint, I looked up and saw her light was still on. For a couple of minutes I stalled at the bottom of the stairs, rethinking my decision, but ultimately found myself knocking on her door. I heard her light footsteps and then saw the peephole move. She then unlocked the door and pulled it open. I had hoped she would be in a long robe or unattractive pajamas…but noooooo. She was wearing a thigh-length tee shirt and was braless.

"The pull-out couch will be fine," I said.

"The Rex didn't work out?"

"Nope. I kept waiting to get set up, but no call came."

"Well, I'm glad it didn't. It will be nice to have your company again for the evening. Come in."

"Thanks. Do you mind if I hit your bathroom? Under a bit of pressure."

"While you're down the hall, I'll get us some wine. Merlot okay?"

"That's what I usually have. I did, however, already have a carafe at the hotel while I was waiting. But, why not?"

I did my ditty and joined her on the couch. Two glasses of the Merlot were on the coffee table. We sat and talked for another hour about what was going on back in the States and I purposely talked a lot about Adrianna to combat Joy's sensuous leg movements. One moment she would draw them up under her, flashing just a smidgeon of pink lace, and the next, stretching them out to where the tee rode up on her thighs ever higher. I did my best to keep my eyes north of her shoulders. I also found myself rattling on incessantly about absolutely nothing to make sure my mind would not find itself focused on anything south.

But then she took over the conversation. "At first I really got *into* this country. I found the people genuine and friendly. Oh, there are a few here and there who act like they resent us Americans. Maybe they were from the north and lost relatives in the war to American bombs. But for the most part, they're warm and courteous. They love us and love our money even more. I don't date any of the Vietnamese guys and like I said, most of the Westerners aren't my cup of tea either, like the guy who was mouthing off tonight. There are some French guys still around and some Russians, but most of them are much older and again, unappealing. So, there. Yes, I'm lonely and will probably go back to the States in a year or so."

"I can understand what you're going through. Up until two years ago, I lived in a Georgetown apartment by myself. Even in a bustling area like D.C. which is flooded with amiable, attractive, single women, I only went out a few times and never cultivated a close relationship."

Joy then laid her hand on my thigh. "Until you met Miss Right."

"Yes, but I didn't meet her in the Washington area."

"Oh, yeah, West Virginia. I forgot."

The hand was still on my thigh, which was beginning to trouble me.

"Yes, and I believe I miss her more *this* trip than at any other time in our marriage."

I think she took that as a signal to remove her hand.

"Well, it's just my luck, you know."

"What is?"

"A handsome devil like you comes to town and stays in my apartment. But he's married and will be hopping back across the Pacific the next day."

I didn't respond. She then lit up a cigarette.

"My smoking doesn't bother you, does it?"

"It's your place."

"Well, just tell me if it's offensive."

It was, but seeing as how she availed her pull-out to me for the night, I could deal with it.

There was a little more small talk, then she put out the cigarette, took the last couple of sips from her wine glass and announced that the morning would come all too soon. I reminded her it was *already* morning.

"I'll be safe in my bed tonight, won't I?" she jested.

"Absolutely."

"Oh, drats," she laughed. "But a girl can hope, can't she?"

I didn't respond.

"Anyway, I'll bring you out a pillow and a sheet."

She then went to her bedroom and returned seconds later with the bed linen.

"I'll take it from here," I said.

"Well, night then."

"Good night, Joy. And thanks again."

With that, she went back to her room and closed the door.

I put my half-consumed glass of wine down the drain and set it on the sink. Picking up my kit bag, I scooted off to the bathroom and brushed my teeth. I'd shower in the morning. When I put my toothbrush back into the bag, I had a sudden revelation. I remembered that on my last trip across the pond with the team, I had pulled a twenty from the pocket of a dirty pair of jeans before I washed them out and put the bill in the zip part of the kit bag. It was still there. I was suddenly a man with money.

I started to just lay down on the couch and plop my

head on the pillow, but then thought the better of it. The cushions then came off and I pulled the bed out of the sofa. It popped and groaned until it up-righted on the floor. I wouldn't really need the sheet over me, since the apartment had no air conditioning, so I tucked it in around the flimsy mattress.

Stripping down to my boxers, I donned a clean tee shirt and laid my frame onto the bed. The metal support bar that ran underneath the middle of the mattress dug uncomfortably into the small of my back and I then immediately re-assessed my decision to not just fall asleep on the couch. I thought it would take me a while to pass out, but after saying a prayer for the Mrs. and my daughter, I was soon in lullaby land.

Sometime during the night I had the dream again…the one where I had propelled the M-79 round through the hooch that killed the child and her mother. And why *wouldn't* I have it. I had been through a rather harrowing experience a couple of days before in the very venue where the subject of the dream had taken place. But this night the dream was deeper and more vivid than before. This time I actually smelled the hooch burning when it finally lit up following the exploded round.

I sat up and looked at the red neon numbers on Joy's clock that sat on her bar. I read four-ten. But for some reason, I was still smelling the smoke. It then took me a few moments to realize that it was not smoke from the smoldering hooch, but from a cigarette. In the dim light of a sign outside of Joy's living room window, I made out her form sitting in a sofa chair opposite the couch smoking the cigarette.

"Holy shit, Joy! You scared the hell out of me. Anything wrong?"

She didn't immediately respond, but just kept drawing the smoke into her lungs. Her feet were perched on the rim of the chair and her knees were tucked up under her chin.

"Nothing's wrong. I just couldn't sleep, that's all," she replied.

I sat up fully and leaned back on my hands. "Why not?"

"I was just thinking of you lying out here on this very uncomfortable mattress." Her cigarette then took on a fiery glow when she drew more smoke into her lungs. "Come sleep with me, Bruce."

The words hit me like an electric shock. "That's not going to happen, Joy."

"Like I said...there are thousands of miles between you and your wife tonight. Only you and I will know it happened."

"You, me and my conscience. Sorry, Joy." I then slid off the bed and slipped on my jeans. "I knew this was a bad idea. As much as I appreciate the bed, I don't appreciate the come-on."

Joy sat without word for a moment, then crushed her cigarette out in the ash tray on the coffee table and went back to her bedroom. I allowed the incident to digest for a moment, then put my shirt back on, retracted the bed, picked up my travel bag and twisted the lock on my way out the door.

*   *   *   *

I had about four hours until the Consulate's office opened, so I walked around in the dark for several blocks in search of some all-night coffee shop in which to park my buns and wait. The streets were empty as one would imagine, but I made sure I jumped out of sight whenever a police sedan cruised by. At just before five, I turned a corner and saw the lights of a Westernized-looking diner. The name of the establishment was simply *Jack's Back*. As I drew near to the building, I saw through the large picture window that there was a single Vietnamese male sitting at one of the booths and an American-looking chap behind the counter. And I had a twenty dollar bill in my pocket.

When I opened the door, I suddenly realized what a small world it actually was. As luck would have it…bad luck…the guy behind the counter was one of the men sitting at the next table to mine at the Queen Bee…the friend of the bozo I had left drinking from the urinal. But I walked on in, anyway, and immediately saw there were two more men sitting off to the side drinking hot tea or coffee. Two Vietnamese soldiers. Neither turned to take notice of me. Of course, it was the *police* who were looking for me, not Uncle Ho's men, so I went ahead and made my way to the counter.

I waited a while for the man behind the counter to come by with some coffee, but he appeared to be taking his good old time. And then I thought maybe he recognized me from the night before and was going to ignore me. So, I pushed the envelope.

"Good morning, *Vietnam!*" I called out with my best impression of Robin Williams from the movie.

He then turned around. "Sorry, Mac. I didn't see you come in. Coffee?"

"Yes, please."

As he turned to retrieve a coffee mug and pour in the steaming, black nectar of the gods, I watched closely to be sure he didn't slip something in it to put me away for taking down his friend. He then walked back and set the cup down in front of me. And that's when I realized he actually might not have remembered me. He gave me a quick nod along with a gruff smile and went back to the griddle where he was frying a couple of eggs.

The place was indeed Americanized. There were Army patches and photos in frames on the wall all over the joint. Encased in a larger frame was a khaki shirt of the 1960s military vintage with a blue infantry cord around the right shoulder, buck sergeant stripes on the sleeves and two rows of ribbons and a Combat Infantryman's Badge over the left breast pocket. The black nametag on the right pocket read *Culver*.

The counter guy was about five-nine and balding with a short-cropped white beard and a size forty beer gut. In a moment he turned back to me and as I was stirring a little cream in my coffee, said "Want somethin' to eat with that?"

I looked at the glass cake container on the counter beside me and replied, "How about one of those chocolate donuts?"

He then lifted the glass top from the pedestal and pulled one out with a set of tongs and placed it on a saucer in front of me.

"Are you the guy on the shirt?" I asked.

"Yeah," he replied, proudly glancing over at the framed garment. "I'm Jack...Jack Culver. I own the place." He wiped his hand on his apron and held it out. I shook it. Maybe he *didn't* remember my face.

He stood for a few seconds looking me over and then said, "You're the guy from the Queen Bee last night, aren't you?"

Well, I was wrong again. I wondered then if we were now going to fight.

"I was there. The guy with the lady your friend referred

to as a whore.”

“You know you didn’t have to break Mooney’s wrists and leave him like that. I know he likes to start things up when he’s had a few and is as obnoxious as hell, but sober, he’s actually a pretty good guy.”

“I gave him a chance, Jack. I told him I didn’t want any trouble, but he kept it going.”

“Yeah, I know. He can get like that. But good God, he’s a damn big fella and an ex middle heavyweight boxer, and you’re…well, *not.*”

“Sorry it happened, Jack. How’s he doing?”

“I guess he’s sleepin’ it off. We took him to the medical clinic where they put his arms in casts. What was that you did, some kind of karate move or somethin’?”

“Or something.”

“Who are you, anyway?”

“My name’s Bruce McGowan. Here on business. So how long have you had this diner?”

“Oh, goin’ on fifteen years now, I expect. I’m kinda an icon around here with the Viets. Even with the commies like those guys over there. Nobody seems to have any hard feelin’s. So, are you a vet?”

“Yes. I was here in ’69 to ’71 with the SF up in the Central Highlands.”

“Well, let me shake your hand again.” Which he did. “My wife died back in ’88 and well, I tell ya, I just felt lost. I didn’t know what to do with my life after that. Sold my air conditionin’ business and my house and lit out for over here. Even though I hated my tour here with the 1st Cav every day I was humpin’ the boonies, I told myself that those were some of the best, most excitin’ days of my life. I never felt more alive, doin' what we did here. You might not understand that, but it's the truth. When they started openin' up the country to Americans again, I bought this little place and said I'd make it a little taste of America for these people. They love my hot dogs and hamburgers, not to mention my eggs and hash browns for breakfast. They'll be pilin' in here in an hour or so."

"Well, I'm glad you made a go of it and wish you continued success."

"Thanks, Mr. McGowan."

"Bruce."

"Okay…Bruce."

"Look, Jack. Tell your friend Mooney I'm sorry about his injury. If it had just been *me* last night, hell, I might have joined you guys. But I didn't go for his disrespecting the lady."

"I'm with you there, Bruce. Hey, you want a *real* breakfast? On the house. Anything you want."

"Naw. Thanks, Jack. Just the donut will do. I'm not a big breakfast eater."

"You're missin' out. Best hash browns in Southeast Asia."

"I'm sure. They smell great, too. But, no, I'm good. I probably have to get on. As your place will be filling up soon with real customers, I don't want to take up your counter space."

"No problem with that. Stay as long as you like. It's a privilege gettin' to know a fellow Vietnam vet like yourself, especially the Special Forces type. God bless you, man." He shook my hand again.

I then shelled out the twenty to pay for the coffee and donut.

"Your money's no good in here, Bruce. Like I said, on the house."

"Well, I appreciate it. I might see you again at lunch for one of those hot dogs."f

"Okay, friend," he replied. "Come on back."

I had had a nice conversation with an old vet, gotten a free breakfast and still had my twenty.
I wondered if the rest of the day would be as good.

CHAPTER FOURTEEN

---

*I been gone a long time, so far away from home. And I hear it callin'
me back from my aimless roam. But I know I can't go back-there's
nothin' there to find. 'Cause I know the past is only in the mind.*

*Do you ever feel kind of cold inside, 'cause the joy of life has finally
died. And you can't love anybody' cause there's no blood in a stone.
Well, brother, if you feel that way, you ain't alone.*

Richard A. Morris
You Ain't Alone

I had heard that song some time back and it just seemed
to fit Jack…a man who was kind of a lost soul after the
war, but fortunately had found purpose in his life back
in the same country he probably hated a few decades before,
just like the rest of us.

No sooner had I stepped out of the *Jack's Back Diner,*
my cell phone went off…the first time in a week.

"Good morning, Bruce."

"Good morning to *you,* Lionel. So what the hell
happened to my room at the Rex?"

"It got a bit complicated. The Vietnamese government

had already contacted the Consulate's office there asking about an American fugitive named Bruce McGowan. Your little indiscretion in Pleiku has turned out to be a full-blown international incident. The Viet government wants answers, knowing that you are a State Department employee. The word *spy* has been mentioned and now I'm taking heat from the Secretary of State."

"Obviously, the Secretary doesn't know about my business here. Can't Eagle One put out the fire?"

"I think he's shut it down for the time being, but we have to get you out of there…and soon."

"When the bird gets here, I'm gone. So, I was never going to get that room."

"I'm dealing with your handiwork and you're still miffed you didn't have a place to lay your bones for the night?"

"Well, hell, I need my beauty sleep."

There was no response. I guessed it didn't merit one.

"Eagle One personally called the Consulate General and told him the situation is being handled and to see that you are put on the Department jet. And by the way, your money should be there."

"Oh, I don't need it now. I won't have to pay my airfare back and I'm sure somebody will feed me somewhere over the Pacific."

"Take it anyway. It's five hundred dollars and I want to see vouchers for every penny spent."

"What time will the plane arrive?"

"You are to be at Tan Son Nhut at 1500 hours sharp. I have arranged to get you a new passport."

"What name is on it? I'm sure it won't be the one I

own."

"I'll let you guess. The Deputy Consulate has it. Don't be late at the tarmac. See you back here the day after tomorrow." The line then went dead.

I still had a couple of hours to roam about before the Consulate's office opened, so I found a picturesque little park a couple of blocks down from Jack's. As soon as I planted my buns on a bench, the pigeons flew at me in drones. I thought for a moment I had just stepped into a scene from *The Birds*. But after they figured out I didn't have a morsel on me, they spotted a little old man with a bag of peanuts on another bench and took off in his direction.

When I sit, especially when I'm bored or just waiting around, my brain goes into over-drive. And I was starting to experience some guilt. Not about Adrianna, but about Joy. It was raining down on me like hail. Okay, she did want to take me to her bed in the worst way, but she also bought me dinner and drinks, took me in like a lost mongrel and gave me a place to sleep. I had thanked her by walking out a couple of hours before like a bumptious ingrate. And okay, she had a moment of weakness like we all do, being lonely, sex-starved and all, but I disrespected her and her hospitality. So, considering the time I had left, I decided to go back to Joy's apartment to not only see that she was all right, but to apologize.

In twenty minutes I was at her door. I knocked twice softly the first time around and then with a little more force the second. I saw the peephole cover lift again and she opened the door. I could see in her face that I had awakened her. She was now wearing a short silk pajama top, but the same pink undies. After giving me a look that was something between hurt and embarrassment, she gestured for me to come in, then turned away toward the kitchen.

"I'll make you some coffee."

"Thanks."

I set my bag down and walked over to the window where the morning sun was now up and reflecting off the glass in the building behind her apartment.

"Can we clear the air, Joy?"

She didn't answer immediately, but continued to work up the coffee. Once it began pouring in a small stream into the glass pot, she went to her bedroom and returned to the living room in the silk bottoms that went with the top. She definitely did me a favor.

"What's there to clear up, Bruce?"

"Sorry I left like I did."

"Why *did* you leave?"

"I don't know. Guess I was scared."

She posted a slight smile. "Somehow you don't seem like the kind of man who scares easily."

"Generally not, except where it comes to women."

Her smile broadened. "So, I scare you, huh?"

"More than you know."

The coffee pot had by now quit percolating and she returned to the kitchen to pour two cups. She then came back and put one of them in my hand.

"I'm sorry, Bruce. It was unfair for me to push myself on you last night. You made it abundantly clear that you love your wife and would do nothing to violate her trust."

"I will say this, though," I replied, "if I *were* the cheating kind, be assured that I would be all over you in a skinny minute. You are a *very* lovely woman."

"Thanks. At least that tells me I was not unappealing. That would crush my ego."

I smiled back at her, but didn't reply.

"You just don't know how difficult it is for a single woman in a foreign country with no real friends or romantic interests."

"If you only gave it sometime…"

"It hasn't happened in the two years that I've been here, so I'm convinced it never will."

"I'm sure they're out there. You just haven't connected."

"I'm really not looking for anybody. But I would like to go out once in a while with a good-looking, cultured guy. You see, the problem is, I'm very selective where it comes to men."

She took one last sip of her coffee and then looked at the clock on the bar. "I've got to hit the shower and get ready or I'll be late for work. You can have the bathroom after I'm out."

She finished up in less than twenty minutes and then I went in to shower and shave. I took half the time and threw on a clean khaki shirt. I had to smile when I thought of how I stood naked as a jay bird while Co Dong scarped up all my clothes to wash and press them. The shirt, which she had neatly folded and placed in my bag, looked good on me, if I do say so myself.

But Joy looked good as well. With her long, blonde hair pinned up and dressed quite differently in a two piece gray suit and white blouse with a ruffled collar, she did not look like the same woman I met the day before. She could have been mistaken for a lady lawyer or a corporate executive.

And she knew she looked good.

"Well, we'd better scoot," she said.

After she locked the door and we negotiated the stairs to the street, I followed her along the sidewalk into the ever-thickening crowd, trying in vain to keep my eyes off her. I supposed it didn't hurt to look, considering I had passed the ultimate test...the test of marital fidelity.

We arrived at the American Consulate building a few minutes before eight and Joy led me past Mr. Sanborn who I'm sure was wondering whether we spent the night together. In fact, I was sure it was actually *gnawing* at him. I didn't speak to him, but allowed my impish grin to make him wonder about the two of us all the more.

When we entered Joy's office, a tall, broad shouldered man resembling Mr. Clean with a completely shaved head and square jaw stood waiting on us. Joy lifted her hand in his direction to introduce us to one another, "This is my boss, the Deputy General Consulate, Averill Peters. Mr. Peters, this is..."

"The troublesome Mr. McGowan, I presume," Peters interjected.

From the get-go, I knew I wasn't going to like the smug bastard. After he shook my hand, he placed both of his behind him and pompously began rocking back and forth on his heels.

"That would be me, Mr. Peters."

"Well, I must say, it appears you are indeed in a heap of trouble." He looked down on me over a very long nose.

"How so?" I replied, trying to sound ignorant, which was not all that difficult for me.

"Oh? You haven't figured it out? Surely you jest, Mr.

McGowan."

I could tell the man had some serious delusions of adequacy.

"You mean that little thing up in the Highlands."

"The Vietnamese National police have reported to us that an American by the name of Bruce McGowan was taken into custody by a police detachment in Pleiku Province along with a Vietnamese dissident, but then killed a police captain, seriously assaulted two other officers and shot and wounded the detachment chief, one Major Vann. The man, McGowan, then stole a police vehicle and escaped, evading several police units which gave chase. Does that sound about right?"

"You left out the part where the cops beat an innocent man to death and were prepared to put me six feet under if I didn't sign a drummed-up confession."

Joy gasped. "Then it's true, Bruce? What you told Mr. Byrd on the phone was *not* a joke."

"It all sounds pretty sinister the way *he* said it."

"Oh my God." She then sat down and placed her hand over her breasts in apparent shock. I'm sure she was thinking about how she invited a murderer and fugitive from justice to sleep with her.

Peters continued. "And, Mr. McGowan, you are also a suspect in the murders of three Vietnamese citizens further north of there in the Highlands whose bodies were discovered just yesterday. The police major you shot said you and your Vietnamese sidekick had been in that vicinity."

"Yeah, this guy Vann said something about them missing. But no, I didn't kill them or anyone else."

"Uh *huh*. You know I am bound to turn you over to the

authorities, McGowan."

"Mmmm, not going to happen, Mr. Peters."

"Okay then, why won't it happen?"

"Well, the State Department will be calling here for you to arrange my transportation to the airport so that I can board a Department jet for the States. You will find that I have diplomatic immunity."

"You're wrong about that, Mr. McGowan."

"Wait for the call, Mr. Peters." I could be smug as well.

"Okay, let's say someone does call. How will I know that person is legit?"

"Just ask your boss, the Consulate General. He's already received a call from somebody bigger than the lot of us. Occupies a big white residence in Washington, D.C. Go on, check with him."

"Oh I will, Mr. McGowan. And while I'm doing that, I am going to put you in a secure room under guard."

"Suit yourself. Do I get my one phone call?"

"You're not under arrest…yet. You can call whomever you want."

"How about *two* calls?"

He sighed. "Make as many as you want, Mr. McGowan. You can make a dozen for all I care. By the way, you're not armed, are you?"

"Not anymore. I got rid of it so I wouldn't be compelled to kill someone else." I glared at him menacingly.

He then backed away and stared at me.

"Relax, Mr. Peters. You can have me searched if you want."

"Just…what do you do for the State Department…some kind of government assassin?"

I chuckled. "Get real, Mr. Peters. You've obviously been watching too many Bond movies. No, I'm not an assassin."

He didn't choose to pursue his line of questioning any further as he seemed to be edging further away and out the door.

"I will have Mr. Sanborn come in and place you in the room I spoke about."

"Fine. And I promise that I will not be any trouble while I'm here."

"That would make us *all* very happy, Mr. McGowan. By the way, don't bank on getting back to the States anytime soon. If your people don't come through, which I'd bet a month's pay they won't, you get handed over to the Vietnamese. I think then your smart-ass attitude will quickly change."

"A month's pay, huh? I'll take you up on that."

When Peters left the room, Joy shook her head and said, "I…I just don't know what to say, Bruce. It seems an international man of mystery stayed at my place last night."

"Yeah, Baby," I replied in my best Austin Powers British accent.

She laughed, but it was a guarded laugh, the kind that told me she was no longer very sure about me.

In a few moments, Sanborn came into Joy's office to retrieve me. He said "Come with me, Mr. McGowan" and I followed him to a hospitality room of sorts with a small kitchenette and a fridge full of bottled water and soft drinks. There was a round table with four chairs where people could sit and have a snack or have their concerns addressed as needed. But I found a comfortable seat in a cushy chair that sat against a wall where I could cat nap or watch CNN if I chose.

Birdman hadn't called back with my arrangements, so I called his cell.

"What's the verdict," I said. "Everything a go for me getting out of here?"

"Like I said, 1500 hours. Be there. And about the passport, the Consulate's office is now manufacturing a new one. See the man named Peters there."

"I already have. A real putz."

"Right. Anything else, Bruce?"

"I guess not. You okay? You sound a little strange."

"I'm alright. I'm just mulling over something alarming about this case that affects this office."

"Are you at liberty to tell me?" I asked.

"Not at this time. I haven't pinned it down."

"Sounds austere."

"It's…troubling."

His answer disturbed me and I knew this man didn't get rattled about anything.

"Okay, Boss. You can fill me in when I see you. It's what…Saturday night there? Guess I'll see you Monday morning which is my tomorrow. I'll be glad when I get back so that I can tell time again."

He chuckled.

"Thanks for getting me out of this scrape, Lionel."

"You're a good man, Bruce, and I know what happened

to you wasn't your own making." He paused for a moment and I could hear him breathing on the other end. The atmosphere between us was unlike anything I had ever experienced before and I knew something was not right. "Have a good flight," he finally said.

"Good bye, Boss."

I laid my phone down on the arm of the couch, closed my eyes and put my brain to work. What was it? What about this mission was bothering Byrd? He made it sound like there was something going on about the team. And that made me *doubly* anxious to get back.

At just after eleven Peters came into the room, looking like he had just had to swallow a belly full of pride. Obviously, his boss got hold of him and read the gospel to him…the gospel of the President of the United States. Peters had been salivating at the thought of turning me over to the Vietnamese, even though his job was to look after the interests of American citizens caught up in adversity. He threw my new passport down on the table, pulled up a chair and locked eyes with me. He was starting to grow on me like a colony of E coli.

"Well, Mr. McGowan, I will preface my conversation with you by saying I don't like what's happening here. And as a matter of fact, I don't much like *you*, either. I think you're some kind of rogue who thinks he has a license to violate the system and break the law any time you feel like it. If I had my way…"

"Which you don't, Peters, so get to the point."

He leaned back in his chair and glared contemptuously.

"This office is not in the business of cover-ups and betraying the confidence of our host country. It is a scenario such as this that can lead to a mistrust between countries and a severing of good relations, such as we've been trying to maintain."

"Would you please dispense with the lecture and get on with it?" I barked.

He then folded his arms pompously and puffed up like a toad. The overhead fluorescent light caused the sweat on his big, bald head to glisten kind of like nostril hair does after a sneeze.

"It seems that somebody very high up has demanded that we get you through airport security and on that State Department jet that's coming for you." He then pushed the passport across the table. "And here is your new identity and the money your office wired. I am to ask you no further questions, which is fine with me. The least I have to do with you, the better."

"Ditto here, Mister Clean." I added, "Hey, aren't you missing an earring?"

I could tell that Peters didn't take kindly to the insult by the way a blue vein formed in his right temple.

"You would do me and this office a great service by leaving this building for the rest of the day until it's time for our driver to get you to the airport. He will meet you at one-thirty in front of the building. Another of our staff, Bob Dufford, will be in front of the terminal entrance to see that you get through security and on the plane. So, unless you have any questions, I want your sorry ass out of the building in the next ten minutes. Good bye, Mr. Krebs."

"Krebs?"

"Your new name," he replied. He then turned and without further word stomped out.

"Oh, Mr. Peters?"

He stopped. "What?"

"Do I get your month's pay?"

If looks could kill, I would have been drawing my last breath.

I looked at my passport. The scanned-in picture of me, e-mailed by Byrd to the Consulate's office, was my official State Department photo. The name below it though was *Woodrow Krebs*. I thought it must be Peters' scornful attempt at payback for him having to eat crow. I didn't think Byrd would have come up with it as a joke. But as Lionel did have a wry sense of humor beneath his all-business exterior, I wouldn't put it past him.

On the way out, I stopped back by Joy's office and asked her if she wanted to catch some lunch. I would not only be paying her back for last night's dinner, but I felt perhaps there were things that may have been left unsaid. Maybe one of us needed closure.

"Well, it seems to be a nice day for a walk, so why not?"

"How would you like to eat at an All-American diner just down the street?"

"You mean that place called *Jack's* something or other?"

""Yeah, *Jack's Back Diner.*"

"You know I've been wanting to go there, but I'm usually careful about what I eat. I stay away from fast food. Looks like a burger joint," she said.

"Hey, a good burger once every couple of years won't hurt *anybody,* no matter how perfect the body is."

"Well, I'll admit I've been craving a good old American hot dog lately."

"That's the spirit. Come on."

It was already steamy at eleven-thirty and as we walked together down Do Rahn Street, the more moist her skin became and the more her nylon suit skirt clung to every vivacious curve of her body. I *desperately* had to get home.

In less than ten minutes we had covered the dozen or so short blocks to *Jack's*. The place was not just busy; there were several people standing in line for booths and seats at the counter. Jack saw us come in and waved one of his Vietnamese employees to go pick us up. We were then offered the next booth ahead of perhaps twenty people waiting. I shook my head and said we would wait our turn, but the server would not hear of it. I figured the preferential treatment might run some of the customers off, but the American food was such a tasty change from their traditional Asian diet, nobody was going to complain. When we passed on by them, they smiled and nodded graciously. But then I wondered what was really going on inside of their heads.

After Joy had slid her buns onto the red vinyl seat, I sat down opposite her. Momentarily, Jack came to the table to greet us and personally take our order.

"I said I'd be back, Jack. By the way, this is Joy."

He smiled. "The lady from last night. Ma'am, I have to apologize for our friend at the table. He really didn't mean no disrespect. He's just full of himself when he's drinkin', that's all."

"Thank you, Jack," she replied. "No apology necessary."

"I'm glad you ain't mad. So, what'll you folks have?"

I gestured to Joy to go first. "I think I'd like a couple of your hot dogs with chili, slaw and mustard, and a glass of Coke."

"You got it. Okay, how about you, Bruce?"

"That sounds good. The same for me, but add some fries."

"You won't be disappointed…either of you. It'll be as good as anything you'll have back in the States.

When Jack went to the kitchen to put the order in, I pulled out five twenties and handed them to Joy. "I don't know what the dinner and drinks cost last night, but hopefully this will cover it."

"No, no. My treat. It was just good being with a clean-cut, good-looking American guy for a change."

"I insist, Joy. You don't need to put out that kind of money." I picked up her hand, placed the bills in her palm and closed it with mine.

"Well, it's not necessary."

"Yeah it is. Keep it. Is it enough to cover last night?"

"Yes, just right." She then smiled and put the bills in her purse.

"Okay, Bruce, we're not at the Consulate's office anymore and you'll be leaving soon. I've got to know. Why did you assault those policemen and end up killing one of them?"

"Why do you have to know? What difference does it make?"

"I don't know. It's just something I'd like to know the answer to…so that I can have a good feeling about you…or not…after you do leave."

I didn't respond for a few seconds, mulling over how I would answer that. "They provoked me and one of them had a gun to my head. He wanted me to sign a confession about the deaths of three Vietnamese men with whom we had met a couple of days before. And they beat my Vietnamese friend to death earlier."

"Oh, God, that's horrible. How did the three men you just mentioned die? Did you kill them?"

"No, I did not."

"You met with them and then they were dead."

"Actually, my friend killed them. They were about to shoot *us*."

"So, it was basically self-defense." She paused a moment and I could almost hear the wheels turning in her head. "Can you tell me why you were with the men to begin with?"

"No, I can't."

"Oh," she replied.

"Let's just say it was government business. I was securing some very important information to take back to some very important people in the States. I need to just leave it at that."

"Okay. It was rude of me to pry."

"No, it wasn't," I remarked. "I'm not so sure if the shoe was on the other foot that I wouldn't be inquisitive."

In about fifteen minutes Jack returned with our dogs. I could feel my arteries hardening just in smelling those All-American beauties.

"Enjoy," he said. "I'll be back to check on you."

I dug into mine ravenously while Joy took small bites with the social grace and manners of Emily Post. I had both of mine down along with half my fries before she was halfway through her first. As I leaned back slovenly in my seat and tried to stave off a belch, Joy continued her dainty assault on her last hot dog, chewing each bite slowly. She hadn't said much during the meal and I wondered if she was thinking that perhaps I had committed a more heinous crime than I let on. Maybe I *had* killed them all and wasn't being honest with her. Maybe I was some kind of government assassin…a nice, clean-cut guy as she said, but only on the surface. Inside, I might be a psychopath. Maybe she was thinking how glad she was that the same hands that had committed murder hadn't groped her body.

"Are you okay with me, Joy?'

"What do you mean?

"Well, a couple of things. First, I hope you don't think ill of me for the trouble that I've gotten myself in since I've been here. And I definitely don't want you to think I just go around killing people at the drop of a hat. Just understand that the jobs that I have had over the years involved a certain amount of danger. Unfortunately, I have had to make some decisions that ended the lives of some very bad people. Unfortunate for *them*. But believe me, I am not a murderer or a rogue as Mr. Peters calls me."

"Why do you believe I think badly of you?"

"Oh, I don't know. It just seems that after we talked more about what happened to me a few days ago, you became awfully quiet. Or is it about what happened or didn't happen last night? If so, I want to clear the air. You've been extremely good to me and you don't know how much I appreciate that."

She smiled. "You're very perceptive, Bruce. But you've actually misread my actions. I'm sorry if I appeared to be brooding, but actually, I'm not. It's not at all about people…bad guys…ending up dead because you made them that way." She paused and took a deep breath. "I'm a little embarrassed to tell you this, but…although I've only known you less than twenty-four hours, in just this small bit of time I've become very fond of you…attracted to you. I know you're married, but I can't help it. In a few hours you'll be gone and it will seem like a little piece of my heart will go with you." She grinned, sheepishly. "Again, I'm very embarrassed and now I regret even telling you that."

I patted her hand across the table. "Joy, I really don't know how to respond to that. I *am* very flattered you think of me that way, but I'm very happy with my life *and* my wife. And I can never say that I wish things were different. Yeah, if I weren't married, I'd be interested. Very interested. You are a very sweet and lovely woman, and I'll never forget you."

She smiled again. "Thank you for saying that. I didn't intend to unload on you, but I consider myself a very frank and honest person and usually say what's on my mind. I hope it didn't make you feel uncomfortable."

"Don't worry about it."

"I'll still miss you."

I dropped my eyes and didn't respond, except with a nod.

Jack saw that we were done and came over to our table. He didn't have a bill with him. "Did you enjoy your lunch?"

"Excellent, Jack. Best dogs ever," I said. "No wonder the Vietnamese love to patronize your diner. Does the Vietnamese government know you're trying to Americanize its people?"

He laughed. "I think a lot of the people that come in here *are* government officials."

"By the way, do you have our bill?"

"A fellow GI's money is no good in here."

"No, Jack, not this time. I'm going to pay for our lunch. I pretty much know how much it all was and I believe this will cover it to include a very nice tip." I then shoved two twenties in his shirt pocket."

"Naw, come on, Bruce." He groped his pocket for the money, but I placed my hand over his.

"Please," I said.

"Okay, then, but ma'am, if you come back here…and I hope you do…I'd like to buy you another hot dog."

"That would be nice, Jack. I'd like that."

I slid out first and shook Jack's hand. "It was good to see a nice, friendly American face around here for a change and am glad I stumbled onto your place, Jack."

"And good to meet you, old boy. I guess you're shovin' off today, eh?"

"In a couple of hours."

He smiled and shook my hand. "Have a good trip back to the World."

As Joy and I walked back to her office, she made a point to gig me about the comment I made to Jack. "So, was my face not a friendly one?"

"I'm sorry, what?"

"You told Jack it was good to see a friendly American face for a change."

"Oh, that. I didn't mean it that way. Of course, you have a friendly face…and might I add, beautiful."

"Uh huh. Keep digging yourself out of that hole."

It was about one-twenty when we arrived at the front door of the Consulate building. As I assumed I was no longer welcome inside, I stopped at the door. It was one of those uncomfortable moments when neither Joy or I knew what to say. I had my head down and kicked at a pebble on the sidewalk. She looked to her left down the street and picked at a fingernail.

Finally, she said, "Well, goodbye, Bruce. I enjoyed hanging out with you."

"Likewise," I replied. "Thanks for looking out after me."

She smiled. "Another time, another universe, huh?"

"Yeah."

She then leaned in and planted a light kiss on my cheek.

"Take care of yourself, Bruce. If you're ever back in town…"

"I'll give you a call. And at such time you go back home to the States…"

"Right."

I squeezed her hand right about the time a large-bodied guy with dark hair and glasses exited the Consulate building and walked toward us.

"Joy, is this the man I'm supposed to take to the airport?"

"Yes. Herbie, this is Bruce."

I shook his hand.

"Hello, Bruce. Is that bag all you have?"

"It is."

"Okay, then, are you ready to go?"

"I am."

I then looked at Joy who was stepping away toward the door. All the talk about crossing paths again…we knew it would never happen. She gave me a parting smile and went on inside.

Herbie and I walked to the other side of the building where we found his car in one of the spots that had been marked *American Consulate Parking Only*, as though most Vietnamese could read English.

"We should be there in under a half hour," my chauffeur said.

Obviously, Herbie had not been trained or mentored by the obnoxious Mr. Peters as I found him very cordial and down-right amiable. I couldn't imagine the two of them got along very well. Herbie called ahead on his cell and he pulled into the curb, literally, at the passenger drop-off point, a man in a dark suit and aqua tie stepped out from the doorway, tossed a cigarette into the road, popped in some chewing gum and opened my passenger's side door.

"Name's Dufford. You McGowan?"

"Yes."

"Then follow me." He then looked into the car at Herbie. "Okay to return on back. Catch you later."

I shook Herbie's hand and thanked him, then exited the car and trailed after Dufford into the terminal. I always wondered about the word *terminal*. If flying is so safe, why do they call the building you leave from *terminal?*

We walked past ticketing and then he pointed off to his right. "Security is in that direction, Mr. McGowan."

I held up my index finger to my lips and went, "Shhh. The name's Krebs, Mr. Dufford."

"Oh, yes. I forgot. And you can call me Bob…or

Duffy."

We talked as we walked. "So, how *is* it, working for the anal Mister play-by-the-rules Peters?"

He looked at me and gave me a wry smile. "Makes for an interesting day. You know he would have rather taken a sharp stick in the eye than set this deal up for you. I haven't seen him this pissed off since he was passed-over for the Consulate General appointment a couple years ago."

"Couldn't have happened to a nicer guy."

"Hey, did you really kill a bunch of cops and make off with one of their jeeps, Mr. McGowan?"

"Krebs, Bob. And no I did not."

"Whew, that's good to hear." He brushed his hand across his forehead to feign wiping the sweat off.

I waited a dramatic five seconds before adding, "I just killed one of them. I shot another and assaulted two more."

He almost stopped in his tracks. When I saw his eyes bug out, I thought he had swallowed his gum.

"You…you actually did?"

I nodded. "But let's let this be our little secret, okay?"

He nodded once back at me. "Over there's security. I have some documents here for them to look at."

Dufford moved on ahead of me and showed his Consulate ID to a uniformed agent who happened to be a commie Army sergeant. He then showed the sergeant a State Department order endorsed by the Consulate General that would pass me through to the tarmac and the awaiting Department jet. The commie skimmed over the document as though he could actually read and understand it and motioned me over. He then glared at me. "Passport."

I pulled it from my bag and handed it to him. When he opened it, he kept looking at the photo and my face to assure they were a match.

"I was younger then," I said with a smile.

After studying the passport some more, he finally said, "This no good."

"And why the hell not?"

"No stamp show where you came to Vietnam. How you get here without stamp?"

"My passport was stolen, genius. I was issued a replacement."

"What your business here?" he barked.

"Government business. Mine with yours. I went through these same questions when I came into this country."

"You have government ID?"

"Also stolen. That's why this man from the American Consulate's office is here to vouch for me."

"How come stolen?"

"Because this is a city of low-life vermin who like to break into hotel rooms and steal things," I lied.

"Easy, Mr. Krebs," Duffy said in a low voice.

The sergeant then went back to looking at my photo.

"It's me, believe it. I know we Americans all look alike and you have trouble telling us apart."

"Mr. Kre-ebs," Duffy said in a sing-song voice. "Don't push the envelope."

Finally, appearing satisfied that I wasn't Tom Selleck

masquerading as Woodrow Krebs, the sergeant nodded to another guard who had gone through my bag to let me through.

Duffy stopped there and gave me a faux salute. "Have a good flight, Woody."

Woody, huh? And then I had to chuckle. That name would probably be appropriate in a couple of days when I got back to Wolf Laurel.

"Thanks, Duff," I replied. "Appreciate the lift."

CHAPTER FIFTEEN

I slept most of the way on the Gulfstream V SP from our stopover in Guam until we crossed the International Date Line. It was just the State Department pilot, co-pilot and me. No sweet little flight attendant to serve me a dinner of chicken or steak and all I wanted to drink. When I had boarded, the co-pilot gave me a couple of ham sandwiches, a bag of chips and some bottled water. Hell, even Delta serves me all the Rum and Cokes I want to drink when I'm traveling abroad on commercial flights. The fourteen to seventeen-hour flights across the big drink can get mighty boring, especially when there are no in-flight movies and the view out the window is nothing but clouds and water. At least there were a half-dozen magazines to read, except the last traveler must have been a woman. *Redbook, Better Homes and Garden, Cosmopolitan and Southern Living.*

After the aircraft dropped down for an hour in Honolulu for fuel and my gut got re-fueled at a Chili's-to Go, we set sail the last five hours to San Francisco. We had to lay over for the evening, though. Some nonsense about aviators not being able to stay in the air but so long. Screw the F.A.A. So, I would be delayed another twelve hours before getting back to my honey of a wife. And the Birdman was wrong about the day I'd be back. It was Tuesday and not Monday that I would see him.

I took a few minutes before retiring in my room at the Airport Marriott to call Adrianna who was pleasantly surprised and elated at the same time that I was back on American soil. And so was I. It was now fully sinking in. It had been a harrowing week…or was it more. I had avoided death and imprisonment, but seemingly more important to me was that I had avoided, even defeated temptation of the carnal persuasion. I wasn't altogether pleased with myself for having thought about it, but I *was* pleased that I hadn't given in to it. My conscience and my self-respect were intact.

After I had eaten the steak I ordered from room service and destroyed a carafe of red wine, I crashed on the over-stuffed pillows stacked against the headboard, belched a bit and was prepared to feast on some Sunday night football. At least I *thought* it was Sunday night. I would have to re-program the clock in my head and recalibrate my circadian rhythm. Ahhh, but it didn't matter. I was vegetating like an over-stuffed couch potato. American food, American TV and a heavenly American bed. I was out in three minutes.

*   *   *   *

It had taken over twenty-seven hours and three stop-overs to fly from Tan Son Nhut to the tiny county airport in Eastern West Virginia. And it was just after three on Monday afternoon when we dropped out of the sky. On the way in, one of my aviator buds made the call for me to one Mrs. McGowan, the captor of my heart and vanquisher of all my temptations.

No sooner than I deplaned, I saw her standing on the deck. Her long, dark hair flowed gently across her shoulders in the afternoon breeze and she was as stunning in the sunlight as any forty-five year old vision I had ever seen. It had been a long and uncertain week and a half for her. I was sure that as she ran to greet me, all the anxiety and fear that had built up in her had now dissipated. She sprang onto me like a cheetah, then squeezed the stuffing out of me like a python. I could imagine what she would have done had I been gone a month.

"Don't you ever do this to me again, Skip McGowan. I had the most terrible thoughts running through my head." She then took a step back and looked me all over. I knew what she was doing…checking for bandages. It seems that while with the Special Forces in combat and later as an FBI agent, I had collected four bullet holes. I picked up two more along the way after I met her. I came to the conclusion long ago it must be my 'magnetic' personality.

I laughed. "No. No one shot me this time."

"Well, that's good. Now let's go home. I have your favorite dinner simmering."

"Spaghetti and meatballs?"

She nodded.

"And cherry pie?"

"The cherry pie is cooling as we speak."

"Why do I ever leave you?"

"You're asking the very person who has been asking *you* that same question for over two years?"

"Touché, my dear."

We had dinner at five-thirty, dessert and coffee at seven and a romantic dessert at nine. I had tactfully waited, after experiencing *all* the goodies, to tell her that the mission was not over until I gave Lionel Byrd my in-person report and delivered to him the written statements of Thanh and Siu. I would have to be in his office first thing the next morning. But I was sure that as soon as we had our pow wow, I'd be driving back the same evening. She surprised me by saying she could deal with that…up and back the same day, no danger, no uncertainties.

I was up early on Tuesday morning, but found that Adrianna had already been up for an hour preparing breakfast for the full house of guests we had at the B&B. There was no time for a morning run, even though as I had been away from the pavement entirely too long, my body needed it. There was also no time to wait around for Adrianna's mouth-watering blueberry muffins as well. They would be coming out of the oven in fifteen minutes. I kissed the Lady of the Inn goodbye and told her I hoped to be back around seven, barring any unforeseen complications. She reminded me that even though my job was supposed to be part-time, there seemed to always be 'unforeseen complications.'

Anyway, I set out in my Suburban around six-thirty. I had told Byrd I would be there at ten and believed I had more than enough time to make it. It felt good to have all my toys with me once again, such as my Winchester 700, my .40 caliber Glock holstered under my left arm and my .380 inside my boot.

As Birdman wasn't much for donuts, I knew there would be no pastries on site, so I grabbed a lo-cal gooey, iced honey bun and cup of coffee at the Stop-n-Go off I-66 on the way into D.C. When I got back on, it did not take me long to hit the I-66 parking lot. Apparently, somebody had spun out and hit another vehicle a mile ahead. Had I not stopped at the minute-saver, I would have been ahead of it.

I started to call Byrd to let him know, but he would probably make some snide comment like, "You have to anticipate problems on the Washington beltways and plan accordingly, Bruce." I thought I'd rather be sitting directly in front of him, looking him squarely in the eyes when he chided me.

However, the interstate mess didn't make me all that late. At ten after ten I pulled off Lyon Street into the driveway that led to the rear parking lot at Terminal Enterprises, AKA to us as CTT HQ. Another black Suburban with blacked-out windows pulled from a parking space and came to an abrupt stop within a dozen feet from my vehicle. I thought the driver might be waiting for me to clear the narrow driveway before he passed by; but to my alarm as I came around, he suddenly gunned the SUV directly into my path. Not the kind of driver to play chicken, I swerved off the asphalt, nearly sideswiping a tree.

"Son-of-a *bitch*!" I yelled out. The vehicle then slowed and just as I saw the rear passenger window slide down, the barrel of an assault rifle came out. By instinct, I grabbed my Glock and fell into the passenger's seat just as the gunman unloaded a good portion of his magazine into my driver's side glass. He must have fired a dozen rounds, most of which I felt zing past my body, but two of which creased my left shoulder blade and scalp above my left ear. I then pushed out the passenger side door handle and fell into some weeds. Quickly, I moved around in front of my Suburban's grille and fired seven or eight well-placed rounds into the passing vehicle's side and rear glass. The gunman's truck then laid rubber as it pulled from the driveway onto Lyon and out of sight.

I was not only dazed from the shock of the ambush on our very grounds, but my brain had been rattled by the head wound. My scalp was bleeding profusely onto my shirt. I took out a handkerchief and pressed it firmly against my skull. I then ran from my vehicle to the rear of the building. The door was standing wide open. A sense of dread hit me before I even passed through the entrance.

I inserted another clip and allowed the Glock to lead me cautiously through the hallway where I first saw our receptionist, Marina, slumped over her desk with a bullet wound on the left side of her head and her eyes still open in death. Blood oozed down her cheek and into her gaped open mouth.

When I turned the corner, Palmer's dead body lay in the hallway that led to all our offices. His Walther, still in his hand, had been pulled out seconds too late. My Marine buddy, Candellera, was lying on the floor in his office with several rounds having been pumped into his chest. A large amount of bright red blood had pooled beneath his body. And then I found Ty Marshall's body in the kitchenette. He had been pouring himself a cup of coffee. Both the coffee and blood splatters were still draining down the white cabinets. His body had fallen over the snack table and turned it over.

I then checked Chuck's office, where I set up as well a few days of the month, but thank God he was not there. I figured he was off for the day or Byrd had sent him out on something.

Across from the kitchen, was Virginia's office where I found her leaning back in her chair with her eyes closed, looking as though she were asleep. One could have easily come to that conclusion had it not been for the two wounds just below her breasts. I checked her pulse, but felt no throb. Birdman's Girl Friday and my Moneypenny…gone. She was to retire at the end of the year.

I was suddenly reeling and in my shock, I didn't know whether I needed to cry or throw up. I thought both would happen. I then took a deep breath and turned to go to the end of the hallway to Lionel Byrd's corner office. I started to shake, fearing what I would find. His door was closed. Was he in there at all? Cradling my Glock with my right hand, I turned the knob with my left. After pushing the door open, I swept the pistol around the room. He wasn't at his desk, so I wondered if he or anyone else was in the small toilet room off to the left. I kicked the door open, but found no one.

But when I rounded the corner of his large desk, I saw him. Lionel was lying face up on the floor by his chair. His white shirt and yellow tie were splattered with his blood. There was a single bullet wound in his chest near his heart. His eyes were still partially open. Further sickened, I steadied myself, thinking I would heave the contents of my stomach all over his desk.

But then I saw him blink. Quickly, I laid my Glock on his desk and knelt down to him. New, bright blood was pumping out of his chest with every beat of his heart. I pulled his blazer off the coat rack behind me and pressed it hard against his chest at the entry wound.

"Lionel. Can you speak?"

He lifted his right hand and motioned for me to bend down to him. His mouth opened just a little to speak, but blood spurted out instead. I heard him gurgle so I turned his head to the left to keep him from choking on his blood.

"My God, Lionel. Who did this? How did they get in?"

He tried to form words, but I was having a difficult time making out what he was trying to say. Finally, he succeeded. He said one name and after coughing out more blood, he said another. After getting out the second name, he then told me one more thing. It caused my own blood to burn like the fire of Hades and a pang of anger hit me in the chest. Lionel's voice began to trail away into a whisper as he asked me to tell his wife Miriam something. After he took one long, last breath, I heard the rattle. And then he was still.

"Lionel?" I called. I then felt his neck below the jaw line and there was no pulse. I knew there was no use in trying CPR.

My tears came so quickly, I began to choke on them. As my knees were weak and wobbly, I had trouble standing back up. Still, I managed to get to my feet and steadied myself against his desk. For the first time in my life I was so confused that I had no idea what to do next. I did know I had to call somebody…but who?

I knew I couldn't call Lionel's wife as protocol and common decency dictated that in this case, someone from the Executive Office would go by her house. And I couldn't call 911 and have the D.C. cops running all through the crime scene, asking questions about who we were and what we did. Clearly ninety-five percent of the State Department for whom we worked didn't even know we existed. So, I dialed 411 and asked the operator for the Office of the Secret Service.

When the Secret Service operator came on the line, I identified myself and said, "My name is Bruce McGowan and this is an emergency."

"What is your emergency, sir?"

"Please have someone to tell the President that I am at Lionel Byrd's office and our location at Terminal Enterprises has been compromised. The team has been hit. No survivors. I must impress upon you the urgency of the matter and tell the President I need an investigative team to get here immediately. Have someone call me right away at…"

"I see your number, sir. Just a moment. I will convey this to an agent presently standing by."

In less than twenty seconds a man's voice came on the line. "This is Peter Wyman. With whom am I speaking?"

"Bruce McGowan, Special Operative with Terminal Enterprises."

"What is your code name, Mr. McGowan?"

"Scorpion."

"Okay, and your ID number?"

"Alpha Romeo four six four two one."

"Just a moment." And he took one.

"You check out. Okay, you said your location has been compromised?"

"Yes."

"Casualties?"

"All."

"Any fatal?"

"All," I replied. "Another thing, Wyman, I pulled in about the time the bad guys were leaving. They shot me up as well."

"Did you get a good look at them and their vehicle?"

"Not really. I was trying to get out the way of a hail of automatic weapons fire."

"Were you hit?"

"Slightly. Minor wounds to my head and left shoulder."

"Another moment, please."

I could hear him speaking with someone else, maybe on another phone. Shortly, he got back to me.

"Have you secured the site?"

"Yes."

"Then remain there and I'll send a clean-up team."

"How will I know you?"

"You can trust me, McGowan. I just spoke with Eagle One."

Eagle One was what I needed to hear.

"Then I'll be here."

"Will be there in one-five (fifteen minutes)."

I was shaking as though I was standing somewhere in Antarctica in Bermuda shorts and a tee shirt. Now knowing what I knew, straight from the lips of a dying man, I wasn't sure I could trust *anyone*. But as I had contacted the Secret Service who protected the President, I had no choice *but* to trust them. There was no one else.

After canvassing the scene, making sure I watched where I stepped and touched nothing, I revisited each of the bodies. They had all apparently died quick deaths considering the well-placed rounds. It was a professional hit all right and it had gone down like clockwork. Now digesting what Lionel had told me, I knew not only how they got in, but why they were murdered. They were actually after Lionel. The others were just collateral damage because they happened to work there. But if they just wanted *him* taken out, I wondered why they didn't just hit him somewhere off-site. When I passed Virginia's office again and saw that her right hand was lying in an open desk drawer atop her .380, I knew that the feisty old gal had intended not to go down without a fight. But she was no match for professional hitmen. I was as much shaken about her as I was Lionel. We had had a lot of laughs and teasing over the past four-plus-years and I would miss her deeply.

Then suddenly a revelation struck me between the eyes. The killers had intended to hit *me* as well. It only made sense considering what Lionel had told me. I was supposed to have already been there; but as I had stopped for a pastry and became tied up in wreck traffic, I missed the ambush by mere minutes. I then wondered why the assassins continued on without closing the deal on me. There were obviously more of them than the one of me. Maybe they knew that I would not go down easily considering who I was and there would in fact be another day. Maybe through the crosshairs of a sniper's rifle the shooter would watch my head explode.

Aftershocks continued to rattle my body and I started to shake. Slowly, the horror of it all was beginning to sink in. Gone. The only friends I had in this world were gone. CTT Washington had ceased to exist. I allowed my back to slide down the hallway wall until I touched bottom. My wounded brain tried to deny it, but my heart knew it was all too real. I sat for what was probably five minutes in one spot without moving. The place was deadly quiet. Dead for real. I thought about Lionel lying on the floor in his office, his red blood oozing into the gold carpet. His spirit gone.

After taking a deep breath and regaining a small degree of composure, I stood again. I then thought to check Marina's security program adjacent to her desk that taped the film that Voyeur, the exterior camera system, shot this morning. After opening the cartridge, I saw that it was empty. There would be no filmed record of the intruders. Scurrying again on back to Lionel's office, I checked his desk. His computer was gone and so was his briefcase. The safe had been emptied out of all classified documents, some of which would have been Top Secret. I looked down again at Lionel and began to choke up. I loved the man as much as I had even loved my own father. The strange thing about it was that I had only known him for less than five years.

It was a clean, well-planned executive take-down. And now I not only knew who did it and why...but who had ordered the hit.

CHAPTER SIXTEEN

lmost on the mark, within fifteen minutes, a black Excursion and black Lincoln Town Car pulled up in the rear parking lot. Out poured four men and two women, all dressed in black or gray business suits and all carting Uzis. A little late for the guns, people. I met them at the back door and held up my State Department ID so they could see it and not drill holes in me.

I blocked their entry momentarily to demand, "Your identification, please."

They looked at me as if to say "Who is this guy kidding?" considering a badge hung from their breast pockets. But each pulled from his or her inside coat pocket an ID. A tall, thin, serious-looking man who resembled Joe Friday in the face and definitely looked the part said, "McGowan?"

"Yes."

"I'm Wyman."

"This way," I said.

Immediately, they all donned surgical gloves and placed paper slippers over their shoes and moved on in.

"Stay here, McGowan," said Wyman. "We'll sweep the building and then I'll return to ask you some questions. First, I need to check your firearm."

I pulled my Glock from its holster and gave it to him. He hit the release, dropped the clip into his hand, checked for a round in the chamber and sniffed the gun.

"This weapon has been fired."

"You didn't notice that big black Suburban sitting back there all shot up? Did you think I was just going to put my head in the ditch and not return fire?"

"Easy, McGowan. I know you're upset about losing your team. I'm just doing my job here."

I nodded and took a deep breath. "Sorry. I know you are. You're not the bad guys."

He placed a hand on my shoulder...the shoulder that had a chunk out of it. I flinched and he drew back his gloved hand, smeared with my blood.

"I have a trained medic on my team. I'll have him look at that."

"Don't worry about it right now. I'll take care of it. Do what you need to do."

"I'll need to keep your Glock," he said. "It will be run through ballistics, as you know."

"I expected that. When will I get it back? I plan to use it."

He gave me a cockeyed look, understanding what I intended to do with it.

"Do you have another piece?"

"I have a boot gun...a .380. It has *not* been fired. I also have a Winchester 700 in the rear compartment of my

SUV."

"All right. Let me see the .380."

I pulled the gun from the boot holster and turned it over. He checked the clip, smelled it and then handed it back to me.

"I'll be back to you in a few minutes. Suggest you get bandaged up."

I went to the men's room which was adjacent to Palmer's crumpled body and pulled out the First Aid kit that was located in the storage unit beneath the sink. I then ripped off my left shirt sleeve to get to the shoulder wound. The sleeve itself had been torn by the bullet. Finding some disinfectant, I poured it liberally on the wound and winced. It burnt clean through to the bone. I then took out a compress and some surgical tape and nailed them down tightly to my shoulder. I knew I needed stitches, but there was no way I was going to take the time to go to the emergency room. I had been shot up worse than that.

My head was also still bleeding and it probably required stitches as well. The blood that had streamed down my face had soaked the entire left side of my shirt. I looked at the pitiful face in the mirror, a face filled with both anger and sorrow, and told myself that none of this was my fault, even though the eyes said *guilty*. I had missed being killed by minutes and should have been lying there in the team house with my friends. They call it survivor's guilt. Lionel Byrd and I had even talked about that. He, Virginia and others on our team were in the World Trade Center when the towers went down. He always thought that fate had marked them for death, but they had escaped it. He had compared it with scenarios like when one person survives a plane crash where three hundred others were killed. He actually believed that when you manage to cheat certain death, when you should have died by all logic, the Grim Reaper will still find you sooner or later…another time, another place. I don't know why I stood before the mirror and thought about that. But, I did know one thing…death had certainly found *him*. Now, would I be on *its* hit list?

I found a towel, wet it, wiped the oozing and dried blood from my left temple and pressed it against the scalp for several minutes. When I released the pressure, the bleeding had all but stopped. I then found a large, square Band-aid and stuck it on. Continuing to look at myself in the glass, I saw that I was not symmetrical, so I ripped off my right sleeve at the seam.

When I exited the men's room, Wyman caught up with me again.

"Is this your entire team?"

"No," I replied. "Chuck Robinson is missing."

"Do you know where he is?"

"No."

"We'll need his contact information. I assume you have his cell number and address."

"I do."

"I note that Mr. Byrd's safe door is open and there's nothing in it. I also assume there were classified documents in there."

"I'm sure. But I don't know what."

"There's no briefcase in there and his desk top computer seems to be missing."

"I saw that."

"I also saw cameras on the roof when we came in. Where is the computer that holds the tapes?"

"On the receptionist's desk and in Virginia DeHussey's office as well. The tapes have been removed."

"Appears they covered all their bases," he commented. "Very professional hit. When exactly did this go down?"

"I pulled in at ten minutes past ten. Probably anywhere from nine-fifty to ten."

"Any speculation on who may have done the hit?"

I shook my head. "We are a covert, counter-terrorist unit, Mr. Wyman. We could be the target of a number of foreign or domestic terrorist factions who somehow found out who and where we are."

"You come under the State Department, right?"

"On paper and administratively, yes," I said. "But Mr. Byrd was directed by and answered to a higher power. I think you know who."

He just stared at me with his steel-gray eyes and didn't respond.

I continued. "How will you take care of things here?"

"A Federal CSI team is right behind us. They will do their work and handle the bodies. Next of kin will be immediately notified personally. I *will* need their personnel records."

"They would be in the filing cabinet in Mrs. DeHussey's office."

"Okay, then. You need to leave. Here's my card, but *I'll* call *you* when we've run everything through our and the CSI team's lab. You can come by my location indicated there on the card to retrieve your Glock." He then gave me a piercing look. "Unless of course we find this gun was involved. Then *we'll* be retrieving *you*."

I threw a laser beam back at him. "Don't insult me, Mr. Wyman. You *know* I had nothing to do with this hit."

"Again, I meant nothing personal. I'm covering all the bases, that's all."

"I only ask one thing of you," I said.

"What's that?"

"That you personally go by the Byrd address and tell his widow what happened. And then I want the President himself to speak to her and offer his condolences."

"I will do my best to see that it happens."

I nodded and then left out of the back door. I looked at my shattered vehicle, then opened the driver's door to take account of all the glass in the seat and floor. Finding my work gloves in the rear compartment, I began picking out the shards of glass and tossed them in the weeds. When I was convinced there were no large pieces of glass left in the seat that could give me a new flesh wound on my ass, I cranked the Suburban, made a turn in the back parking lot and pulled out onto Lyon. I looked up and down the street to see if the perps' vehicle was parked anywhere nearby where the bad guys would be able to take another crack at me. But it appeared they were long gone.

A couple of miles down the street, I found an Exxon station and vacuumed the remainder of the glass from the interior of my vehicle. I was still vacuuming with probably a half-minute remaining when I found myself sobbing. My tears had blinded me so completely that I could no longer see what I was or was not picking up, so I hung up the nozzle. I placed my bottom back in the driver's side seat and sat with my forehead on the steering wheel. It was then I realized that the tears were just as much from my anger than from sadness.

I took out my cell phone and dialed the number, hoping the voice of betrayal would answer. After four rings, he did.

"Bruce, my man. How goes it? Are you back?"

"Where are you, Chuck?" I said in a low, hateful tone.

"Out on assignment. Are you back at the office?"

"You know goddamn well I'm back, Chuck." I paused a few seconds to keep my heart from springing out of my chest. ""I've got one question for you, Chuck…why?"

"What's got into you, Bruce? What do you mean, *why?*"

I grit my teeth and grasped the steering wheel as though I was choking it. "Lionel Byrd did not die before placing your name on his lips. You didn't check to see that he was dead before you left, you son-of-a-bitch. You let that hit team in the back door and took part in the massacre of our team."

There was a long pause and I could hear his sharp breaths.

"So where do we go from here, Bruce?"

"Where do we go? Well, it's like this, Chuck…I'm coming for you and *you're* going to *Hell.* Then *I'm* going *home.*"

Another pause.

"Who knows, Bruce?"

"You mean about you? Just me, right now. We're going to meet up, Chuck. Just you and me. And one of us is going down."

"If we do that, how will I know you won't bring the Bureau down on me?"

"You have my word, prick. And how do I know you

won't bring the rest of your new friends down on *me?*"

"My word as well."

"Sure, Chuck. The word of a traitor? The word of a sniveling piece of shit who betrayed his friends? You take me for a moron?"

"I'm being straight with you, Bruce. Just you and me."

"Uh huh. When was it that you got into Congressman Randall's pocket, Chuck?"

"So, you know about Jonathan Randall. But, of course you do. You just returned from Vietnam where you got the low-down on him."

"We all know he's running for President, and now I know it was a young Captain Jack Randall who was paid a chunk of dough by an ARVN colonel to massacre a complete village and burn it to the ground. It would be that kind of story, if it ever got out, that would kill his chances for the nomination, wouldn't you think? How long have you been working for the bastard, Chuck?"

"Long enough."

"Then I guess it was you who killed Berryhill and help stage several other murders before that to look like suicides. So did you plan to kill them all?"

"No, Bruce. Randall didn't have to. His people just scared the hell out of the rest of them. A man has to really do some thinking when somebody threatens to kill his wife and kids."

"You're a goddamn piece of shit, Chuck."

He didn't respond.

I continued. "So then you found out I was going to Vietnam from Marina, put two-and-two together and informed Randall. He then knew somebody high up was onto the story."

"We knew Berryhill went to the President. The Congressman has a man loyal to him that sits on the right hand of His Majesty. And of course you know Randall was the former CIA Director. He still has a pack of wolves from the Cold War on his payroll that controlled the story *and* the rifle company alumni. And yes, I'm one of them. Is there anything else you want to know before I kill you, Bruce?"

"Yeah, when do we do this?"

"Any time, Bruce. The Congressman has a cabin west of the Shenandoah between McDowell and Monterey on Highway 250. You come alone. You'll find me there."

"Alone?"

"Alone."

"Name the day and time."

"Tomorrow. Twelve o'clock high. And, oh, Bruce. If you go to the press or the FBI, two things will happen."

"What?"

"I work for a man who has long arms. Arms that extend well beyond the State of Virginia. The lovely Mrs. McGowan back in West Virginia will die a horrible, painful death and then after that, your sweet little daughter out in Colorado will have an unfortunate, fatal accident. You see, we're good at making things look like accidents."

I gripped the steering wheel even harder with my left hand. Just hearing the words sent a chill through my spine. "Oh, I don't intend to tell anybody, Chuck…especially about my plan to kill you."

"I'll be waiting, Bruce. Tomorrow. The address is 3

Mountain Road, just off Highway 250 about six miles west of McDowell."

"I guess you'll try to ambush me as I'm coming down the road, eh Chuck?"

"No, Bruce. I'll walk right out from the cabin to meet you. It'll be face-to-face…like the OK Corral. You'll be armed and so will I. The best man will be left standing."

"Like I can believe you and your merry band of murderers won't ambush me."

"You have no choice, Bruce. Tomorrow." He then clicked me off.

As I sat there behind the wheel fielding the myriad of thoughts and emotional pangs torturing my brain, I also wondered if this would indeed be the end of CTT. We had teams in Chicago, L.A., Miami and New York numbering a total of twenty men and two women. But Lionel Byrd was the guru, the founder and developer of the Zulu concept. The remainder of our team was out there without contact and direction.

The FBI, CIA and NSA had their own counter-terrorist teams integrated within their organized structure…the key word being *structure*. But we were a different breed. We didn't play well with others. Rogues, scoundrels, assassins, we were a unique team. We didn't make the effort to advise the terrorist of his rights before we acted as judge, jury and executioner, because he *had* no rights. Now, one of us had gone bad…had betrayed us. A man with no conscience or soul. It had to be all about money. Why else would he turn on his friends? Perhaps he traded that soul for a cool million. It would be a drop in the bucket to a billionaire many times over like Jonathan Perryman Randall.

Murder was not foreign to the congressman. Human life

meant nothing to him when he was a young Army officer and it still didn't. The members of his own unit he did not kill, he threatened to kill. He would do anything to not only save his name, but his ass from going to jail over the village massacre. And that dirty little business in Vietnam would definitely be the land mine he would hit on the political highway to the Presidency. Somehow, he had managed to make a connection with one of our very best operatives to take out Lionel Byrd…and me when I returned from my fact-finding mission. I then wondered if it was only money that motivated Chuck Robinson to join up with the likes of Congressman John Randall. It sure as hell wasn't love of country.

I again contemplated as to why Chuck and his goons didn't just leap out of their vehicle and waste me in the parking lot when they had the chance. Of course Chuck knew that I was dead accurate with anything that spit out bullets and I was planting them in every piece of glass in their SUV as fast as I could get through the clip. He also knew that automatic weapons fire or not, I would pick each one of them off as soon as I saw a head emerge. He was smart to call it off. He didn't figure I would suspect him. He knew he had my confidence and trusted him with my life. It would then make it easy for him to then take me down at any time. If he didn't pick me off at a hundred yards via a sniper rifle, it might go like this: he and I would be sitting having a beer at somewhere on a park bench in the Virginia highlands far from the madding crowd, lamenting the loss of our friends and that we should have been there. And then while I was taking a swig from my Rolling Rock, he would simply pull out his piece and cut me down. I wouldn't be expecting it. But the latter scenario wouldn't happen, now that I knew he had turned traitor.

It was a fact that I had no intention of taking my

information to the Bureau or the U.S. Attorney General. I was taking no chances on Chuck and the congressman escaping prosecution due to lack of connecting evidence. I still had Thanh's and Sue's statements which may serve to discredit Randall and he may even have to withdraw from the race. But connecting him to Berryhill's and the others' deaths as well as the massacre of Team Zulu would be a stretch. I also doubted that the members of his unit who were still living nervous lives would come forward, considering the threats already leveled against them and their families. Randall with his money would still have the 'long-reaching arms', as Chuck said, and the men of Charlie Company would remain fearful for their families.

Chuck and the rest of Randall's mob were professionals and had made sure there were no clues left at the team house. It was all part of a very solid plan. He would materialize in a day or so and then be compelled to divulge who CTT was and what we were about…and he would say that Mr. Byrd had sent him on assignment the day before. He regretted that he was not there to try stopping it. Perhaps the killers, most likely a foreign terrorist element such as al Qaeda had found out about the State Department's Counter-terrorist Team, and in taking it down they would score one for their people. The finger would then be pointed back at the most powerful man in the world and he would be found out. The world would know that CTT, a covert organization that operated contrary to the Constitution and law of the land, was of his own design. His challenger, Congressman Randall, known as Jack Randall back in his younger days, would have a field day with the media over it and the President himself would be seen as a rogue and a despot.

But now the plan had to be altered. I had found Chuck out. If tomorrow didn't go down, I knew that he would follow through with his threat regarding Adrianna. She and

Caroline were his aces in the hole. As fear suddenly raced through my arteries just thinking about it, I realized I still had an old friend's number in my cell phone contact list from three years ago. Only six weeks ago I had played golf with him at the Elks Country Club. State Police Lieutenant Harlan Williams.

He answered right away. "Bruce. How're you doing, man? Are you in D.C. or around the corner?"

"D.C., Harlan. Listen, I don't have much time. I have a personal favor to ask."

"Sure. What is it?"

"I won't be back home for a day or so and I need you to put a couple of troopers in an unmarked car outside of the B&B."

"Why? What's going on?"

"I have good reason to believe Adrianna is in danger. There's somebody out there who has made terroristic threats against me *and* her."

"Who?"

"Again, I don't have time to explain. Can you do this for me? Just two days, that's all I ask. Day and night."

"How many times are we going to go through this? Wolf Laurel has certainly had its share of tragedy the last couple of years."

"Please, Harlan. I *will* explain when I get back home."

"Okay, Bruce. I'll put a couple of guys there. But when you get back, you be sure to see me first thing."

"I promise, Harlan. Thanks. Also, make sure they're armed with assault rifles."

"What the hell? Assault rifles?"

"Yes. Please, just trust me on this."

"We're not going to have a big shoot out like went down in 2001, are we?"

"No. This is just a precaution. Are you okay with this?"

"Yeah, but…"

"Thanks, Harlan. This is a load off my mind."

He let out a long sigh. "We were mighty peaceful around here until you decided to come back home to live. But…don't worry. I'll look out for the little lady. See me first thing. Understood?"

"We'll talk. Goodbye, Harlan."

I did feel a lot better, but then again, I knew that a professional would spot the cop car instantly and may even take it out, still getting to Adrianna. Speaking of the wife, I needed to call her, not to alert her as to any danger, but to let her know I would not be back for a day or two.

"Hey, sweetheart, you remember when I promised I'd be home this evening? Well, I ran into a problem.

"Of course you did, Skip. What is it this time? Did Mr. Byrd put you on something else?"

"The de-briefing is taking a little longer and we have a meeting planned later in the afternoon," I lied.

She was quiet for a moment…the kind of quiet I don't much care for…the kind where she's steaming.

"When will this business ever end for you, Skip?"

"This is my last deal with the team, Adrianna. I'm not going back."

"Uh huh. Are you just saying that because you know I'm

a bit ticked off right now?"

"I'm saying it because it's true. I've officially pulled my last mission with the team."

"Then I'm officially not mad anymore."

"That's good. Look, uh, sweetheart, I…just want you to know that I always miss you when I'm gone, and…I want you to know I'll always love you."

She was quiet again. "What's wrong, Skip. You sound strange. You generally don't say those things."

"I'm fine, Adrianna. Don't worry."

"You also sound very down…almost like you lost your best friend."

If only she knew.

"I'm all right," I replied with a smile in my voice. "I'm great. I just look forward to getting back to you, that's all. I think that last trip across the water took a lot out of me. But remember, that's all behind us."

"I hope so."

"Bye, sweetheart. See you in a day or so."

It was then noon. There were exactly twenty-four hours between Chuck and me. One of us was going to die.

CHAPTER SEVENTEEN

In less than twenty minutes I had broken from the ever-busy D.C. noonday traffic and made I-66. At four, I pulled off at Staunton and checked into a small roadside motel on U.S. 250. So that my shot-up Suburban wouldn't be a spectacle to the other guests nor spotted by any of Randall's men on their way to his cabin, which I fully expected to happen, I parked in the rear. Since the vehicle was no longer secure what with the missing door glass on both sides, I had to take in all my gear which included a set of binoculars, a hand-held listening device, a survival knife and kit. When I was pretty sure no one was in proximity, I also took in my Remington 700 and a spare Glock I kept on the floorboard under the mat along with three clips of .40 caliber hollow points.

As the door to my room looked a bit flimsy and there were gouge marks on the frame where someone had broken in or at least tried, I wasn't about to leave the room to get something to eat. Even though I was pretty damn famished having only had the honey bun earlier in the morning, the queasiness in my gut was attempting to overpower my hunger pangs. Still, I needed to keep up my strength, so I ordered a Domino's pizza.

While waiting for delivery, I cleaned up my blood-crusted face again and pulled the bandage off to check the wound on my scalp. I really needed stitches up there and had to keep the wound cleaned up with peroxide to keep it from getting infected. I then took the bandage off my shoulder and saw that a hunk of meat was missing. It was also sore as hell. In my survival kit I found some Neosporin which I liberally applied to my head *and* shoulder. I replaced the shoulder gauze and re-taped it to my skin. I then applied a large Band-Aid to my temple area to assure I wouldn't wake up in the morning with my head stuck to the pillowcase. Looking at the poor bastard in the mirror, I knew one thing…I was getting pretty damn tired of being a blood donor. And when this was over, the only blood I'd be giving would be an occasional nick on the chin from my razor.

After half the pizza went down with a Diet Coke, I tried to take my mind off the day's tragedy by lying on the bed and watching TV. The movie playing on AMC ironically was *Three Days of the Condor* where Robert Redford, a CIA analyst, came back from picking up coffee for his team and found that a mailman had wiped out his entire unit. How coincidental, not to mention freaky, was that? I quickly switched channels to the national news. The incident, as I expected, had been totally contained. There was no mention of a mass murder of State Department employees or anyone else in Washington, D.C. It was inevitable, however, that the story would break in the next couple of days once it was determined by the Executive and State Departments what information would be released. The families would demand it, along with answers. But there would be no mention of what our team was about. They were merely employees of Terminal Enterprises, an import-export business who effected government contracts with civilian vendors manufacturing the latest in weapons systems. It could have been a robbery gone badly where the perps mistakenly thought money was kept on hand or foreign nationals whose terrorist agenda it was to either steal plans, disrupt any future deals or simply send a message. Some sharp investigative reporter may even uncover the fact that Terminal Enterprises was actually a covert counter-terrorist element. I expected the remnants of our team in the other locations would be reassigned to other government positions. But as I laid there and thought about it, it really didn't matter anymore.

I closed my eyes and thought about Lionel's wife and adult children. Candellera, Palmer and Marshall were not married, nor had they any children, but I was sure their mothers were having a rough time about now. And then there was young Marina, about whom I knew very little. And Virginia. I closed my eyes tighter and saw her face. She was so affable and full of life. Tom would be devastated. And when all this was over, when I had killed the enemy, and when I finally became the sedentary, non-action figure that Adriana wanted in a husband, I would then realize how big the hole in my heart actually was. But for now, I couldn't think about it. Chuck Robinson and undoubtedly several of Randall's men were out there waiting for me…waiting to kill me as soon as I stepped into their cross-hairs. Tomorrow I would go on the biggest hunting expedition of my life…and when the day was over, I intended to be the one to walk away. The predators would then become my prey.

At nine-thirty, about the time my lights were fading, my cell phone rang.

"Mr. McGowan?"

"Yes."

"Wyman here. How are you doing?"

"Fine. Trying to get to sleep to make this day-long nightmare go away."

"Are you still in the area?"

"No, but I'm still in Virginia."

"I need to get your Glock back to you. Ballistics cleared you."

"I didn't know I needed to be cleared. I thought checking my gun out was just a formality."

"In situations like this, nobody is above suspicion. By the way, we've contacted all Zulu locations and are bringing them in. We've still not been able to get hold of Robinson."

"He may be out of the country on a mission," I said. Then again, he may not.

"Okay, I'm sure he'll turn up. Tell him to contact me if you happen to speak with him first."

"I will," I lied.

"By the way, there's someone at my location that wants to speak with you. You have two minutes."

Now, I was puzzled.

"Bruce," the voice said. "May I call you *Bruce*?"

My heart skipped a beat. The voice was unmistakable.

"Yes, Mr. President."

"I just want to tell you how sorry I am about your comrades, especially Mr. Byrd who I greatly admired and respected. I don't mind tellin' you that he was my friend."

"He was mine as well, sir."

"It had to be traumatic for you to find them like that. I can't imagine."

"Yes, sir." I swallowed a sob.

"I want you to know that I was delivered your message

and I personally offered my condolences to Mrs. Byrd. When you get a chance, I'd like you to stop by. Mr. Wyman will arrange it."

"I would consider it a privilege, sir."

He paused a few seconds. "Did you obtain the information I asked for?"

"I did, sir."

"I will need the originals to get them to the Attorney General accordingly. Do we assume the same character you investigated had a hand in today's incident?"

"I'm convinced that is the case, sir, and I am taking it upon myself to personally eradicate the problem."

"Let the system do that, Bruce."

"I understand."

"Well, thank you for your years of service, Bruce. Not just your current dealings, but with the Army and Bureau as well. I didn't ever get the word to you, but I am also grateful for the work you did there in West Virginia on that most terrible of all days. It could have been even worse, if that can be imagined. I'm proud to know you, Bruce, and believe me when I tell you our country owes you a tremendous debt.

"Thank you for saying that, sir. Mr. President, I…"

"He's off the line now, Mr. McGowan," said Wyman. "I trust you'll be able to get some rest tonight. One thing, though…"

"What's that, Mr. Wyman."

"Keep yourself accessible."

"I'll be heading back home tomorrow," I told him. "I just stopped at a motel for the night to clean up and nurse my wounds before seeing my wife. She'll freak out anyway when I come through the door. I also have to clear my head about all this or I won't be worth anything as a husband."

"I understand that, but just don't disappear on me."

"You can always reach me at this number."

"All right. Good night, Mr. McGowan."

"Good night, Mr. Wyman."

*   *   *   *

At eight fifteen on Wednesday morning I saddled up the Suburban, checked my ammo and clips, locked and loaded, and then set out to the west on Highway 250. I had been over the road several times before to see a Vietnam buddy and his wife who live on a beautiful 100 acre farm west of Monterey. Each time I negotiate the winding road I gain a renewed appreciation for the majestic Allegheny countryside. For a while, the terrain rolls and then settles into deep green plateaus where black Angus cattle and dingy white sheep lay under shady groves near mirroring ponds. And then the highway climbs and twists for something over five miles, compelling the transmission to drop down into the next lower gear. After reaching the apex of the first mountain, the road follows the ridgeline down an eight percent grade for several miles until it levels off into a small village where a gurgling creek flows past ancient, white farmhouses and weathered red barns. And then the climb begins again up another, even higher mountain in the Allegheny chain. But this day, I appreciated none of that…not the beauty of the Mountain Laurel, not the feeling of climbing, turning or descending, not the aroma of honeysuckle or the fresh mountain air. I was oblivious to it all. My brain was fixated on one thing…taking out the people who murdered my friends and bringing down Congressman Jonathan Perryman Randall.

It was after McDowell that my GPS voice told me I had one mile to my turnoff point that led me to John Randall's retreat off Highland Turnpike, 3 Mountain Road. When the voice said "Your location is five hundred feet on the left," I slowed the Suburban until I saw a narrow, paved driveway and a gate on which there was a sign that read *Private Property, No Entrance*. I continued on by the driveway for another two-tenths of a mile until I spotted a firebreak also on the left. After throwing my vehicle into four-wheel drive, I jumped the ditch and turned onto the path. When I had cleared sight of U.S. 250, I parked the vehicle in a small clearing. It was eleven-ten.

Well, it was still five months till any hunting season and it would have been my dumb luck to run into a forest ranger while I was groping my way through the woods with my Remington. I would not only have to watch out for him, or her, but Randall's henchmen as well who I knew were set to ambush me. I could have taken Chuck at his word that only he would be at the cabin waiting for me as the minute hand approached high noon; however, I have learned that murderers are anti-social personalities and so are liars. Why would I trust that a killer would also not lie to me?

Finding a piece of high ground at the edge of a tree line, I lifted my binoculars to scan the forest for any glints or movement. One well-placed round fired by a sniper would take out the only person who had knowledge of Chuck Robinson and the evidence of his involvement in the murders of his team, quickly and without any hullabaloo. But I *knew* Chuck. Well, maybe not really; but I knew how he thought. He wanted to come face-to-face with his enemy. He liked to see the face of the man he kills. It was the psychopath in him which I thought was only directed toward bad guys. *Very* bad guys. Now I knew he was actually one of them.

As I began to move forward a little at a time, rifle pointed, stopping to check behind every tree and clump of brush, the field glasses finally fell onto the road that led down downwards to the cabin. I knew they wouldn't be expecting me to just parade down the road, but maybe they thought I would advance parallel to the road. I figured they would be positioned at points just off the road that gave them both cover and concealment.

Suddenly, to my right I heard the snap of a branch. Dropping quickly to my left knee, I took aim, listened and waited. No further sound. Using the scope on the Remington, I scanned back and forth in the direction of the noise. There he was. Standing still between two trees and staring back at me was an eight point buck. I smiled and took my weapon down, then rose to my feet and moved on.

I had trekked along with a great deal of stealth for another seventy-five yards, then saw where the terrain rose dramatically. When I crested the hill, I also saw where the woods ended into a clearing beyond which sat a rustic, but stately two-story log house about a hundred yards further back. A majestic upper deck that jutted out on the right side of the cabin gave the congressman a grand view of the Alleghenies. The place had to be over ten thousand square feet and valued with the land at somewhere in excess of a million dollars. But from what I had read a year ago in the *Post*, the congressman, a billionaire, had three other homes located in Maui, Malibu and Coconut Grove. The cabin was nothing more than a hunting camp to him. Yeah, I follow a little politics from time to time. The thing is, when I heard his name, first out of the mouth of friend Thanh the week before, I hadn't connected Captain Jack Randall to Congressman Jonathan Randall. It was the dying Lionel Byrd who connected the dots. Randall was one of two names on his lips. Chuck's was the other.

I set up in some thick brush in the prone position where I could get a panoramic view of the cabin and its surroundings. At first survey, I didn't see anyone about. But after a minute, a goon about as big as Chuck stepped out on the balcony with a cigarette in his hand. Through the scope I could just about make out his features. I could tell he was muscular and his long, slick, black hair was pulled back and tied off in a pony tail. With his right hand, he brought the cigarette up to his mouth every twenty seconds or so. In his left hand was an Uzi.

Out of the corner of my eye I then caught the movement of another man on the road walking into some brush off the right side. All I could make out about him was that he had a short blonde buzz cut, was wearing a black leather jacket and had an AK-47 in his right hand. He then stopped and looked back at the Steven Seagal character on the deck who waved him on deeper into the thicket to a point about thirty yards in where he could capture me if I so chose to walk down the road. Did they actually think I was going to do that?

From a door beneath the deck then appeared two more men, one with a 30-30 and the other wearing a shoulder holster containing what appeared to be a 44 magnum. The first man was then dispatched by the traffic cop on the deck to the far right toward the rear of the cabin and the second to the far left to take up a position on the edge of the woods behind a split cord of oak.

I checked my watch and it was now eleven-thirty five. I'd have thought Chuck and gang would have set up well before now, perhaps even as early as ten o'clock back there just off the highway. They should have anticipated I would get there early to recon the area and feel my way in. But again, I wondered if the guards were just being positioned to signal that I was coming in since Chuck had to face me. He would not have had me ambushed if that were the case. But, in order to gain the element of surprise with Chuck, I had to take *all* these guys out.

I started to crawl out of position to take down the nearest man who was within fifty yards below me, when two more figures appeared on the balcony. I trained my scope on their faces. I recognized both. One was Chuck Robinson, the Judas bastard, and I recognized the other man from his appearance on his TV commercials and debates. John Randall. Finally, a third person stepped out from the open French doors…a petite woman in her low thirties with long blonde hair that fluttered around her head in the late spring breeze. I had seen pictures of Mrs. Randall standing beside the congressman on TV in campaign events and the woman on the balcony was not her by a long shot. And as the blonde hung onto Randall, teasing his ear with her lips, it told me she was not his daughter either.

The Steven Seagal guy then began pointing to the positions where he had posted his men and I saw Chuck nod. Chuck appeared to be the man in charge. In a couple of minutes, Randall, his paramour and Chuck then turned to go back inside, leaving the body guard to lean against the banister and finish the cigarette.

From my pocket I took out my silencer and screwed it into the barrel of the Remington. I then low-crawled down through the thicket toward the man closest to me. Once I was positioned within about ten feet of him, I think he felt my presence and turned in my direction. Pushing off against the ground with my left hand, I sprang to my feet and whacked the guy on the chin with the butt of my rifle just as he wheeled around. The sickening crack told me that I had shattered his jaw into pieces. I was surprised that the man was still conscious as he was going for the AK that he had dropped. From the sheath on my belt I quickly pulled out my Ranger knife that had been my close-combat friend since Vietnam and drove the blade into his abdomen just below the rib cage. Blood from the ruptured artery spurted immediately and the man exhaled a groan after he had taken his last breath. One down.

The man who was crouched about a hundred yards to my left behind the wood pile was stocky, dressed in a red checkered shirt and wore mirrored sun glasses. As I didn't feel like crawling all that distance, I decided to just lift my Winchester, put the cross-hairs on his upper chest near the throat while I had a clean shot and pull the trigger. When the bullet struck him, his body was thrown backwards behind the pile of wood about six feet, still out of sight of the man on the balcony. His damaged neurological system caused his body to jerk several times and then he was still. His 30-30 lay across him.

I knew it would probably take me another fifteen minutes or so to envelop the third man in the woods and I needed to do so as quickly as I could. If they had radios to communicate with one another and Chuck or the man on the deck couldn't raise the two I just eliminated, they would then realize their numbers had been cut in half. That would make them ever the more vigilant. Of course, there could be more of them somewhere else in the woods or inside. But Chuck knew me and he knew he needed every last one of them.

I didn't want to take out the guard on the balcony from where I was lying in the bush. At a hundred fifty yards I could still plant a bullet between his eyes, but I knew the force of the round tearing through skull would send the man spiraling backwards through the double French doors into the room where I had seen Chuck and the congressman disappear. The element of surprise would be gone.

Back-tracking into the woods, I then ran at a crouch

through some terribly thick brush and briers that tore at my arms and legs, toward the area where I had seen the third man enter the tree line. Stopping to take another look through my binoculars I zeroed in on every tree and potential hiding position, but did not see the man. I thought perhaps while I had been busy knocking off his buddies he had either moved further on down the slope or moved further back toward the road. But it was neither. Behind me I suddenly heard the alarming click of a hammer being cocked. He had instead enveloped *me*. When I turned to face the man, I saw the muzzle of a 44 magnum pointed at my head.

"We've been expecting you, McGowan. I didn't know you'd make it this easy."

Neither did I.

"Drop your weapon!" he barked.

Slowly I laid the Remington down in the weeds and lifted my hands. The man turned up his lip in an Elvis-style snarl and nodded. "Now get moving."

And then behind the gunman I saw it not twenty feet away.

"You didn't think I'd come here alone, did you? My partner is right behind you," I said.

"Do I look stupid? You really think I would fall for that old trick?"

My friend, the buck, had re-surfaced. He just stood there watching us without moving.

"Oh, he's there all right." And then I yelled out "Haaaw!"

The deer suddenly bolted, making enough noise for the man to turn and swing the pistol in the buck's direction.

Fortunately, he did not fire, but then seeing that it was only a deer, he turned and wheeled around back toward me just in time to see the blade of my Ranger knife flying toward his throat. After the thud, he dropped the pistol and clutched at the handle of the knife. While blood gushed from his neck just below his Adam's apple, he made a gurgling sound and fell to his knees. As I moved in on him, his body then tumbled forward and he fell on his face, driving the blade further through flesh and bone out the back of his neck. I took a moment to reflect on the incident. Maybe God had sent the buck to follow me and to ultimately distract the man who would have paraded me on in to the cabin. Divine providence? Perhaps.

Three down.

By the time I had made my way back down the slope to a point where I could flank the man on the deck and get off the well-placed shot that would send his body reeling off the balcony, he was gone. I knew that somehow I needed to find the man and take him down so that it would just be Chuck and me…that is if there was no one else inside except the puny congressman and his whore. I stayed well back out of sight for another ten minutes, finally checking my watch to discover it was five minutes to twelve. The people inside would be getting antsy. I saw that on the south side of the house there were no windows except what was probably a small bathroom window on the upper floor. Just as I had made my mind up to blitz the twenty yards or so to that side of the house, the man with the ponytail appeared on the deck again. This time he had a walkie-talkie in his hand. I was close enough to hear him talk into it and then he looked toward each of his men's positions. After not being able to immediately raise anyone, for obvious reasons, he flipped the cover on the radio to check the batteries. He then tried again and I heard him say "Come in, goddammit!"

I knew if I didn't take him out right away, he would come to the conclusion that his men had been compromised and that would drive him back inside. He and Chuck would then take up positions to intercept me, guns ready. The man made it easy for me. When he stepped up to the railing and leaned over to look at the ground below him, I pumped the one round into the side of his head just above the ear that caused his body to tumble from the balcony onto the concrete patio below. So now he wouldn't be lying on the deck in full view of anyone inside who might come out to check on him.

It was time to move in. Running at a full clip from the edge of the woods to a basement door under the three story deck, I made it in about ten seconds. I then tried the doorknob, but it was locked. Peering inside the door glass, I saw that it was a work-out room of sorts with a treadmill, elliptical machine and free weights. Across the large room were a billiard table and a bar. As I couldn't be sure that no one was in the room, I knew I was taking a chance on walking into an ambush. However, I took the butt of my Winchester and knocked out the bottom left glass, shards of which fell silently onto the room's thick carpet. Clicking open the dead bolt, I then turned the exterior knob and stepped quickly inside. I immediately threw the rifle into a ready position and slowly edged my way in. Knowing I could take a bullet at any time from someone who lay in wait, I continued at a crouch, allowing the Winchester to lead me forward. After searching the room quickly, I was then satisfied there was no one else in the basement.

I found that the other half of the basement was actually another level of living quarters complete with three small bedrooms, two baths, a den and elaborate kitchen. When I passed a heat register, I heard both the woman's voice somewhere upstairs along with the unrecognizable drone of a man's voice. Between the large gym room and the living area was a short hallway with walls on either side on which was a collection of framed photos of the congressman with former Presidents, movie and rock stars, and even one where a flock of Hooters girls lounged around him. There was another of him perhaps ten years before when he was the Director of the CIA standing with two Latino guerrilla types in what appeared to be a South American jungle setting. And then I saw a photo of young Captain Randall shaking hands with a young Colonel Bao, obviously about the time they were scheming to massacre the people of Dak Trang. Thinking that it might add a little substance and credibility to the Dak Trang story along with the statements, I took the frame down, separated out the photo and rolled the slick paper up to stick into my back jean pocket. It might not look like much when I got it back, but although crumpled and creased, the image of the two men would still be there.

At the end of the hallway was a set of carpeted stairs to the upper floor. Stepping gingerly all the way up, I crested the top stair without making any noise. I then turned the knob slowly and pushed open the door, hoping that the hinges had recently been oiled. The door led directly into the hallway of the main floor. As I slid along the wall with the 700 still leading the way, I could now hear the voices more clearly. They appeared to be coming from the closest room on my right. As I edged ever closer, I could see the large entranceway from the hall to the room. I kept checking behind me as well as ahead to see if I could detect any shadows, but except for the voices of Randall and his mistress there appeared to be no one else on that floor. Either Chuck was in the same room listening to their conversation or he was elsewhere on the floor waiting to get the drop on me.

As I peered into the room within a foot of the door

facing, the first thing I saw was the head of a six point buck that I was sure Randall had bagged out of season. It would have been ironic if the buck that saved my life only moments before was the son or grandson of the head on the wall. Very quickly I poked my head around the door facing and then back in, catching a glimpse of the congressman yukking it up with Miss January. I did not see Chuck Robinson.

I waited a few moments to see if I could hear Chuck somewhere else in the building. It was possible he had gone out onto the upper deck on the reverse side of the house where he would *not* find his second in command…that is unless he looked straight down. He would then see that the man's head had been split open like a ripe watermelon by a sixty-seven cent round. Finally, I decided to swiftly move in on the love birds which prompted a scream from the blonde. Randall did not flinch. Instead, he remained on the white, soft leather couch in a semi-reclined position and smiled.

"Ah, Mr. McGowan, I presume. We've been expecting you."

"Where's Robinson?" I shot back.

And it was at that very moment I felt Chuck's presence behind me.

"Don't turn around, Bruce. And don't try anything. Now drop the rifle and take out your Glock with two fingers of your left hand. You know me and what I'm capable of."

I took a deep breath and sighed. I *did* know what he was capable of. And he was almost as good as me. I knew I should have first done a room-to-room search of every room before showing myself, hindsight being 20-20.

"Now, take out that .380 from your boot, sport, and

remove the knife."

I followed his order and laid both weapons on the white carpet.

Randall eyed the knife and saw that blood from the blade had already stained the carpet.

"Tsk, tsk, McGowan," he said. "I suppose that blood belongs to one of my men."

"Two to be exact, Congressman."

"You killed them all?"

"All of them."

"Including the man on the deck?"

"Including Steven Seagal," I said.

"That grieves me, Mr. McGowan. He had been with me for years. Like a brother."

I just glared at him without a response.

Chuck stuck the muzzle of his pistol into my back and said, "Now move over toward the fireplace where I can look into your eyes when I kill you."

After stepping around the couch and ottoman, I went to the mantle and turned around. Chuck still stood in the doorway with his XD 45 pointed at me.

"I *figured* you would get here early and take out my men. And you did that very nicely. You're *good*, Bruce, and I knew that. But not good enough."

"And I guess I under-estimated you, Chuck, not to mention that I thought you could never betray your country and your friends. How long have you been Randall's whore?"

He laughed. "Interesting word. But I'm nobody's whore,

Bruce. I'm just an independent contractor. I re-joined ranks with the congressman about a year ago. I owe him a lot from the CIA days. And he pays well. Maybe he would've taken you in too if you weren't so goddamn patriotic."

I then looked over at Randall. "And this son-of-bitch doesn't have a patriotic bone in his body. Congressman, you're nothing but a self-serving, sociopathic prick who uses your office to garner only power and personal gain. It makes me wonder how many other assholes like you are representing the American people."

Randall chuckled. "Mighty sharp tongue you have there, McGowan. Too bad my man Chuck here is about to silence it."

I lifted my lip in a snarl as though I had just picked up the stench of monkey shit. "Tell me, Randall, how did it feel thirty-three years ago when you cut through that Montagnard village, killing women and babies?"

He smiled sarcastically and jutted out his chin. "It felt unbelievably powerful while it was happening… like having the best piece of ass ever. When it was over and I looked down at all the bodies, I stood there, smokin a cigar and said, "I did this." The small fortune in my pocket felt pretty good, too."

I looked back at Chuck. "You were ex-military. And although you were also combat hardened, does it not make you sick to be working for a prick like this who would murder an entire village for money, and then to keep his own command from talking it up at reunions, systematically kill them? What do you say, Chuck…huh?"

He diverted his eyes and didn't reply.

I then nodded. "Of course it makes no difference to you. You did the same thing. Even worse. You and those dead goons out there wiped out your own team…your friends who alongside you risked their lives to take down terrorists so that your fellow Americans could live safe lives. You're *worse* than Randall is."

I sensed I was getting to him. His eyes were back on mine, piercing and terse. "Shut the hell up, Bruce. Like you're not cut out of the same mold? I've seen you take people down, executing them rather than bringing them in. 'I'm saving the system the cost of a trial,' you say. So, what's the difference? Murder is murder. No degrees to murder."

"That's where you're wrong, Chuck. I kill people who need killing…like you…not the innocent. And I sure as hell don't kill my friends."

His fingers tightened around the grip of the XD and I knew my words were penetrating his conscience like poison darts.

"Lionel Byrd was a good man. The best. Did you not have any conscience about pulling the trigger on him? And how about Virginia, who thought as much about you as she did any of us? None of them deserved to die like that."

Chuck curled his upper lip into a malignant smile. "People die all the time."

I glared at him contemptuously. "You're a low-life son-of-a bitch. It makes me physically ill to think I actually considered you my friend."

He glared back at me, but did not respond.

"So, how did you find out I was investigating the Dak Trang massacre?" I asked him.

"I guess since you're about to die, there's no harm in telling you. Congressman Randall was at the National Prayer Breakfast and saw the old sergeant-major talking with the

President. And when the congressman saw both of them looking in his direction, Mr. Randall sent his aide over within earshot to see if he could pick up some of the dialogue. When the words Dak Trang were uttered, the congressman knew he had to do something about it. And then when I found out from Marina that she had booked you on a flight to Vietnam, I put two and two together. I then knew that the President had talked to Byrd about engaging someone to gather evidence. Why else would you be going anywhere without the rest of the team? We've never worked that way."

"Pretty coincidental that somebody who's moonlighting for this asshole is…was…a member of the same team as somebody who would be investigating him," I said.

"Ironic, isn't it?" His evil smile returned.

Randall finally broke in. "You *know* it's all about politics. I'm running against an incumbent President. And he will be seen as someone who will resort to dirty tactics to defame a man who actually has a good chance of beating him. The good people will see him for what he is."

"And what the hell are *you*, Randall, but a murdering piece of shit who brings nothing but disgrace to the congress. Killing scores of good patriots just to further your goddamn political ambition. As President of the United States how could look at yourself in the mirror every day with that black heart of yours?"

"Ah, there he goes again, Chuck. Why don't you just go ahead and take Mr. McGowan out in the woods and make crow bait out of him?"

Before Chuck could take a step forward, I thought I'd press Randall's button one more time. "What do you think I found out in Vietnam about your thirty year old secret?"

"I know about the Degar girl…that she was a survivor of the raid. I suppose you got her statement."

"I did."

"So, let me see here. She was a mere child back then, never saw any soldier's face, especially mine, and she suddenly resurfaces after all this time with some cock-and-bull story about Americans massacring her village?"

"I have her statement, Randall, but that's not all. I also have the statement of a former ARVN soldier who over-heard you plotting with Colonel Bao."

"And how credible will *he* be? My word against his. And the good old sergeant-major went and hanged himself. He's no longer alive to sustain either the woman's or the Vietnamese guy's fable. You wasted your trip, McGowan."

"But I have a third statement, Randall," I lied. "We found Colonel Bao and may I tell you how cooperative he was just before we killed him. He spilled it all, Bozo. I have him on tape. You're going down."

"You forget that you are about to die, Mr. McGowan. Dead men tell no tales."

"You might kill me today, Randall, but believe me, those statements will hit the press and the Attorney General's Office tomorrow whether I'm alive *or* dead. Oh yeah, the statements are in a friend's hands as we speak. I don't return tonight, the story hits tomorrow. You'll be investigated for war crimes by the Ethics Committee. How does Kansas sound to you, Congressman…Leavenworth, Kansas?"

"You're bluffing."

"You think? Try me."

Randall pushed his blonde toy aside and picked himself up off the couch. He then walked toward the window with his hands behind his back and stood for a long moment. I realized I had him worried, now. He knew if I didn't resurface, maybe somebody *would* turn over all three statements. Of course, he didn't know Bao's statement didn't really exist and the statements from Thanh and Siu were in my glove compartment a half mile away. Without turning to face me, he said, "How does a million sound?"

I let out a low whistle. "A million, huh? Is that what he's paying *you*, Chuck?" I figured he wasn't.

Chuck didn't answer, but I knew he was agitated. His eyes said so.

I then started pushing *his* buttons. "Come on, Chuck. What kind of money would make you turn on your friends like you did yesterday?"

He looked at Randall and scowled. "So, what about that, Congressman? McGowan has a point here."

Randall wheeled around. "Wait a minute, Chuck. You're not falling for his little game, are you? He's trying to play *you* against *me*."

Chuck then stepped further into the room and approached to within five feet of Randall. "Maybe he is, Congressman, but you only promised me a half-million bonus if I took down Byrd and McGowan."

I laughed. "A half-million? Come on, Randall. You can do better than that. Chuckie here put his life on the line for you."

"Shut up, McGowan!" Randall shot back. "Go ahead, Chuck. I don't give a damn about those statements. They still don't prove anything. The people will see it as only a smear tactic. Waste this guy. I'll make it worth your while."

"Sure, Chuck," I said. "What do you think...another

hundred grand? I would have made a cool million if I turned over the statements and went away."

"Either kill this bastard or give me the gun, Chuck!" Randall shouted. His face was now scarlet.

Barbie Doll on the couch appeared to be freaking out. She scooted down to the end of the sofa and began balling up. "Johnny, I don't like this. Please don't do this."

"Shut up, Princess." He then looked back at Chuck. "So, do it…now."

Chuck nodded. "Sure, Congressman. But first, make me the same deal you were going to make McGowan or I don't shoot. I let him walk…straight to the Attorney General. How much *is* his life worth to you?"

"Are you trying to shake *me* down, Robinson? A former CIA Director and a member of the House of Representatives?"

It was exactly what I wanted to happen. If I could get them at each other's throat, maybe I'd have the opportunity to make my move.

As they stood there glaring at one another, I threw out another card. "And, Mr. Congressman. You've got a young lady there on the couch who's scared out of her gourd. Do you want her to see my brains scattered all over the fireplace? But then you'd have to kill her, too. Can't have an unreliable witness on your hands."

Princess then started screaming. *"Johnny, are you going to kill me?!"*

"I said shut up! Shut up all of you! Shoot the man now, Robinson! That's an order! Then shoot the bitch!"

The girl sprang from the couch and screamed out again, "No! *No!*"

Randall slapped her hard across the mouth, knocking her to the floor. He then picked her up by her long, blonde hair and flung her into Chuck. The impact between them caused the gun to go off and the report was deafening. The bullet traveled through her abdomen and out her back, harmlessly into the wall to my left. As she fell, she raked her long nails across his face, one of which caught his right eyeball. When Chuck yelped in pain, I seized the opportunity I had been looking for. I grabbed the fireplace poker and sprang onto him, coming down hard on the left side of his head. It caused him to plant another round in the trey ceiling. I then hit him between the eyes with the poker which knocked him to the floor. When he went down and started bringing the XD up, I grabbed his powerful hand with both of mine and turned the weapon in toward him. The gun then exploded a third time, propelling the bullet into his left temple. I heard him utter one word...*God*...before he took his last breath. Ironically enough, Chuck would be standing before Him in merely a split second.

Randall tried to break past me, but I threw a forearm into his throat and he dropped like a brick to the floor. When I picked up Chuck's XD and pointed it at him, he scooted all the way back against the base of the couch on his hands and butt and cowered.

"Please, McGowan. Please don't kill me. I'll give you anything you want. Even half of my fortune...whatever it takes."

"What are you going to do, write me a check?"

"No...no. I,..I'll take you from here directly to the bank and get them to give you a cashier's check."

I dropped my hand that held the pistol down to my side and I think he took that to mean maybe we had a deal.

"Are you good with that…Bruce?"

"Oh, now you want us to be on a first name basis, eh Johnny?"

"I will be the best friend you ever had if that's what it takes."

"Yeah, I know. We'd be friends for about five minutes and when I turn my back you'll make a call to one of your other goons and put a hit out on me."

"No sir. I wouldn't do that. Believe me…my word's my bond."

I actually laughed out loud which prompted him to form a nervous grin.

"Tell you what, *Johnny*. You're going to leave here handcuffed to my dash. We're driving straight to the U.S. Attorney General's Office where you're going to confess not only to the Dak Trang massacre, but also to the murders of my friends. You will write that confession before we leave here and then deliver it personally to the A.G."

His grin faded to a mulish scowl. "I can't do that. I *won't* do that. You either take me up on my offer or we have a good old-fashioned Mexican standoff."

I was actually surprised at his defiance, me holding the gun and all.

"If you don't, Randall, I will kill you where you sit."

A smirk then formed on his face. "I know your type, McGowan. You won't do that. You won't commit cold-blooded murder. You might take out bad guys, but you won't…"

I quickly raised the pistol from my side and fired a single shot into his brain.

"You're right, Johnny boy. I only take out bad guys." I then thought of something I heard Clint Eastwood say in an old *Dirty Harry* movie and added, "A man's got to know his limitations."

That moment that I stood there over Randall's body staring at the face that still bore the look of surprise, I was amazed there was no spiritual warfare going on between my ears. No internal battle for my mind and soul. No remorse. It was a cold-blooded killing, but I didn't care. The bastard had ordered the murder of my friends…and scores of other innocent people. Maybe it scared me a little of whom I had become, feeling nothing like I did. But, one thing for sure; I knew I'd get over it in about ten seconds. And then when I got home, ate, showered and made love to my wife, I'd sleep like a baby.

I pulled a handkerchief from my pocket, wiped my prints off the poker and the XD, then placed the gun back into Chuck's hand. The poker found its way into Randall's hand. Paraffin on Chuck's sleeve and ballistics tests would prove that the fatal wounds to the congressman and his mistress were fired from Chuck's gun.

After retrieving my weapons, I retraced my steps, stopping to wipe my prints off the door knob at the top of the basement stairs as well as the outside door. I was sure I had not touched anything else.

At such time the FBI came onto the scene, it would hopefully go down like this: a State Department employee, Chuck Robinson, had gone renegade and taken up with Congressman Randall, whose myriad of illicit dealings would soon be uncovered. On Randall's order, Robinson and several of the congressman's loyalists put a hit on a department director Lionel Byrd and his staff who had been investigating the Dak Trang massacre. Afterwards, Robinson fell out with Randall and then demanded payment; but obviously he and the congressman couldn't come to terms over the money. Subsequently, Randall and several of his body guards took off for the Western Virginia hideaway for a little fun with the mistress. Robinson followed them and when the lovers had settled in, he over-powered and killed Randall's men outside the cabin. Robinson then broke in and confronted Randall. They argued and Randall hit Robinson with a fireplace poker. In a fit of rage, Robinson shot and killed both the congressman and the girl. Now despondent over losing the fortune promised to him and feeling the guilt from having murdered his fellow operatives, he put a bullet in his own head. That's what I would make sure the Bureau put out to the media, with Wymans' help. I was never there, of course. It would clear up the mystery surrounding the murders of the six State Department employees on Lyon Street and expose the conniving, womanizing, and murderous Presidential candidate, Jonathan Perryman Randall, once and for all, God rest his soul.

After back-tracking through the woods, I re-joined my Suburban, thankful that I didn't get a parking ticket from a forest ranger. I continued on west through Monterey and Hightown, past my buddy's farm, and on into West Virginia where by two-thirty I had done a full day's work and was heading south on 219 toward home. For some reason I had missed lunch and was a bit famished. Killing bad guys *always* makes me hungry. Even though I'm normally a light and healthy eater, I stopped at a McDonald's in Marlinton and ordered a Big Mac combo. In a strange way, it seemed as though it was the best, most satisfying cheeseburger I had ever had.

CHAPTER EIGHTEEN

When I walked up the steps to the front door of our inn, I knew I looked like hell, still wearing the same mangy and blood-crusted khaki shirt with the ripped-out sleeves, a bandage on my left shoulder and a piece of scalp missing from near my left temple. I was hoping Adrianna wasn't home so that I could shower, shave and put on some fresh clothes. Although I had taken note of her van in the driveway, I further hoped a friend might have picked her up for lunch, which happened once or twice a week, and would be dropping her off later on. But no such luck. When I stepped through the doorway with my Remington 700 in hand, my holstered Glock hanging off my left shoulder and grungy travel bag in hand, Adrianna was in the sitting room talking with three lady guests while partaking of some hot ginger cookies and freshly-made lemonade.

"Well, look what the cat dragged in," she said. "Dear ladies, this man who looks like the Terminator is my husband." She then gave me one of those "How could you embarrass me like this" looks.

"Good afternoon, ladies," I greeted. "I hope you're having a pleasant stay here. But, if you'll excuse me, I've had a tough couple of days at the office and need to get cleaned up."

The expressions on their faces, what with their taking account of all the hardware, was priceless.

I hit the shower immediately after which I replaced the bandage on my shoulder. The wound was looking better, but the hot shower water caused it and the place on my head to start bleeding again. When I stepped out of the steamy bathroom, Adrianna was standing in the living room waiting with her arms folded.

"Well, if you aren't a sight for sore eyes. What happened this time? And how may bullet holes are you wearing?"

I dropped my head and didn't answer right away. Her comment was all I needed for the day's tears to finally come. I bit my lip hard to keep from sobbing.

"Skip, what's the matter." She practically ran to me and placed her arms around my naked back. "I've never *seen* you like this. Did somebody…"

"Die?" I said, finishing her question. "Sit down with me, Adrianna. I need to tell you something."

I prefaced my soliloquy by telling her what the back-to-Vietnam mission was all about, including a play-by-play of everything that happened, except my night at Joy's place. I told her why I was sent there and what I needed to acquire to get the goods on Jonathan Randall. And that led me to yesterday's gruesome findings at CTT. The words were scarcely out of my mouth when she placed her hand over her breasts and gasped.

"My God. Mr. Byrd is dead?"

"He died while I was with him. They're all dead."

She put her arms around me tightly, bringing my head into her bosom, and then began to cry. We held each other for a few moments without saying anything. Finally, I broke from her arms and sat on the edge of the couch with my face in my hands.

Adrianna then placed her fingertips to the Band-aid on my scalp. "Are you okay?"

"Yeah. This time fortunately just flesh wounds. I'll heal." My psychological wounds were another thing.

"What will you do now?"

"This is the end of it all for me, Adrianna. No more. No more work for the government." I then looked up at her and gave her a half-smile. "Looks like I'll be underfoot here every day of our lives from now on. You'll get sick of me in a hurry."

She kissed me on the forehead. "No, Mr. McGowan, I will never be sick of you. It will make me very happy."

I waited until the next morning before making the phone call I dreaded the most. A young woman answered the phone and I identified myself. I then heard a second woman's broken voice come on the line.

"Bruce?"

"Yes, it's me."

"I..." And then she began sobbing.

"Miriam, I just don't have the words to express how sorry I am. I want you to know that even though Lionel was not that much older than me, I thought of him as a father. I never worked for or with anyone else in all my service with the government I loved and respected as much. He was the best man I ever knew."

"You were with him when he died I understand."

"Yes. And Miriam..."

"Yes?"

"He told me to tell you he loved you and the girls. He said that you were the one true love of his life."

She didn't reply, but she had apparently removed her phone from her face as I heard her crying in the background. In a moment she regained her composure.

"Bruce, the funeral will be Sunday at the First Presbyterian Church. He will be laid to rest at Arlington. I hope you will be there."

"Adrianna and I will be there, Miriam. If you need any help with the arrangements or need me to do anything to help put his affairs in order, you let me know and I'll be there."

"Thank you, Bruce. My girls and I will manage. And Lionel's brother is here to help out as well. Lionel always spoke well of you, you know. He said you were the best at what you do."

And that's when I started to choke up.

"But Bruce, there is one thing you can do."

"Sure. Anything, Miriam. What is it?"

"You find those bastards that did this."

I paused a moment to consider how I would respond. "You may want to check the papers and national news in a day or so, Miriam. A prominent political figure will be found with others in a cabin in Western Virginia. You will then remember our conversation today and know that Lionel's death has already been vindicated. I can't further elaborate."

"I understand, Bruce. Thank you for telling me that. And thanks for thinking of me."

"Take care, Miriam. Good bye for now."

I knew I had taken a chance in giving her that sketchy bit of information since anyone on either side of the law could have tapped Lionel's phone. But she had to know and the funeral was not the place to talk about it. If there were still remnants of Randall's mob out there with designs on me, just bring it on.

Adrianna said she would certainly go with me to Lionel's funeral. She would however prefer that we leave to go on Sunday morning and return the same day since she was expecting more guests. She would ask her friend and part-time assistant, Linda White, to sub for her during the day.

I was up early on Saturday morning doing something I had not done in over two weeks. I went for a run. The air, cool and fresh, electrified my lungs, but also served to help release some of the anxiety, sadness and anger that had plagued me over the previous two weeks. In taking account of those perilous days, it seemed that I had been caught up into some kind of surreal whirlwind, a mighty rush of wind that had sucked itself into my body to a point where I felt as though I would explode. That hateful wind, as Sue had metaphorically described, that began long ago had continued to blow through the years, ultimately finding its way to the little house on Lyon Street where it devoured our team. But in the end, I had rechanneled its course to wreak its deadly force onto those who created it. All of its victims, both good and bad, had perished. I alone had survived.

A morning run always helps me clear the cobwebs. When I finally directed my Nikes down Seven Bridges Road and into the parking lot at Wolf Laurel, I felt no pain in these old bones. Only release.

The lovely Adrianna had prepared my favorite breakfast…the hoe cake with butter and molasses, which of course would serve to put back into my system the same calories I had burned in my four mile run. But I didn't care.

The TV on the wall in the dining area was tuned to Fox News and the three ladies from the afternoon before were taking in the events of the morning while waiting on their breakfast. I greeted them cordially as I whisked by on my way to the shower. However, before I reached the hallway that led to the stairs to our apartment, I heard one of them gasp over the chatter of the other two.

My God!" she exclaimed. "Someone found Congressman Randall dead with several others at his cabin over in Virginia."

I stalled and then turned to listen to the broadcast. There was film of State Troopers all over the grounds talking with one another as body bags were being carted on gurneys on their way to the coroner's wagon. Adrianna then came out of the kitchen to watch as well. When she had digested what was happening, her astonished and condemning eyes fell onto mine. I stared back at her blankly, but said nothing. I then knew that *she* knew.

I quickly showered, donned a pair of Bermudas and a white polo, then returned to have breakfast with our guests. Adrianna brought out the hoe cake along with some thick, crisp bacon and fruit, but did not say anything to me. Generally, she did not join her guests for breakfast, content only with being their server. This morning was no different. After going back to the kitchen a second time, she returned with some fresh coffee to pour into my favorite Ranger cup. It was her only acknowledgement that I was even in the room.

"Won't you join us for breakfast this morning,

sweetheart? You've been on your feet all morning."

"Yes, dear," the eldest of the ladies echoed. "Sit and enjoy the wonderful food you've prepared."

She shot me a quick glance and replied, "I guess I can sit for a moment. Suddenly, I need a cup of coffee."

The ladies then turned their attention back to the news. "I can't believe what this world is coming to," said the same woman. "Poor John Randall."

My handiwork, ladies.

"Such a good family man," another said. "I was going to vote for him."

I had just taken a gulp of the coffee and thought I might spew it all over the table.

"Well, generally," I said. "when a prominent man like this is found dead with bodies lying all over the place to include that of a pretty young woman, sometimes we find that a person is not as squeaky-clean as he appeared to be."

Now, the condemning eyes were *theirs*. I had spoken ill of the dead who had to be a man they obviously admired. That's why I thought it best to not add further comment. I definitely didn't want to run Adrianna's new guests off. I added, "But then again, who am I to speculate."

Adrianna took a few sips of her coffee, gave me a look I had not seen before from her beautiful peepers, and then she said, "Excuse me if you will. I have to go upstairs for a moment. Please help yourself to seconds."

After I heard her feet on the stairs, I knew I couldn't let the morning continue to go south, so I said, "Pardon me, ladies," then pushed away from the table. I zipped up the steps rather quickly and nearly beat Adrianna into our apartment. When I entered the living room, I found her standing by the window, arms folded and looking out over the massive pink dogwood below. She heard me come in, but did not turn around.

I walked up behind her and placed my arms around her tiny waist. She felt rigid and cold.

"Was that you, Skip? Did you kill those people?"

"I've never lied to you, Adrianna, and I'm not going to start now. I told you it was Chuck Robinson and John Randall who hit our team. If I had been there fifteen minutes earlier, maybe I'd be dead as well. What Lionel Byrd's dying lips told me was in essence the same as a judge and jury deciding their fate…"

"And then you took it upon yourself to become their executioner. You couldn't turn it all over to the FBI?"

"And have these people escape on a lack of tangible evidence or because it was all hearsay? No. They got what was coming to them."

She turned around and searched my eyes with hers. "What kind of a man carries out something like this? I'm not sure I even know you now."

"You knew who I was when we got married, Adrianna. You witnessed me taking down people that were prepared to kill us right here in this house…people who were about to blow up thousands of innocent Americans."

"But you did these things either out of self-defense or because it was part of your job. Yes, you saved me from certain death at the hands of that Islamic professor. But what you did up there in Virginia at that cabin was premeditated murder."

"No, Adrianna. If I hadn't gone for them, they were coming for me. Maybe even coming here for you. Chuck

Robinson threatened that, if I didn't face him."

"All I know is that the man who shares my bed is capable of doing some very heinous things, Skip, and that makes me very afraid."

I placed my hands on her shoulders. "Wait a minute here. You can't think I'd ever hurt you."

"I'm not saying that, Skip. I know you wouldn't. But it's what is inside you…the wrath, the demons, the terrible fury that you are capable of unleashing at the blink of an eye, that troubles me."

"I promised you on the phone the other day as well as yesterday afternoon that I was done with all this. I am ready to be nothing more than teacher, gardener and husband Bruce McGowan. You will never again have to worry about danger being any part of my life."

She dropped her eyes for a moment…a long moment, then returned them to mine. "Can I get that in writing?" Her tone was a bit sardonic.

I smiled at her. "I would prefer to seal the contract with a little body-to-body contact."

She didn't smile back or succumb to my frivolous chagrins. And as I held her, I found her body uncharacteristically rigid. I knew it would take her a little time to digest what she had just found out. In a way I didn't blame her. She had now learned that there was a more dangerous even malignant side of me than she thought. But I hoped that once she had slept on all this, I would again be in her loving graces.

Indeed, as the day progressed, I saw that she had loosened up a bit. Her smile even came out a couple of times like the sun after a cold rain. And when night came and we turned in, she slowly began to warm up to me.

Enough to where she actually allowed me to do impious and perverted things to her body. That's when I knew the vexations were pretty much out of her system. But, I also pondered the image that must have been ravaging her mind of the massacre I committed at Randall's cabin. There may even be days in our future that when I touched her, she might stare at my hands, visualizing what they were capable of.

*   *   *   *

We left Wolf Laurel just after five-thirty the next morning in my Austin Healey which would put us at the First Presbyterian Church around ten, well in time for the eleven o'clock service. I pulled off the interstate in Fairfax to pick up a copy of the *Washington Post* to see if members of my team were in the obituary. The only two I could find were Lionel's and Virginia's. Her funeral was also on Sunday at the same time. I could only be there in spirit. I had never met her husband Tom, but felt I knew him through her. Perhaps I could visit him one day and tell him how much I loved her.

I did find an article on page two about the killings. Apparently, the FBI under orders from the President had told the press just enough to keep the story white-washed so that the true function of CTT would not be divulged.

Funeral Services Today for Murdered Civil Servant

(Associated Press) "Washington, D.C. The FBI has continued to keep the lid on its investigation into the shooting deaths of a long time public servant and five others at the Terminal Enterprises location on Lyon Street Wednesday. As the motive of the shootings has yet to be determined, FBI Agent-in-Charge, Frederick Baines, speculated it could have been robbery. Terminal Enterprises, a government contractor that develops proprietary security software, all but ceased its operation after the murders of its key personnel. Lionel Byrd, manager and Director of Operations, had a long and distinguished career with the FBI and CIA, prior to starting up the business. His funeral is today at the First Presbyterian Church on Donaldson Avenue at 11:00 AM. A grave site service will follow at Arlington Cemetery."

Of course, the Randall story had dominated the front page of the *Post* and every other newspaper in the country for the past three days. Investigative reporters for the major TV news networks and tabloid rags were having a field day speculating about the mystery mistress found at the Senator's cabin. And then, who was the alleged murderer, Charles Robinson? There were also bodies of three men found on the grounds outside of the cabin. As Randall, a Presidential candidate, was assigned Secret Service protection, there was dialogue about the dead being government agents. The White House quickly put that speculation to rest by stating that Randall had refused agent protection. It had been public knowledge from the very beginning. Of course, I knew why he had refused the Secret Service. With all of Randall's shady dealings, he definitely didn't want any agents anywhere in proximity.

Remarkable stories were also starting to break about members of Randall's Vietnam unit coming forward to talk about a My Lai type raid where a total village was wiped out. Randall allegedly used strong arm tactics to keep the story quiet. The majority of Randall's infantry company had died mysteriously or had disappeared without a trace. Reporters were also digging into Randall's connection to the Mafia and his dubious rise to fame and fortune. Then there were the women…and not just the woman with whom he was found dead. Two mistresses had already surfaced, eager to convey to the highest bidder about their relationships with the congressman. The same press that had supported and touted the man who would be President was going to be ruthless. It would be open season on a man who had not yet even been buried. But there was one thing for sure…they would continue to 'bury' him in words day after day for months on end.

We arrived at the church around ten-thirty and were greeted warmly by one of Lionel's adult daughters who then directed us to where her mother and other family members had gathered. When Miriam saw me she hugged my neck, getting the collar of my shirt all wet from her tears.

"Thanks for being here, Bruce. You look so handsome in that dark suit."

"Miriam, this is my wife, Adrianna."

"Hi, dear," she greeted. "My but you are even prettier than Lionel described. He always understated everything, which was his way. He…" She suddenly broke into a series of sobs and I placed my arm around her shoulder without saying anything.

She then quickly recovered and dried her eyes, needlessly apologizing for her tears. Lionel's brother, an older look-alike, but certainly not as refined, approached and shook my hand. I also met Miriam's other daughter, a glamorous mother of three who was pretty much a basket case.

In a few minutes we were escorted to the sanctuary where we were deposited about half-way back on the right side of the aisle. Lionel's coffin sat parked at the altar with an American flag draped over it.

For a man who led a mostly private life, given the nature

of his vocational history, I was surprised that the church was nearly packed. I suspected many were from various branches of government service, both still active and retired, while others were merely curiosity seekers…the kind that feed ravenously off of the National Enquirer and Jerry Springer. I was sure that when Randall's funeral took place in a couple of days in his home state, the mob of media and paparazzi would extend out the door and into the street.

Off to the left of the aisle I recognized Carlos from the Chicago CTT element sitting among a dozen or so other men I assumed to be from CTT locations throughout the country I had never met. They all looked like they ate nails for breakfast. Carlos had apparently seen me come in and when I looked in his direction, he nodded once. I acknowledged with a nod of my own.

The service was solemn and traditional as the minister dressed in a black robe basically preached a dry, philosophical sermon using profound and scholarly words that I wasn't sure were even in the dictionary. There was singing by the choir and the congregational reading of the scripture, and then it was over in forty minutes. When the Marine Honor Guard marched smartly down the aisle and took charge of the coffin to wheel it from the sanctuary, piped in music played Barber's *Adagio for Strings*, a real weeper of a symphony with its melancholic carpet of violins. I didn't even know Lionel had served with the Marines way back when. But I'm sure there was a lot that I didn't know about this very secretive man.

We were about twenty cars back in the long funeral procession that took about a half hour to reach Arlington. By the time we exited our car, the Honor Guard was already carrying Lionel's coffin up the small incline past the symmetrical rows of crosses toward the open grave at the top of the hill. When most of the mourners were in place, a stoic-looking chap in a black suit and sunglasses stepped up to the minister and whispered something to him. For perhaps five minutes we all stood in place waiting for the preacher to say something, wondering what the deal was.

Finally, we heard the roar of four motorcycles on the roadway below us and turned our heads to see two SUVs and a black Lincoln pulling up behind the bikes. First, four men also in black suits and sunglasses exited the two Expeditions and scanned the area. A few moments later, one of them opened the rear door of the Lincoln and out stepped a familiar face…the President of the United States. Walking at a quick-step, he and the Secret Service Agents reached the gravesite in less than thirty seconds and then stood not fifteen feet from Adrianna and me.

After a five minute service, the Marine Guard fired three volleys of blanks and I saw Miriam flinch each time the guns went off. The President then stepped forward and when the Marines had finished folding the American flag, it was first given to the Commander of the Guard who then handed it off to the President. Walking smartly to where Miriam Byrd was sitting, he bent at the waist and handed the flag to her. For nearly a half minute he whispered something to her, then leaned in to kiss her on the forehead.

When the President turned to leave, his eyes fell on mine. I thought I saw a slight nod to which I acknowledged with one of my own. And then he was gone in a flash.

Adrianna and I worked our way through those who remained to express their sympathy until we finally reached her and her two daughters. There was little more for me to say to her and her to me. She did thank us again for being there and as she knew we would probably never see each other again, she smiled and squeezed my hand.

As we turned to go back down the hill to the Healey,

two men in black approached us. The youngest one touched me on the sleeve and said, "Mr. McGowan, we'd like you to come with us."

"And you would be who?"

They both flashed their Secret Service badges and then the young one said again, "Now, will you please come with us?"

"My wife is with me and we are in that green car there. I go nowhere without her. What is it you want with me?"

"It is not *us* who want anything with you, sir. You are asked to accompany us to the White House."

"All right. I'll follow you, but will not ride with you. And she goes too."

He nodded. "Okay, but stay close to our vehicle."

I then looked at Adrianna. "Are you okay with this?"

"The White House? Sure."

I guessed that the President wanted to have a dialogue with me and further assumed they would escort Adrianna to a separate room. They would make sure she was accommodated. If you can't trust the President of the United States and his staff with your wife, then who *can* you trust?

It took less than ten minutes to cover the distance between Arlington and 1600 Pennsylvania Avenue. The driver of the black SUV stopped at the gate to speak with the guard who then looked back at us. Then we were all waved through.

"The White House, Adrianna," I remarked, looking at the stately building as though we were on the grounds of royalty. "Did you ever think you'd be getting your own special tour of the place?"

"Well, *I'm* certainly excited," she replied. "And I can see *you* are."

"You know something? All the time I was with the Bureau and lately with CTT, I have never been inside this place…not even on a tour."

I followed the SUV into a small parking lot and pulled the Healey up beside it. The men in black were out of their vehicle quickly and the young agent that had been doing the talking then approached us.

"Are you armed, sir?"

"Yes. I have a Glock in my shoulder holster and a .380 strapped to my leg."

"I'll need them, sir."

Understandably and without protest, I handed both weapons over.

"Are you armed, ma'am?"

She laughed. "No, of course not."

"May I check your purse anyway?"

"Yes," she replied. "Here."

After he had searched through it, he gave her a half smile. "Follow me, please." I presumed one had to go to a special school to learn how to be that stiff and stoic. But then again, I remember my early years with the Bureau and how anal *I* was.

We were led down a long corridor past stunning original portraits of former Presidents and First Ladies and after making several left and right turns, we were approached by a young lady who I took to be the President's personal assistant.

"Mrs. McGowan, if you will follow me, I will escort you to one of the sitting rooms where you will meet with the First Lady. Mr. McGowan, would you please follow Agent Pavlowski?"

I thought Adrianna was going to fall apart as I saw her knees buckle slightly. And I thought perhaps we would one day have to have that goofy smile surgically removed from her face.

I parted ways with her and followed Pavlowski to a door where he stopped to rap twice.

"Come in, Brian," called the voice from inside.

When we entered the Oval Office, the President immediately stepped forward to shake my hand. I wondered later if he had noticed how sweaty my palm was.

"Would you like something to drink, Bruce?"

There was a sudden catch in my voice. "N…no, sir. No thank you."

"Well then, please have a seat."

I could have been my usual funny self and asked, "Where? Over there behind the desk?" But we weren't that good of friends yet.

He motioned with his hand for me to sit in one of the comfy wingback chairs near the center of the room and then he sat down opposite me. He then became solemn and sighed. "Pretty sad deal, Bruce…Mr. Byrd's death and the others. I called him my friend, you know."

"Yes, sir. I had inklings that may have been the case."

"Got to know him fairly well these past few years. A good and moral sort of man."

"Yes, sir.

"Let me get to the point, Bruce. You don't mind if I call you by your first name?"

"Not at all, Mr. President."

"Good. Well, I do appreciate you jumpin' in on such short notice to secure the information we were lookin' for. I know it wasn't an easy thing for you to do. You had to cover a lot of ground."

"Yes, sir." I knew he had to be rather worn out with my saying nothing but "yes, sir."

"You did make contact with the Vietnamese man and Degar woman?"

"Yes, I secured their statements. They proved fruitful."

"And I understand you had some difficulties getting out of country…something about killin' a cop?"

I think I may have turned a peculiar shade of scarlet. "That would be correct, sir…unfortunately."

"Well then, tell me the particulars of your trip there, and don't leave anything out."

I told him everything…every minute detail. Including Thanh's shooting of Bao and his guards, and of my being jailed for having been at least an accomplice in the killings. Of course, I left out the part about Joy taking me in. The less said about that, the better. And then I told him about arriving at CTT and finding the bodies of our team and staff.

"You probably know, Mr. President, that Lionel Byrd was not dead when I got to him. These were his last feeble words he whispered: "Bruce, Chuck went bad. He did this. He and three others came here and killed us. And the Army captain who raided that village was Jonathan Randall. *Congressman* Jonathan Randall. I found out Chuck had been working for him. Randall ordered the hit because we were getting too close. The President knows. Go to the President, Bruce. And be careful. They will be looking for you." And then he said, "Tell Miriam I love her and…" I began to well up. The President then reached across and placed his hand on my shoulder.

"And then Lionel began choking on his blood. Those were his last words."

The President nodded and was quiet for a moment. "I know this was difficult for you, Bruce. Are you sure you don't want a Coke or something?"

"I'm good, sir." Actually, I didn't want to take the risk of spilling anything on his white rug beneath our feet.

He settled back in his chair and rested his chin reflectively on his fingertips, keeping his steely eyes on mine.

"Bruce, unless you crawled into one of those caves back there in Greenbrier County, you know that Randall and several others were found dead at his cabin out there in Western Virginia. They say it wasn't a pretty scene. A young woman was also killed."

"It's been all over the news, twenty-four seven, yes, sir."

"Seems everybody speculates how the killins' went down inside the cabin…a murder-suicide carried out by Robinson. Of course, no one, except you, me and the Secret Service, knows who Robinson was. Word going around is that he was a disgruntled employee of Randall's and they fell out in a big way. Maybe Robinson had some psychological problems and went off. Then when it was over, he had remorse about it and ended his own life."

"I read that, sir. I guess it could have gone down like that."

"But, there were also bodies of three armed men found on the grounds as well. Obviously, he took them out one by one on the way in."

I squirmed some more, but didn't respond.

He continued. "My scene experts doubt all this, though. If Robinson *was* one of Randall's men, he could have been waved right in."

"Maybe he had planned to just take everybody out."

"Maybe. But, contrary to what was put out to the media, we believe it was an expert hit by a professional. And whoever killed these men staged the killins' inside to look like a murder-suicide. If that's the case, the real killer was not only a dangerous and violent man, but cunning as well."

I shuffled nervously again in my chair.

He continued. "That bein' the case, regardless of what Randall and Robinson did, we'd have to bring this man to justice."

"It would be the right thing to do, sir."

"A man can't take the law into his own hands even when he thinks it's the only righteous thing to do."

"No, sir."

He sighed again. "The problem is, the Bureau and the Virginia State Police are stumped. No other fingerprints or clues were found to prove any different from what's been speculated." He then looked up and around the room, thoughtfully. "If there *is* somebody like this still out there that's dangerous, we have to find out who it is. Of course, this guy could even be playin' both sides of the fence…a kind of rogue contractor. *You* even might be in danger, Bruce. I'd be very careful."

"If the incident went down like a few are speculating,

Mr. President, I'd say he wouldn't be after *me*. I think he would be satisfied he accomplished his mission and would all but disappear."

"I expect you're right about that, Bruce. If I were this man, I'd never again surface."

Both of us then became quiet and reflective-like.

"On the previous matter, Bruce, do you have the statements? Not that it now matters."

"I have them, sir. They're at home in my safe."

"Then I will ask that you make them available to me. I can have one of the agents come by to see you in a few days."

"That will be fine, sir."

He then rose to his feet and I followed suit. "Well, I just wanted to have an opportunity to chat personally with you, Bruce, and tell you how much I value your service to this country. And I appreciate not only your loyalty, but your patriotism. I've been followin' you since that big take down of the subversives on 9-11. This country owes you a big debt, my friend."

"Thank you, sir."

"One more thing, though."

"What's that, Mr. President."

"I'll be lookin' to replace Mr. Byrd soon. I believe in the concept of CTT and it needs to continue its work. We need to reorganize the team, add some people perhaps, and put in place a new director. I can't think of anyone else to put in there, Bruce, if you'd like to be considered."

I smiled. "I appreciate your confidence in me, Mr. President, but I've been licking my wounds lately, literally, and have promised my lovely bride that I would give up government service. She needs me and I need to be with her. With your permission, I'd like to just fade away. Old soldiers do that, you know."

"I thought you might say that. And of course you *should* retire, considering your long and brilliant service. But you'd be missed, Bruce. Byrd told me you were the best he'd ever worked with. And I believe that. If you ever change your mind…"

"I won't, sir. The country would have to be in dire straits and grandmas going to fight wars before I'd pick up a gun again."

He laughed. "Well, let's hope we never get to that point." He then held out his hand. "Go with God, Bruce."

"Every day, sir."

"I'd also like to shake Mrs. McGowan's hand as well before you leave."

"She would consider that an honor."

He then went to his phone…not the red one…and buzzed his assistant. "Please have Mrs. McGowan stop by. Thanks."

In scantly ten seconds there was a rap on the door and the President opened it.

"Mrs. McGowan, thank you for agreeing to come here with your husband today." He took her hand and kissed it, the true gentleman that he was *and* politician. "I want you to know how much we appreciate Bruce's service to his country…and you have given up a lot these two years of your marriage to allow him to do it."

I wondered how he knew we had only been married two years. But, of course, he was the most powerful man in the world and there was nothing he couldn't find out.

Adrianna smiled. "I had a nice conversation with your wife, sir. She is such a delightful lady and I will remember this day as long as I live."

"Maybe someday we'll come down to your quaint little inn there in Greenbrier County. Wolf Laurel, isn't it?"

"Yes, sir. We would consider that an honor. Only a hundred seventy a night."

He laughed loudly and I flushed. Obviously, Adrianna had been living with *me* too long, but she *did* have a great business head.

"Why don't we get the White House photographer to take a picture of the four of us," the President said. He nodded to his assistant and she scrambled to go find the guy.

After the photographer had taken four or five shots, the President shook my hand again and said, "I'll have copies sent to you, Bruce."

"We appreciate that, sir."

As we walked down the hallway a piece, the President kept his hand on my shoulder, then stopped and said, "Think it over anyway, Bruce," And then he winked.

"Grandmas in combat, sir."

He laughed. "Okay, Bruce. Have a safe trip back home."

As young Agent Pavlowski escorted us out, he handed me back my weapons. "Don't you think it's about time to put these in mothballs, old man?" There was that half smile again.

"Since when did they start making snot-nosed brats Secret Service Agents?" I asked, smiling back.

He didn't reply. He just shook his head.

I held the door open for Mrs. McGowan as she slid her small frame onto the tan leather seat of the Healey. Her head was still in the clouds having just spent twenty minutes with the First Lady. And me? Although still wearing a heavy heart from seeing my friend and mentor being laid to rest earlier in the day, I was feeling pretty important myself. I had actually sat in the Oval Office and had a conversation with the President of the United States. Furthermore, he had known all along who I was for the past three years. *And* he had offered me the job of running CTT. How cool was that?

As we took a different route back home, down through the beautiful Virginia countryside, Adrianna laid her pretty head back against the seat, closed her eyes and smiled.

"I love you, Skip McGowan. You're mine. All mine now. I don't have to share you with anyone or any*thing*. No more danger. Nobody shooting at you. I can't tell you how good that makes me feel. I couldn't imagine life without you."

I looked at the woman I loved and smiled back. "I know," I whispered. I then placed my arm around her and drew her into me. It had been a long time since I had seen her so relaxed and happy. And that is why it was not the right time for me to tell her what I was thinking.

AFTERWORD

We hope you have enjoyed **A Hateful Wind**, the third book in the McGowan Collection. Before you continue on to the next book in this chronology, the author suggests you first read or listen to **The Justice Club** where he introduces hit man Atticus Steed who will be featured in the collection's fourth book, **Killing the Viper**.